"Alexis Morgan lets her imagination soar to create characters who steal your heart while their personal story deeply touches you. . . . Magically adventurous and fervently romantic."

—Single Titles

"The vivid, edgy scenes [Morgan] paints for the reader make the story come alive. . . . If you're looking for a paranormal series layered with danger, intrigue and romance then you'll want to run out and get Alexis Morgan's Talion series. It's a definite keeper!"

—Fallen Angel Reviews

"A quick and exciting read."

—A Romance Review

DARK WARRIOR UNLEASHED

"Red-hot talent Morgan kicks off another supernatural series, the Talions. In setting up the challenges and unique characteristics of her protagonists, she ensures that there will be more adventures to come. This is great stuff!"

—*Romantic Times*

"This book sucked me in, and I didn't want to stop reading."

—Queue My Review

"A book that must go to the top of your must-read-as-soon-as-you-get-it list."

—*Simply Romance Reviews*

Dark Warrior
UNTAMED

ALEXIS MORGAN

Pocket Star Books
New York London Toronto Sydney

Pocket Star Books
A Division of Simon & Schuster, Inc.
1230 Avenue of the Americas
New York, NY 10020

This book is a work of fiction. Names, characters, places, and incidents either are products of the author's imagination or are used fictitiously. Any resemblance to actual events or locales or persons, living or dead, is entirely coincidental.

Copyright © 2010 by Patricia L. Pritchard

First Pocket Star Books paperback edition August 2010

POCKET STAR BOOKS and colophon are registered trademarks of Simon & Schuster, Inc.

For information about special discounts for bulk purchases, please contact Simon & Schuster Special Sales at 1-866-506-1949 or business@simonandschuster.com.

The Simon & Schuster Speakers Bureau can bring authors to your live event. For more information or to book an event contact the Simon & Schuster Speakers Bureau at 1-866-248-3049 or visit our website at www.simonspeakers.com.

Cover design by Lisa Litwack.
Illustration by Craig White.

Manufactured in the United States of America

10 9 8 7 6 5 4 3 2 1

ISBN 978-1-4391-7592-7
ISBN 978-1-4391-7596-5 (ebook)

This book is dedicated to my mother,
Ethel Potts Rodgers.
Mom, thanks for teaching me that playing with words
was a fun thing to do. We miss you.

Acknowledgments

A special thanks to all my friends who help keep me sane in this crazy business—you know who you are, and I hope you know how much you mean to me. Just knowing you're out there at the other end of a phone call or e-mail is a gift that I cherish so much.

Chapter 1

"*W*ho the bloody hell are you?"

Piper looked up from her computer screen and studied the irate male glaring at her from the doorway. Her stomach did a little rock-and-roll number. He was, without a doubt, the guy they'd warned her about—Greyhill Danby. She'd been hired while he'd been in England, and she knew for a fact that no one expected him back yet.

"I suppose I could ask you the same question— but I'd like to think I would've been a little more polite." Her smile wasn't meant to be nice; rude was always the best response to rude.

His eyes, an incredible shade of bright blue, narrowed as he walked into the cramped room. That fierce gaze wouldn't miss much. She was willing to bet he'd committed every detail to memory the moment he entered, from the pictures on the wall to the number of buttons on her blouse. He certainly wouldn't have missed the pink and purple highlights in her dark hair, much less the tattoo on her right arm. And he clearly didn't approve of any of it.

When he didn't respond, she continued. "Well, since you've obviously forgotten how to speak, I'll answer for both of us. I'm Piper Ryan, the Dame's new assistant. This is my office, and you must be Greyhill Danby."

It took some effort to tear her eyes away from all that masculine intensity, but she managed. Barely.

"Now since the pleasantries are over, you'll have to excuse me, Mr. Danby. One of us has important work to do."

Her fingers flew across her keyboard to make her point. She'd delete the gibberish she was typing after he left. *If* he left. He'd widened his stance and crossed his arms over his chest, clearly intending to take root.

She hit the save button and then looked up, sighing loudly. "Is there something else I can help you with, Mr. Danby? I really am very busy."

His lips tightened. She'd definitely pushed too far.

"I can see that you're busy, ah . . . Miss Ryan, was it?" His eyebrows snapped down over those bright blue eyes as he stared at her. "And I'm sure whatever you're doing is important to someone, somewhere. However, since this is actually *my* office, you'll understand why you need to go do your little job somewhere else."

Apparently no one had told him that they'd be

sharing the space until the workmen finished remodeling the rooms upstairs into offices for her and Kerry Thorsen.

Thanks a lot, Sandor Kearn. You could have warned me that you left this guy out of the loop.

She turned to face Danby directly. "I'm guessing that you haven't talked to Sandor since your return."

He nodded sharply. "You'd guess right, although I'm not sure what he has to do with you usurping my office."

Piper laughed, fueling the flames. Holding her hand up in apology, she finally managed to speak.

"Sorry, Mr. Danby, but with that British accent of yours, it sounds like this is 1776 all over again and I'm one of those pesky American rebels. But I assure you, sir, I didn't dump your precious tea in Puget Sound. It's over there on the cabinet right next to my coffee."

He scrutinized the clutter with a slight sneer before turning back to her. "My advice to you, Miss Ryan, is not to get too comfortable here."

He stalked out, taking most of the oxygen in the room with him. That was the only reason she could come up with for why she suddenly felt so breathless. Yes, that had to be it. Slowly the pressure in her chest eased, leaving her to figure out how she was going to share such a confined space with that uptight jerk. Sexy, but a jerk nonetheless.

Turning back to her computer, she deleted the nonsense lines. She'd manage somehow. She always did.

Out in the hall, Grey pinched the bridge of his nose
and wished he could rewind and try that whole mess
again. Maybe he should take a lap around the rose
garden—or half a dozen—before seeking out either
Sandor Kearn or the Dame herself.

Granted, neither one of them were particularly
happy to have Grey around, but to stick a spy—especially that flit of brunette—in his private office was
too much. How was he supposed to work with her in
there? She'd already turned his neat and tidy office
into complete chaos.

What else had changed in the short time he'd
been out of the country? Although Dame Kerry had
told him to take his time moving to Seattle, he hadn't
wanted to give her the chance to rethink her decision
to appoint him as her Chief Talion and enforcer.

He'd worked around the clock to close up his flat
in London and make arrangements to ship his belongings to the States. He'd finished in record time, and it
had been exhausting. It also didn't help his mood that
his departure had been delayed for over six hours because of weather, followed by a flight full of screaming infants and heavy turbulence.

So he was seriously jet-lagged and short-tempered.
He'd only intended to stop by the Dame's home long
enough to let her know that he was back and to drop
off a few things in his office. Which, as it turned out,
was evidently no longer just his.

Exactly who was this Piper Ryan? And more importantly, how had she managed to worm her way into the Thorsen household so quickly? The last he'd heard, he was supposed to be in charge of security, which included vetting potential employees. Obviously someone had also usurped his job while he was away.

The most likely culprit was Sandor Kearn, Grey's predecessor as Chief Talion. Even though Sandor had happily relinquished the role, he'd probably felt obligated to continue his former duties until Grey returned. That was all well and good, but why hadn't he kept Grey in the loop?

The answer was obvious. Sandor had guessed how Grey would react to finding someone else ensconced in his office. And not just someone, but Piper Ryan. Her image filled his head, another reason to curse his gift of almost perfect recall. Her dark hair appeared to have been cut with grass clippers with no intention other than drawing attention to streaks of purple and bright pink that clashed with her bright red lipstick and nail polish.

Her dark eyes had a faint tilt to them, hinting at an interesting ancestry. And those full lips with that small mole at the corner of her mouth made him wonder. . . . Better not go there.

He stepped out into the garden, breathing deeply to draw in the damp mist that was often part of a Seattle morning. It was the one thing that his new home had in common with his old one. What London didn't have were the towering peaks of the Cascades and the Olympics that framed the Puget Sound area. Then there was the impressive presence of Mt. Rainier, the snow-covered volcanic peak that served as a backdrop to the city itself.

He could come to like it here, provided the Dame and her Consort would trust him enough to do his job. If they couldn't, he'd be banished to serve the Dame at a distance, most likely from London or perhaps Scandinavia. His skin crawled as he remembered the sharp bite of Nordic winters.

Speaking of Europe, Grey needed to check in. Not that he wanted to, as tired as he was, but it was politic of him to do so. Pulling out his cell phone, he dialed the familiar number. After a handful of rings, the call clicked over to voicemail. Considering his mood, that was for the best.

"You wanted to know when I got back to Seattle. Now you know. So far, no new developments. E-mail me if you have any questions. I might even answer if the mood strikes me."

He hung up, thankful he didn't have to speak to a man he could barely tolerate. A common interest forced them to be civil, but it wouldn't last past the resolution of the current situation. That was just fine with Grey. Plus, he agreed with that old saying about keeping your friends close and your enemies closer.

"Greyhill, I hadn't heard you were back!"

He automatically snapped to attention as he turned to face the new Grand Dame of the Kyth, Kerry Thorsen. His training demanded he bow to honor his ruler, but he held himself back. Kerry had made it clear that she preferred a more casual relationship with her

Talions than her predecessor had. Besides, courtly behavior seemed out of place when the Dame was wearing a faded T-shirt and jeans that had more than one hole in them.

The radical change in the royal court was only one of many things Grey struggled to come to terms with since the death of their previous ruler. Although Dame Judith had chosen to live out her last years in the Pacific Northwest, she'd kept many of the customs that had held her in good stead for the thousand-plus years of her reign. The entire Kyth world had been rocked by the combined shock of her death and her choice of successor. It was that last one that had brought Grey to Seattle in the first place.

"Grey?"

The puzzled note in Kerry's voice made him realize that he'd been staring at her. He shook his head to clear it.

"I'm sorry, Dame Kerry. After a long, hectic trip, I'm afraid I'm not back up to full speed yet. Please let me take those flowers for you." He looked around, searching the garden for some sign of her guards. "Where is everybody? Are you alone out here?"

"For once." Kerry smiled as she handed Grey the basket of roses. She stripped off her gardening gloves and dropped them, along with her pruning shears, on the table beside the door.

"I believe Ranulf is out hunting down some parts for his pet Packard. Sandor has taken the kids shopping before they head to the airport to meet Lena's flight. I don't expect them back before dinner tonight."

Grey still studied the garden behind her. "May I ask where you left your guard?" Discreet was one thing; invisible was quite another.

She shrugged, obviously not concerned. "Sandor mentioned something about assigning someone to follow me around. I told him not to bother."

Bloody hell. Sandor shouldn't have allowed her the option of refusing. It was the duty of the Talions to protect the Dame. If Kerry wouldn't let them stay nearby, how were they supposed to keep her safe?

"I will ensure any guards assigned to you will be as unobtrusive as possible."

"But I've never needed one before." Kerry wrinkled her nose and frowned. "Well, unless you count when Ranulf and Sandor get it in their heads to hover."

"We're all concerned for your safety, my lady."

"I'll think about it," she said dismissively. But that was all right—he could be stubborn, too.

Kerry started toward the house. "You must be tired. Why don't you come in and have a seat while I get those flowers in water?"

As they stepped inside, she asked, "Care to join me for an early lunch?"

Since it gave him the perfect excuse to stand guard over her, Grey didn't hesitate. "Gladly. Why don't I let Hughes know?"

"Thanks. I'll wash up and grab a vase."

Kerry disappeared down the hall toward her private quarters while Grey cursed under his breath.

Damn it all! What was Sandor thinking? No matter what Kerry thought, the Talions should stand guard 24/7 to protect the Grand Dame of the Kyth. Like it or not, Kerry was the ruler of their people, one of the few to possess the rare combination of powers that qualified her for the job.

Her ability to heal was crucial to the well-being of those who served her. By all reports, Kerry also wielded an impressive arsenal of combat gifts, but even she wasn't impervious to attack.

She needed to be protected. Not everyone was thrilled that she'd ascended the throne. Most of the American Kyth simply seemed curious, but some of their Old World kindred were fuming. They'd had their own plans for the succession, and Kerry wasn't what they'd had in mind.

A small but vocal faction claimed that Judith had meant to give Kerry her memories only as a temporary measure to keep them from being lost forever. If Kerry didn't step down soon, they might very well attempt to take matters into their own hands.

Well, Grey would certainly be having words with Sandor. Granted, the Dame *was* married to Ranulf Thorsen, a powerful Talion in his own right. The Viking was perfectly capable of protecting Kerry by himself, but only if he was actually *with* her. When Ranulf couldn't be by her side, another Talion should be. Dame Judith had slacked off on security and look where that had gotten her: murdered by a Talion warrior who'd gone renegade.

Ranulf and Sandor had obviously let Kerry have her way too often. As Chief Talion, it was Grey's honor and his duty to keep her safe. Now if she'd just trust him enough to let him to do his job.

For the time being, he'd use the chance to share a meal as an excuse to remain close by until Ranulf could take over. Grey sought out the butler requested a pot of Earl Grey tea and something to eat for them both. When he returned to the dining room, Kerry was already busy arranging her flowers.

"Hughes will be in shortly."

"Good. I'm famished." She shoved the last rose into the vase and stood back to admire her handiwork. "Perfect."

To Grey, the arrangement looked a bit haphazard, but his Dame looked pleased with her efforts. She buried her face in the blossoms and drew a deep breath, then set the vase on the sideboard before sitting at the table.

"So how was your trip, Grey? I had expected you would be gone longer. I hope you didn't rush things on my account."

Was she disappointed that he'd returned so quickly, or only surprised? It was hard to know, but he suspected she'd have been just as happy to have him stay gone indefinitely.

"London was London, so it rained much of the time I was there. There wasn't much to do, other than shut off the utilities and close up my flat. I've arranged to have my things shipped to Seattle, which means I'll have to start looking for a permanent place to live. Until then, I've extended my reservation at the hotel."

Kerry frowned. "Wouldn't you be more comfortable staying here at the house? We've plenty of room."

Kerry's offer seemed sincere, but he couldn't imagine that she'd want another guest imposing on her hospitality. She and Ranulf had recently taken in three Kyth teenagers whom Sandor had rescued from living on the streets.

"I appreciate the offer, but you already have enough extra mouths to feed. How is that going, by the way?"

"It's been an adjustment for all of us, but especially for the kids. Sean and Tara have been on their own for years, so they're not used to taking orders from anyone. God knows, they've had little reason to trust the adults in their lives."

Her smile looked a bit rueful. "Kenny is definitely a handful. He wasn't happy when we told him he had to go back to school, especially since he'll need tutoring to catch up. We're looking into online programs for the older two so they can earn their high school diplomas. After that, who knows?"

Hughes appeared in the doorway with a heavily laden tray. "Ma'am, shall I serve?"

Kerry shook her head. "No, just leave the tray. We'll take it from there."

The butler looked a bit disappointed but did as Kerry asked. Evidently Grey wasn't the only one who would appreciate a little more formality around the place. He wondered how Hughes felt about the newest additions to the household. The teenagers must present a variety of challenges.

Did those three kids have any idea how lucky they were? According to the laws of their people, Kerry would've been within her rights to have ordered them executed for the way they'd been stripping life energy from ordinary humans. Instead, Sandor had convinced the new Dame that mercy should also be part of Kyth law.

Grey didn't necessarily disagree, but he wondered if Kerry's decision had been driven by compassion or cowardice. Only time would tell. For now, he could only watch and wait.

Piper froze. She'd been on her way to get the Dame's signature on a stack of papers only to realize that Kerry talking to Greyhill Danby. She was in no mood to deal with *him* again. Their earlier encounter had been more than enough.

Especially if he started asking a bunch of questions she couldn't afford to answer. She certainly didn't want him to start poking around. Her references and paperwork had stood up well enough to Sandor's inquiries, but she suspected he hadn't looked all that hard. Between the three kids he'd rescued and Lena's whirlwind trip to the East Coast, he'd been distracted.

She checked her watch. Another fifteen minutes and she'd be done for the day. If the bus gods smiled on her, she'd even have time to grab a lunch before heading to class. This was one of her long days; she put several hours working for Kerry, followed by the three classes she was taking to finish her degree.

That thought brightened her mood considerably. She'd be twenty-eight on her next birthday, and she was finally going to graduate. It had been a long haul, but the end was in sight.

Deciding the signatures could wait until tomorrow, she returned back to the office and put the papers into a bright red folder labeled with Kerry's name. If something came up after Piper left, Kerry would know where to look for the documents amidst the clutter.

That had her grinning. She bet Greyhill was an "everything in its place" kind of guy and her clutter would drive him crazy. Poor man, it wasn't like he had any choice about sharing his office. For an instant she considered straightening up a bit before leaving, but rejected the idea. If Greyhill Danby didn't like the mess on her desk, he could get over it.

She logged off the computer and snagged her backpack off the floor. After flipping off the lights, she charged out into the hall toward the front door, only to bounce off a obstacle that hadn't been there a few minutes before.

She stumbled backward and was rescued at the last second when Grey latched onto her arms and jerked her back upright. Despite his obvious impatience, his hands were gentle. She knew she should apologize for almost knocking him down, but her brain and her mouth were seriously out of sync when she spoke.

"Are your eyes really that amazing shade of blue or do you wear contacts?"

Her face flushed hot and then cold as his eyebrows shot up in surprise.

"Thank you for noticing, and yes, they're actually that blue. Do you always say the first thing that pops into your mind Ms. Ryan?"

"I try not to. I'm sorry I ran into you. I've got class."

Okay, that came out wrong. She tried again, hoping to make more sense, but the warmth of his hands against her skin had her brain firing on only half its cylinders.

"What I meant to say is that I'm running late for my classes at the university. But that's no excuse for running down an innocent man."

Those blue eyes suddenly warmed up about a hundred degrees, and his stern lips softened as he smiled. At that moment, innocent was hardly the word to describe Greyhill Danby. Good golly, the man was compelling enough when he was angry. She didn't know what she'd do if he turned out to be charming, too.

His hands dropped away from her arms, leaving her missing his touch as he stepped out of her way.

"You mentioned something about leaving."

Piper blinked twice. "What? Oh. Yeah. I was. Excuse me, please."

She walked down the hallway, feeling his gaze following her each step of the way. It was hard not to turn around and catch him watching.

Just as she was about to turn the corner, a phone

rang. She looked back to see Greyhill flipping his cell open.

His eyes flickered in her direction, and just that quickly, every vestige of warmth disappeared from his expression. He muttered something into the phone and then stared at her until she gave up and walked away.

What was that all about? It wasn't as if she had a burning desire to eavesdrop on his all-important phone call.

She stalked out into the bright sunshine. She was under enough stress working as Kerry's assistant without having to deal with a man who ran hot and cold. She didn't understand him, and wasn't sure she wanted to. Right now she had more important things to do than waste her time thinking about Greyhill Danby.

Piper walked down the street to wait for the bus. Thanks to her encounter with Grey, she'd just missed the last one and had at least twenty minutes to kill before the next arrived. She sat on the bench and pulled out her European history text. Although she was majoring in business, she'd taken the class as an elective.

Today's lecture was on the Vikings. She was having a great time reading up on the adventures of her boss's husband back in the day. There was no mention of Ranulf by name, of course, but he'd definitely been there. She didn't know him well enough to ask him about it; but one of these days she'd corner him and demand some answers.

Heck, maybe she could even use his experiences to write a paper on the true story of his particular tribe leaving Scandinavia. Not that the Kyth would ever let her publish it; they were far too secretive about their existence to allow that.

She stared at the pictures of the artifacts in the book and wondered how people who had created such beautiful things could also have waged war with such passion. But that wasn't a topic she'd take up with Ranulf Thorsen. Nor was *her* past.

He and Kerry had no idea why she'd really sought them out, and she wasn't about to tell them. It was enough that they'd accepted her as one of their kind, even if she wasn't pure-blooded Kyth. The fact that Kerry had offered her a part-time job had just been a bonus.

Although waiting for Sandor to check out her resume had definitely been nerve-wracking, Piper had passed muster. But now that Greyhill Danby had returned, she prayed he didn't get it into his head to do some checking on his own. Sandor might have allowed her to disappear from Kerry's life as quickly as she'd appeared; however, Danby didn't seem to be the type to let someone off that easily. He'd keep digging and digging until he knew the truth.

And that was something she couldn't afford. Not now. Not yet. Maybe not *ever*.

She forced her attention back to the page in front of her. She'd started taking college classes before she'd even graduated from high school, never expecting it would take her so long to finish her degree. She'd always had to fit classes in around her work schedule as she struggled to keep a roof over her head and meals on the table, but the end was finally in sight.

She liked to think her mother would have been proud of her, but it was impossible to guess what her father would have thought. He'd disappeared from her life too long ago for her to have any memories of him.

She ran her finger down the page, looking for where she'd left off. She was quickly drawn into the world the historian described. Picturing Ranulf Thorsen rather than some nameless barbarian helped bring the history alive for her. She was lost in it, and it took her several seconds to notice the purr of a well-tuned engine as it slowed to a stop right in front of her.

When she did look up, she admired the classic lines of the Jaguar before checking out the driver.

Rats! What was *he* doing there? Hadn't their paths crossed enough for one day?

When Grey rolled down the window, Piper shoved her textbook back into her pack and approached the car. She bent down to look in the window.

"Did you need something, Mr. Danby?"

"I thought you might like a ride to the university. I'm going right by there."

He broke off eye contact and stared out the windshield, looking as if he already regretted the offer. Well, he wasn't the only one who had qualms about the two of them being alone in a car together. But her mother hadn't raised her to be a coward.

"I'd love a ride if you're sure it's no inconvenience." She reached for the door handle before he could respond.

She'd barely fastened her seatbelt when he hit the gas hard. Piper braced herself and settled back to enjoy the ride.

Chapter 2

_G_rey glanced at Piper, not quite sure why he was driving her to school. He would like to know how much of his phone call she'd overheard, but he tried not to lie to himself about the reasons behind his decisions, even impulsive ones.

He was pretty sure Piper had been well on her way out of the house before he'd gotten down to the nitty-gritty with Harcourt. Maybe he should've curbed his tongue, but the prick could've given Grey time to settle in before pressing him for details. Granted, Harcourt had good reason to take the ascension of Kerry Thorsen harder than most, but what was done was done.

Now wasn't the time to think about that. He turned his attention to the much more intriguing problem sitting next to him.

"I assume you're going to the main campus."

Piper sat with her eyes at half-mast, a soft smile drawing his attention to her beauty mark. He tried not to think about how kissable that mouth looked, with limited success. She wasn't his type but that didn't seem to matter.

She nodded. "Yes, you can drop me anywhere on Forty-fifth. I can walk from there."

"I can do better than that, Ms. Ryan. Just tell me where you need to go."

"If you're sure you don't mind, turn in the main gate and then I'll show you from there."

She gave him a puzzled look. "Why are you doing this? I got the impression earlier that you weren't exactly pleased to find me ensconced in our office."

"You mean *my* office." He softened the correction with the merest hint of a smile.

"Which it will be again, Mr. Danby," she shot back. "If you hadn't instantly gone on the attack, I would've explained. Two of the rooms on the second floor are being remodeled into offices for Dame Kerry and me, which is why I'm in your office and she's using the dining room. Once everything is done and the new furniture arrives, I'll be moving out of your space. Sandor was hoping you wouldn't be back quite so soon."

Piper frowned. "That came out wrong. I didn't mean he was hoping you wouldn't come back, just that sharing the office wouldn't be a problem."

Or maybe the Dame was having second thoughts about assigning him to work here in Seattle. Had they heard the rumblings of discontent from the European

Kyth and assumed he felt the same? Well, it wouldn't be the first time he'd had to prove himself.

Right now he wasn't thinking all that clearly. He was too busy wondering how it would feel to kiss Piper before she got out of the car. When she gave him a suspicious look, he quickly banked the fires.

She sat up straighter and put her pack on her lap. "You can let me out at the next building."

He pulled over to the curb and stopped. "I suppose I'll see you tomorrow in my office."

"Don't you mean in *our* office?" Piper laughed as she opened the door. She met his gaze with a twinkle in her dark eyes. "Nice car, by the way. It fits you."

"How so?"

She ran her fingers along edge of the leather seat. "It's all sleek lines and class on the surface."

"And beneath the surface?"

"There's a monster of an engine, ready to run down the competition."

She paused clearly waffling about what she was going to say. "In your case, I suspect, underneath that cool exterior beats the heart of a warrior who takes his duty very seriously."

Then she was out of the car. "Thanks for the ride. I'll see you in the morning."

He watched her walk away, taking a long hard look *her* exterior. How much of her quirky style was designed to keep people from noticing her sharp mind? Maybe they had more in common than he thought.

For now, he was going to head back to the hotel for some much-needed sleep. First thing tomorrow, he would start on his growing to-do list—beginning with the puzzle of Piper Ryan.

Lawrence Harcourt paced the room. How dare Greyhill Danby hang up on him! And when he'd called the Talion back, all he'd gotten was voice mail. He knew Grey had just arrived in Seattle, but he could have at least provided a brief update on the situation.

He'd give the man a few days to report back. After that, he'd start the plan in motion himself. The thought of treason didn't sit well with him, but someone had to take a stand before that woman became too firmly entrenched as Grand Dame.

"Father? Is something wrong?"

Lawrence schooled his features before turning to face his daughter. "Not at all, Adele. A minor setback in a business dealing. Nothing for you to worry about."

"If you say so," she replied with a smile.

She resembled her mother so much. He couldn't believe that his daughter was now older than her late mother had been when he'd married her. Sophisticated for her age, Adele had made them both proud. Though she wore jeans and T-shirts to classes, as all the young people did these days, she always honored his request that she dress for dinner.

After pouring himself a drink, Harcourt sat on the sofa and patted the space beside him. "Please come tell me about your day while we wait for dinner."

She sat in one of chairs that faced the sofa instead, which surprised him. It was rare for Adele to defy him, even in such a small way. Yet there was nothing in her expression to suggest she was unhappy with him, so he let it go. He spent so much time trying to outmaneuver his competitors that he sometimes forgot not everyone always had an ulterior motive.

"How are your classes at University going?" he asked when she didn't immediately speak.

"Boring," she answered with a note of amusement in her voice. "You know how much I love higher mathematics—not! Although even that's better than memorizing all the Kyth bloodlines in my spare time. I really don't see why I need to know who among us has the same great-great-great-great grandmother."

Harcourt gave her the same answer he always did. "Because knowledge is power, especially among our kind. Knowing those connections and loyalties helps predict how someone might react in any given situation."

Adele studied her manicure for several seconds. "And why is that important for *me?* It's not like your business interests only involve other Kyth."

"No, but when you're—" he started to say, but she was already shaking her head. "What?"

"Father, I know you're disappointed that Grand Dame Judith chose someone else to succeed her, but what's done is done. My future lies elsewhere now."

Adele's words were spoken softly but with conviction. She kept her gaze on her lap, probably to keep him from seeing something in her eyes that she didn't think he'd like. Something like relief.

He fought down the rush of anger. His daughter had been groomed to ascend to the throne of Grand Dame from the moment her particular gifts had manifested themselves.

Granted, Adele didn't have exactly the same talents as the late Dame, but his daughter had come closer than anyone else had in a very long time. Her gifts, coupled with her impeccable bloodline, made her the obvious candidate. He'd even taken the family to Seattle every year to visit relatives, always making arrangements to call on the Dame and her Consort.

All those plans, all that work, and all for nothing. Now an upstart woman with no pedigree and no right had been declared Grand Dame. Not only that, but she'd managed to ensnare Ranulf Thorsen, which only proved the rumors he'd been hearing for years about the Viking's instability. That didn't explain Sandor Kearn's support of the Dame, though.

Maybe insanity was contagious.

"Father?"

He jerked himself back to the present. "I'm sorry, my dear. You've been most gracious about what's happened. However, nothing is set in stone yet, so we need to continue as we began."

The look she shot his way was puzzling, but before he could pursue the matter any further, a servant appeared in the doorway.

"Excuse me, sir, but dinner is served."

"Thank you. We'll be right in." Harcourt stood up and offered his hand to his daughter. "Shall we?"

"Yes," she said, but she didn't sound happy about it, making him wonder if they were actually talking about dinner at all.

Grey checked the address Sandor had given him against the one on the building. He had the right place, but it certainly wasn't what he'd expected. The door opened and people filed out of the restaurant, bringing the scent of fresh bread and cinnamon along with them. His stomach rumbled. Inside, there wasn't an empty table in sight; hopefully it was a testament to the food.

Sandor stood up at a corner table long enough to catch Grey's attention.

When Grey reached him, Sandor poured him a cup of coffee and handed him a menu. "Good morning. Hope this isn't too early for you."

"Not at all. The eight hour time difference from London still has me a bit off schedule, but I'm adjusting." He studied the menu briefly. "What's good?"

"It's all good, but I always order the spinach and feta omelet with a basket of cinnamon rolls."

The waitress made her way to their table, her notepad at the ready. Grey kept it simple and followed Sandor's lead. As they waited for their meal, they made small talk about mutual friends over cups of the restaurant's special blend of dark roast coffee.

Grey took another sip, waiting for the jolt of caffeine to hit his bloodstream.

"Did Lena make it back all right? Dame Kerry

said you were picking her up at the airport yesterday."

Sandor nodded, clearly pleased by the return of his woman. "She may have to make another trip to finish up, but she got a lot done while she was there. The moving truck will be heading this way by the end of the week."

"I'm sure she'll be glad to stop living out of a suitcase. I know I'll be relieved when the rest of my things arrive."

The waitress came back carrying two plates piled high with food. By unspoken agreement, both men concentrated on their breakfasts. Grey knew after just one bite that he'd be back here soon, perhaps even becoming a regular at the café.

Finally, he pushed his plate away and sat back. "That hit the spot. Thanks for inviting me."

Sandor finished off the last bit of his eggs and then set his fork down. "Glad you liked it. I thought you might prefer to meet away from the Dame's house in case you had any questions."

"I appreciate it. I haven't really had a chance to look over the files you left for me, but I will today." He poured them each more coffee. "I did meet Piper Ryan yesterday though."

Sandor winced. "I'm sorry. I didn't think to warn you about her, but—"

"I know. You didn't expect me back so soon." He was tired of hearing that and let it show.

The other Talion got the message. "I've had a lot going on and let a few things slip. That shouldn't have been one of them."

"You've all been through a lot recently." Grey could afford to be gracious, and besides, he needed Sandor's cooperation on some of the changes he wanted to make.

Where to start? Maybe with the easy stuff.

"So how did Dame Kerry come to hire someone like Piper Ryan as an assistant?"

Damn, he didn't mean to sound like a snob, but there should be standards. A dress code at least. He wasn't above enjoying a short skirt when it showed off such fine legs, but first impressions counted.

He knew Kerry was on trial, even if the others didn't. She was now the head of several foundations dedicated to the education, health, and financial stability of her people. Every decision mattered if Kerry was going to solidify her position. And that included her staff.

Sandor said, "Piper called one day wanting to meet the Dame," said, "She'd recently found out about her own Kyth heritage and wanted to learn more. Since meeting with newly discovered Kyth has always been one of my principle duties, I talked to her first. When I brought her to the house to meet Kerry, the two of them hit it off. One thing led to another, and Kerry offered her the job."

"I assume her credentials checked out?"

"Yes, as far as they went. She's moved around a lot over the years, so there were stretches of time when she wasn't working."

Interesting, but not necessarily suspicious. "Did she say why she moved so often?"

"Apparently because of her mother's job. Even

when Piper was of legal age, she followed her mother because she was the only family Piper had. When her mom passed away, Piper used her inheritance to enroll at the university here to finish her business degree. She'll graduate after this quarter."

Sandor had reasonable answers for Grey's questions, but there was still something that didn't feel right. Maybe he was a suspicious bastard, but then that was his job. He'd have to do some checking of his own.

Now it was time to address another touchy subject. "I take it Dame Kerry didn't like the idea of having guards posted at all times?"

Sandor shook his head. "Hell, no. She did point out that Ranulf is with her most of the time. If the Viking can't keep her safe, no one can."

He gave Grey a considering look. "Something has you wanting to push for this. Mind telling me what it is?"

Grey knew he was treading on thin ice, but he had to let Sandor know where he stood. "Nothing specific, but I can't help thinking that we might not have lost Dame Judith to Bradan if she'd kept her Talion guards closer at hand."

His companion's face went stone cold. "Is that what everyone thinks? That Ranulf and I failed Judith?"

"No, we *all* failed her, Sandor. I wasn't there to protect her when she was taken, either. Even if she had allowed guards to be posted, you and Ranulf couldn't have done it all by yourselves. I don't want us to make the same mistake with Kerry Thorsen."

The tension eased in Sandor's expression. "Judith thought she was still strong enough to protect herself, but her powers started to fail when her Consort died. No one realized how bad things had gotten until it was too late. Even so, Judith could've held Bradan off until we got there, but she burned out most of her energy trying to save Josiah."

"I hadn't heard that part of the story," Grey admitted. It didn't really surprise him though. He'd always suspected that Josiah had been Judith's friend, not just her butler. Once on a visit to Seattle he'd dropped in unexpectedly to find them sitting on the sofa sharing a bowl of popcorn as they watched a baseball game.

"All the more reason to make sure Kerry is never put in the same position. What if someone attacked when she was alone with just those three kids? We could lose them all."

"Don't think I haven't thought about that possibility. It's right at the top of my worst nightmare list." Sandor sighed. "Kerry may have the same talents as Judith, but she's her own woman. She's been used to doing things for herself. Being responsible for so many people has been a major change for her. I think she fears losing what little independence she has left."

Grey laid his cards on the table. "I don't have to tell you that not everyone is pleased with Judith's choice of a replacement. I'm sure you've heard the rumors. As talented as Kerry is, she's still young and inexperienced, especially when it comes to ruling our kind. She wasn't even brought up in Kyth society."

Gold sparks flickered in Sandor's dark eyes. "Damn it, none of that should matter. She was Judith's choice for good reason. Kerry is the only one Judith ever found with the ability to serve as Dame." His voice rose. "You think Judith was strong in her heyday? Kerry can flatten both me *and* Ranulf at the same time. She played a major role in bringing Bradan down."

Sandor's anger was drawing attention, and the last thing they needed was for someone to notice the sparks flashing in the Talion's eyes or the dark energy roiling just under the surface of his fingertips.

Grey gave his companion a pointed look. "We're in public. Calm down."

Sandor immediately hid his hands in his lap and briefly closed his eyes. When they opened again, he was back in control.

"Grey, I know some people thought that the Harcourt girl would inherit the throne, and maybe she *was* Judith's fallback. But no matter what Adele Harcourt's old man thought, she has never tested anywhere near as high as Kerry does."

"I'd heard that." Right from Harcourt himself, but that didn't meant the man was going to back off anytime soon.

Grey checked his watch. "I appreciate your meeting with me, but I'd better go. As I get settled in, I'll be around the office more. Between you, me, and Ranulf, we should be able to keep Kerry safe, but I'd still feel better with someone patrolling the perimeter at all times."

"I'll talk to Kerry again. Maybe she'll at least consider posting a guard at night."

"Don't worry about it for now. I'll wait until I have a better grasp of things and then make my recommendations to her."

As they walked out the door together, Sandor grinned. "Good luck with that. She can be quite stubborn."

"That's all right. So am I."

All he could was present his plan for approval—and then do what needed to be done anyway, even if Kerry said no. Her life just might depend on it.

Piper paused for the third time in the last fifteen minutes, listening to see if the car outside was passing by or turning into the Dame's driveway. Not that she was holding her breath for Greyhill Danby to make an appearance.

Right—of course she was.

Their encounters yesterday had been unsettling to say the least. If he worked at his desk today, she'd have to spend hours alone in this closet of an office with him.

She'd gotten in early enough to straighten things up a bit. She'd even asked Hughes to bring in an electric tea kettle for Grey. As a peace offering, it wasn't much, but at least she'd tried.

The groan of the heavy iron gates rolling open out front caught her attention. She wouldn't stoop to peeking out the window, but it had to be him. Sandor wasn't expected in until sometime that afternoon.

The front door opened and closed, and footsteps were definitely heading Piper's way. She forced herself to keep working. A few seconds later a shadow fell across her desk, forcing her to look up.

"Good morning, Mr. Danby." She was proud of how calm she sounded.

He cocked his head to the side and studied her. "Mr. Danby is a bit formal, don't you think? My friends call me Grey. May I call you Piper?"

"Piper's fine." Then she mimicked his pose and gave him an impudent grin. "But since your friends use Grey, what should I call you?"

He laughed, sounding a bit rusty. "Cute. And here I'd hoped we were over that first rough patch." He held out a small box. "I also thought a little peace offering from a Brit to a colonist might be in order."

"Very cute, Grey." Then she recognized the restaurant's logo and immediately snatched the box from his hand. "I'll have to starve myself the rest of the day if I eat this, but some things are worth the sacrifice. Thank you."

"You're welcome."

"I put fresh water in the kettle if you'd like tea."

"Perfect. Would you like a cup, too? I brought in Darjeeling and a bit of Earl Grey."

"Either would be fine."

She forced her attention back to her computer, trying to ignore her companion. While he fixed the tea, she checked her morning e-mail. Because her work for Kerry required Piper to contact other Kyth, she'd struck up a few online friendships with people all over the world. It was a shame that she'd never get to meet any of them in person, though. Even if she could afford to travel, it was doubtful any of them would want to have anything to do with her if the truth ever came out. Actually, *when* the truth came out. She had no illusions that Grey was going to accept her story at face value.

"Bad news?"

She jumped about a foot and turned to glare at Grey. "Don't sneak up on people like that!"

He gave her a puzzled look and held out her tea. "I wasn't exactly sneaking. I saw how hard you were staring at the screen and wondered if something was wrong."

She forced a smile. "Seems we spend a lot of time apologizing to each other. Sorry, Grey, I didn't mean to snap. And no, it isn't exactly bad news. Just complicated."

"Let me know if I can help." He set the steaming mug next to her computer and returned to his desk.

Sharing a workspace with someone else normally didn't bother her, but now she was hyperaware of every move the man made. The faint scent of his after-shave was even more of a distraction. She'd never get through the morning's work at this rate. Hoping that listening to music would help, she pulled her iPod out of her bag and cranked it up.

Piper scanned her long list of e-mails, making note of the ones she'd need to discuss with Kerry. The rest she either deleted or stuck in a folder to deal with later. Finally, she reached the bottom of the page.

How odd. The Kyth all had e-mail accounts with the same server, but this last one didn't match.

She clicked to open it, and her computer screen went black. A few seconds later, it filled with a pulsating pattern.

Had she just downloaded a virus? Then she realized that the dizzying display was made up of one phrase written over and over again. Her blood ran cold as she shoved her chair back. The words were written in blood red against a black background.

"Uh, Grey, could you come here a minute?"

Damn it, he'd finally been making some headway in a stack of files from when Piper suddenly shot back from her desk, knocking a pile of papers to the floor in the process. His first instinct was to grumble, but then he saw the look on her face.

He might not know Piper all that well, but he'd bet his last dollar that she wasn't easily scared. And right now her face was undeniably pale.

When she turned to face him, a ring of white showed all around her dark irises. Years of training had him reaching for the gun in his shoulder harness, even though his Talion senses didn't detect any immediate physical threat.

"Piper, what's wrong?"

She held out a shaky finger and pointed at her computer screen. "Can you look at this?"

He moved closer. The red and black color scheme made it difficult to read the text. But before he could ask any questions, the screen blinked off. When it came back on, an error message flashed, saying the computer was searching for a solution. He was willing to bet that when it rebooted, there would be no record of what had been written there.

But he'd seen it and so had Piper. Written there in bloodred words, over and over again, were the words: *The day of reckoning is coming.*

Chapter 3

*G*rey holstered his gun and stood back, still trying to make sense of what he'd just seen. "I don't suppose that's one of your friends' sick idea of a joke?"

Piper looked insulted. "Of course not. First of all, I don't use this account for my personal correspondence. I've never given out the address except on behalf of the Dame and her foundations. Secondly, the e-mail address was weird. I've never seen it before."

"Weird how?"

"It's not from the usual e-mail account we all use. As soon as I saw it, I wondered if something was wrong."

"But you opened it anyway." He probably would have too, but he wanted to know what she'd been thinking.

She ran her fingers through her hair, clearly frustrated. "Yes, and maybe I shouldn't have, but I was more curious than worried. Sandor says our system is hacker proof."

"I don't doubt that, but we both know no system is totally safe from attack when someone knows what he's doing and is determined to get in."

He was glad to see some of the color returning to Piper's face. "Why don't you run a full scan on your system while I check my e-mail? Maybe we all got the same message."

"Good idea." Just that quickly, Piper was back to business, but he noted that her fingers hovered over the keys, hesitating before she started typing.

Grey returned to his own computer and did a quick check of his e-mail. Nothing odd there. Next he'd check in with Kerry and Ranulf to see if they'd received anything similar. The cryptic message was clearly a threat. But with no indication for whom it was intended, it was impossible to know how seriously to take it or who might need additional protection.

Piper's reaction had been genuine, if perhaps a bit extreme. It was impossible to tell if she knew more than she was letting on. He tended to think not, or else why would she show the e-mail to him? Too many questions and too few answers. After lunch, when she was gone, he'd start digging into her past. Although part of him wanted to accept her at face value and not delve too deeply, he'd do his job. When he finished, there wouldn't be much about her he didn't know.

"I'll be back in a few minutes, Piper. Yell if something else happens. And let me know what the virus scan shows. I need to check in with Dame Kerry."

"Okay." Piper took a healthy swig of her tea. "I probably overreacted, but that was just so strange. If I find out who did this, I'll show *them* a reckoning."

"I'd pay to see that." He resisted the urge to pat her on the shoulder on his way out. "I'd appreciate it if we kept the specifics of that e-mail between us for now. If it is just a prank, there's no use in getting everyone in an uproar. I'll check with Kerry and Ranulf, though, to see if they've had any problems."

Piper frowned. "All right, but if it happens again, I need to tell Kerry."

"Agreed."

Basking in sunshine, Kerry moved down the row deadheading her favorite roses, stealing a short break from her paperwork. She planned to prune one last stretch before tackling that stack of correspondence piled high on the dining room table. By then, Hughes would have had time to sort the day's mail, so she had that to look forward to as well. *Great.*

When the sliding door opened, she cut another wilted rose and dropped it in her basket before looking up. She'd hoped it was Ranulf, but it was Grey. She hid her disappointment and studied her new Chief Talion.

"Good morning, Grey. How are you settling in?" Something about him made her think he'd never really left the military. Despite his casual sports shirt and khaki pants, he always carried himself as if he were still in uniform. She knew he thought he should bow in her presence and only held back because he knew she wasn't comfortable with such gestures.

"Better, thanks. I met Sandor for breakfast at a wonderful local café this morning, so that got today off to a good start."

"That's great. I'm sure he can give you lots of pointers about the area."

Grey's eyes maintained a constant surveillance of their surroundings. "It's nice that you've kept up the rose garden. It's always been quite a showplace; Dame Judith took great pride in it."

Kerry dropped another handful of rose petals in her basket and looked around. "I'm pretty new at this, but I've consulted a local master gardener on what to do when. I'm thinking about adding a stone bench and fountain in the far corner in Judith's memory. You know, a quiet place to read and enjoy the flowers."

He nodded in approval. "She would've liked that."

Grey silently trailed behind Kerry as she moved from bush to bush. Then she looked back and noticed the lines of tension bracketing his mouth. No doubt her time out here in the garden was about to end.

No use in beating around the bush, rose or otherwise. "Do you want to tell me what's wrong, Grey?"

He took her basket and carried it as they walked back toward the house. "Probably nothing, but someone tried to send Piper a virus or something attached to a strange e-mail. I was wondering if you'd had any similar problems with your computer today."

"I haven't logged on yet, but I was about to head that way. Is Piper's computer all right?"

"She was running a scan when I left her. You might want to do the same." He hesitated and then added, "Or I could do it for you."

He wanted to go messing around in her personal files? "No, that's okay. I'll check my morning messages and then set the system to run a full scan."

"All right. If you need me I'll be my office. I would appreciate knowing if the problem is more widespread than just Piper's computer."

Those fierce blue eyes saw too much, including her reluctance to let him do what was probably just his job. If it had been Sandor making the offer, she wouldn't have hesitated.

Grey hadn't said a word, but she knew she had insulted him without meaning to. Eventually she would have to give him a chance to prove himself and his loyalty. Maybe it was time to get started on that.

"You know, I have several phone calls I need to make this morning. If you have time, perhaps you should run a scan on Ranulf's laptop, as well as mine, since you know what you're looking for. If you're sure you don't mind, that is."

His expression remained distant and chilly. "Not at all. If you'll log on, I'll take it from there. I won't open any of your personal correspondence unless I see an e-mail address similar to the one Piper received. After that, I'll run a complete scan."

Maybe it was time for some frank conversation. "Grey, I know I'm not Judith, nor do I want to be.

I've been on my own since my teens, and it's difficult for me to ask others to do what I'm used to doing myself. I'm still learning to delegate."

His ice blue eyes warmed up several degrees. "I'm afraid I have tendencies in that direction myself."

She grinned and looped her arm through Grey's, surprising them both. "Should make for an interesting working relationship, don't you think?"

He managed a small smile. "I'm sure it will."

The seed was planted. Let them stew over that one for a while. Eventually they'd decide it had been a fluke or maybe even a prank. Then it would be time to launch the next salvo, this time aimed at one of the Dame's most trusted employees. Or better yet, the one who was working so hard to get himself in Kerry's good graces.

That could be fun.

Certainly the attacks would be more effective if they came from multiple directions. If done properly, the Dame and her friends all be spinning in circles and pointing fingers at each other. Since one Talion had gone renegade, it wouldn't take much to convince everyone that it had happened again. Imagine losing two Dames in such a short time.

Such a tragedy. So sad.

It would be a shame to destroy Greyhill Danby. He'd always been a decent sort, but he'd crossed over to the enemy camp. He should have reported in regarding the new Dame's incompetence by now. Instead, nothing but silence. No doubt his overdeveloped sense of duty was getting in the way.

As far as the others, it was widely known that the Viking warrior Ranulf had long been poised to make the leap into full-blown insanity, likely brought on by extreme old age. That he'd mated with the usurper was only further proof of his instability.

But Sandor Kearn's stalwart support of Kerry Thorsen shouldn't have come as a bit of shock. He'd always been charming, all glitz and little substance. Then he'd refused to carry out an execution order, and instead dragged those three mongrels home for Kerry and Ranulf to raise. Purebreds would've been one thing, but mutts? Had they no sense of dignity?

Obviously not.

Time was of the essence, of course, considering the damage being done to the noble heritage of their people. Even so, the destruction the ones conspiring against the legitimate heir required a great deal of care. Once everything was in place, execution of the plan would be fast and swift.

Execution. The word had such a nice ring to it.

Tick tock, they were on the clock.

Too bad they didn't know it.

Grey still hadn't returned from his meeting with Kerry. What was taking him so long? Piper wanted to know if anyone else had gotten the bizarre e-mail, and she was almost off for the day. She'd feel better if she knew she could write the whole thing off as a hiccup in the system.

Maybe it wouldn't hurt to go looking for Grey. If she hurried, she could talk to him and still catch the next bus. She collected the morning's correspondence and slung her book bag over her shoulder. She headed toward the dining room where Kerry did most of her paperwork.

As usual, there were papers scattered all over the table, but Kerry was nowhere in sight. Only Grey sat at the table with two laptops open in front of him, his attention focused on the screens.

"How did the scan go?"

She hadn't realized that he'd noticed her. "All clear. No sign of any damage and no record of the e-mail itself. How is that even possible?"

"I don't know, but I'll find out." He looked up at her. "You're the only one who received it."

Was that accusation in his voice? She gathered her resolve. She was probably just overreacting—again. Darn the man, why did he bring that out in her? There was something about him that made her feel as if he was constantly judging her.

"Look, next time I see Sandor, I'll ask him to do his computer mumbo jumbo on my system. Maybe he can solve the case of the disappearing e-mail."

"No need to bother him with it. I'll see what the scans turn up on the rest of the computers after lunch." He stood up. "Speaking of which, want to grab a bite? I can drop you off at school after."

Okay, *that* she hadn't expected.

"I don't want to inconvenience you, Grey. I can take the bus and get something at school."

"It's up to you." He shrugged before adding, "But I'm going out for lunch anyway, and the university is on the way."

It was difficult enough sharing an office with him. Being in his car again—not to mention sharing a meal—would be even harder. When she didn't answer, he grinned mischievously.

"What's the matter, Piper? Afraid I'll bite?"

Afraid that he *wouldn't* was closer to the truth. The smart thing would be to politely turn him down, but evidently she wasn't feeling all that bright.

"Let me write a quick note for Kerry on a couple of these letters, and I'll be ready to go."

"Either you bribed someone or you are the luckiest man alive. No one finds a parking space this easily in the University District."

Grey gave Piper a look that was just short of a smirk. "Timing is everything."

"Right. Maybe that works for you, but I take the bus because I'm so tired of circling the block a dozen times looking for a place to park."

Grey parallel parked with disgusting ease. If she had been behind the wheel, she would've had to take at least a couple shots at it before she got close enough to the curb.

As he locked up the car, Piper studied the nearby

restaurants. She wasn't picky, but somehow she didn't see him appreciating the places that catered to the local college students. Cheap and greasy didn't seem to fit the image Grey projected, even if he'd dressed more casually today.

"Sandor recommended a deli up the block. He was spot on about the place we ate breakfast, so we'll see if he's as good with lunch."

She fell into step beside Grey. "If it's bad, we can always make him reimburse us."

"Somehow I don't see that happening. But I am supposed to join him and Ranulf for one of their workouts this week. I can always forget to pull a few punches. Ranulf might even help."

Grey kept surprising her. If it weren't for the way his eyes crinkled at the corners, she would have thought he was dead serious. She found it hard to picture him pounding on Sandor, but the Talions were the warrior class, and he had reached for his gun when she got that e-mail. She'd never spent time around men who carried concealed weapons before and wasn't sure how she felt about it.

From day one, she'd found both Sandor and Ranulf easy to talk to. She liked the way they treated Kerry and Lena, as well as the three kids. Grey was a different story though. Oh, there was no mistaking that he could be charming when he wanted to be, but those predator's eyes saw too much and could go from summer sky blue to arctic ice in a heartbeat.

"We're here." Grey snagged her by the strap of her pack and pulled her to a sudden stop.

"Sorry, I wasn't paying attention."

He held the door open for her. "You're thinking awfully hard about something. Want to share?"

Uh, no. That wasn't going to happen, not now and not ever. She settled for an easy lie. "I have a test today." That much was true.

They walked up to the counter and studied the menu on the wall. They placed their orders, and Grey led her to a small table in the back corner. After setting his drink down, he turned the table slightly and chose the seat that put his back to the wall and offered the best view of the small restaurant. She'd noticed Sandor do the same thing before. The possibility of an attack was never far from their minds.

When they were both seated, Grey asked, "In what subject?"

It took her a second to realize he was asking about her test. "European history."

"Is that your major?"

"No, actually. My degree will be in business, but I had room for one more elective. I love history, and the professor really makes it come to life."

"Why European?"

His eyes darted cautiously around the room, yet his attention was somehow still focused on her. She wasn't used to having anyone care that much about what she was doing or why.

"I wanted to learn more about my own ancestry, I guess. And then there's the fact that growing up I read everything I could about ancient warriors—knights, highlanders, Celts, and let's not forget the Vikings."

She leaned closer and made a pretense of making sure no one was listening. "Don't tell Ranulf, but I keep looking for his name to show up in a textbook."

Grey chuckled. "Good luck with that. He hasn't lived this long without knowing something about hiding in plain sight, but let me know if you find anything."

When their number was called, Grey went to pick up their sandwiches, which turned out to be every bit as good as Sandor had promised.

"So, tell me. Should I be looking for Greyhill Danby in my textbooks as well?" she asked as they threw out their garbage. She wasn't sure he was going to answer, but when they walked out into the bright sunshine he finally did. Sort of.

"That depends on the time period you're covering in class." He unlocked the car door for her.

His expression was completely deadpan, leaving her no clue about whether he was serious. Searching for him could be a fool's errand, but she might give it a try. She always loved a challenge.

Lunch had been a nice interlude between the upsetting morning and what would most likely be a tense afternoon as she squeezed in one last study session before her test. At least Grey had proved to be an enjoyable companion, letting his guard down enough to seem younger and more approachable. It was nice.

But then he pulled the car over at the same place where he'd dropped her off the day before.

"So Piper, mind telling me why you wanted to insinuate yourself in the Dame's household?"

Her stomach lurched as if the Jag had just plunged down a sudden dip on a roller coaster.

"That's a rather loaded question, don't you think?"

Before he could respond, she held up her fingers and counted off the points. "Let's see, Kerry and I met and really hit it off. She needs an assistant, one who's good with numbers and has a background in accounting. I need a job that is flexible enough to work around my classes. It's as simple as that. Nothing sinister, no hidden agendas."

She was proud of how calm she sounded even while lying through her teeth.

"Now if you'll excuse me, I don't want to be late."

Grey had deliberately waited to spring the question on Piper, figuring he'd get as much out of her reaction as he would her actual answer. He watched her stalk away, her temper showing in each step.

So, that went well. Not only did he piss off Piper, but he ruined his own good mood at the same time. Damn, it was easy to forget himself when he was with her. He was the new security officer, responsible for making sure the Dame was safe from anyone who might wish her harm. Even Piper.

Instead, he couldn't keep his mind off the angry brunette who'd just disappeared into the building without looking back. Even if she were his type—which she most definitely wasn't—it was far too soon to be wondering how that smart mouth of hers would taste. Maybe it was an indication that he'd been too long without someone to share his bed.

Nothing more.

He slammed the car into gear, and with an apology to his poor clutch, he peeled out of the university driveway and headed for the interstate. He knew he should get back to the office, but right now he needed to let off steam more. Getting Piper Ryan in bed was out of the question for a lot of reasons, so he'd have to make do with tearing up the highway for an hour or two.

"Gee, Grey, that must have been some lunch." Sandor leaned against the doorframe, a knowing smile on his face. "Or did you get lost driving back here from the deli?"

"Go to hell, Sandor. Or at least go somewhere else. I've got work to do."

Grey kept his eyes on his computer screen. Sandor was no fool and damned good at reading people. The last thing Grey needed was for Sandor to think something was going on.

But instead of leaving, Sandor strolled on in and sat down at Piper's desk.

"Kerry tells me that you and Piper had some sort of computer glitch this morning. Need any help with that?"

Grey's first instinct was to say no, but he hadn't been able to get anywhere in tracing the origins of the e-mail. Maybe Sandor would have better luck. He had to trust *somebody*.

Grey drew a deep breath and turned to face Sandor. "I told Kerry that Piper thought someone tried to send her a virus. Which is true, but there's more to it. The e-mail came from an unknown address, one that didn't fit the usual format. Rather than delete it, Piper opened it."

"Not necessarily the wisest choice, but I probably would have done the same thing." Sandor leaned forward, resting his elbows on his knees. "So what happened when it opened?"

"According to Piper, the whole system blanked out for several seconds. When it came back up, the screen had a black background and was covered with one phrase written over and over in red."

Sandor might have a reputation for being charming, but only a fool would miss the intelligence behind that easy smile.

"What did it say?"

Grey dropped the bombshell. *"The day of reckoning is coming."*

Sandor's smile disappeared immediately. "Son of a bitch! What's that supposed to mean? Well, beyond the obvious threat."

"I don't know—yet. But don't worry, I *will* find out."

The gold sparks flickering in Sandor's eyes matched the blue flames in Grey's own. Too bad neither of them had a solid target for their aggression.

"It gets stranger. The message startled Piper and

before I could do more than take a quick look, the screen went blank again. And then the e-mail was gone."

"You mean you couldn't open the message again?"

"No, I mean it was literally gone. It's like the damned thing never existed. I was going to dig deeper when you came in."

"I don't like this." Sandor studied Piper's computer. "I assume she ran a complete scan?"

It wasn't really a question. "First thing. I also ran one on my computer, and then on Kerry's and Ranulf's. No weird e-mails, no viruses."

"Okay, I'll check Piper's system myself."

"Do you need me to get you in?"

Sandor's fingers were already dancing over the keys. "Nope. I set you up with the authority to override any security protocols, but I kept mine as well. I was going to have you change it when you got back, but maybe we should hold off for the moment."

Piper wasn't going to like having the two of them messing around in her files, but too bad. "Let me know what you find or if you need any help."

"Will do."

Half an hour passed with the click and clatter of computer keys filling the air, punctuated only by Sandor muttering obscenities whenever he got frustrated. Grey knew how he felt and added his own curses to the litany. He kept coming up with nothing. The e-mail could've been a prank, but his gut was telling him otherwise.

He was about to give up and heave the CPU

against the wall when Sandor sat up straight and said, "Well, I'll be damned. Grey, you need to look at this."

"Did you find it?"

"Yes, and I also found who sent it." The gold flames were back again, and dark swirls of energy flowed under the skin on Sandor's hand as he pointed at the screen.

"I can't read it from here, and I'm in no mood for games. Who sent the damned thing?"

Sandor pointed at the screen. "According to this, you did. Care to explain that?"

Chapter 4

Sean flopped onto his bed and stared at the ceiling. Where the fuck was Sandor? The man had promised they'd work out together this afternoon, but so far he was a no-show. Okay, maybe something had come up, but he could've at least said so instead of leaving Sean hanging. He would've understood. Shit happens.

Sean had never been any good at waiting, and lately he was a whole lot worse. He held up his hand and stared at the strange swirls of dark blue moving under his skin. Even though he knew that the energy burning there was part of his Kyth nature, it still creeped him out. What kind of freak came with eyes and hands that sported flame jobs?

Him, for one. Ranulf and Sandor, too, because it was evidently standard equipment for Talions. He was willing to bet that snooty British guy, Grey Danby, had some serious mojo going on. From that first night, Sandor's burning eyes had totally freaked

Sean out, but Danby's eyes were ice cold, sending shivers down Sean's spine.

He was pretty damn sure that if it had been up to Grey, Sean would be dead and buried; he definitely wouldn't be living in the Dame's mansion. And all because Sean had lost control of his body's need for energy. Okay, sure, he'd hurt some regular humans and stripped that last guy of nearly every drop of his life energy. But Sean hadn't known any better. None of them had.

He closed his eyes and rested his forearm across his face, blocking out the light—and the memories.

The burn was getting worse. Maybe he should go find Sandor. Sean was up and out his bedroom before he could change his mind. If worse came to worst, he'd head for the basement gym and lift weights.

A deep rumble of voices from the front of the house led him straight to Sandor. Unfortunately, he was with Grey Danby. Sean hesitated outside of the office door, debating whether or not to disturb them.

Deciding Talion business trumped their workout, he started to walk away when Grey appeared in the doorway. The cold-eyed jerk glared at him. "Sean? Why are you sneaking around out here?"

"I wasn't sneaking. I was looking for Sandor. To talk to him."

Grey stepped back out of the way. "So there he is. Talk."

Sandor tore his attention away from the computer screen. When he saw Sean, he looked confused and then checked his watch.

"God, is it that late already? Sean, I didn't mean to forget you, but something came up that needed my attention. Mind if we reschedule?"

Sean did his best to hide his disappointment. "Yeah, sure, whatever."

"Tomorrow? Same time?"

"Fine."

Sandor smiled. "Good, I'll look forward to it. And, Sean, I really am sorry I forgot."

Grey kept his eyes pinned on Sean, looking suspicious. Did the jerk think he was going to steal something or what? Either way, it was obvious Grey wasn't happy to be interrupted, especially by him. It was time to get out of there. Sean stalked off, well aware of Grey watching him until he turned the corner.

Back in his room, Sean kicked the door shut, wishing it was Danby's face. That guy seriously creeped him out. Something about the way Danby was always watching him, like he was just waiting for Sean to screw up. Well, that wasn't going to happen. Not if Sean could help it. Besides, Sandor wouldn't let the bastard hurt him. Not now.

Just then a heavy fist pounded on the door, startling Sean. Maybe Sandor decided to blow Grey off after all.

But instead of Sandor, big, bad Ranulf Thorsen filled the doorway. The redheaded giant was only slightly less scary than Danby. So far the man had given the Sean a fair shake, and he trusted him because Sandor did. That didn't mean Sean didn't have a healthy respect for the man and his temper.

Sean stumbled back a couple of steps. "Sorry, sir, I was expecting Sandor."

Ranulf nodded. "Yeah, well, he sent me because he didn't want you to miss your workout. He's dealing with a computer problem. Let's go."

Holy crap! Sure, he'd been training with Sandor, but he wasn't ready tangle with someone Ranulf's size. Not to mention the man had a thousand years of fighting practice, most of it while wearing animal skins and carrying a sword.

"I'd rather wait for Sandor."

Sean's voice cracked, but he kept his chin up, facing Ranulf head on. It was hard not to squirm under the man's stony glare, but he did his best.

"I didn't hear anyone ask what you'd rather, kid. You agreed to do what you were told. Now prove you're a man of your word."

Ranulf didn't wait to see if Sean was following. He knew Sean wouldn't dare refuse. To back out now would be suicide.

He followed Ranulf downstairs to the training room. Sandor had posted a chart on the wall for Sean to keep track of his workouts. Knowing what to do, Sean headed for the weight bench and got down to business. He quickly worked up a sweat, thanks in part to a good case of nerves. When he stopped to change positions, Ranulf was standing right behind him.

"Good form, kid. Do one more set of reps to warm up. You'll finish the rest of your routine on your own afterward."

Afterward? What did that mean? Sean counted off his reps and set the weights back on the rack.

Ranulf was waiting for him in the center of the room. He'd peeled off his shirt and kicked off his shoes. If anything, he looked even bigger bare chested with only that necklace hanging around his neck. He held a sword in a two-handed grip.

"Is that thing real?" It sure looked like it to Sean's untrained eyes. Sharp and shiny with a leather-wrapped handle.

The Viking nodded. "Yes, it is. Old, too. Have you ever fought with a blade?"

"Yeah, who hasn't?"

Ranulf cocked an eyebrow in disbelief. "Want try that again, punk?"

Sean flushed with embarrassment. "Okay, I've used a knife. Once. Nothing anywhere close to that size."

But, oh man, he wanted to.

Clearly reading Sean's interest, Ranulf stepped closer and held the blade out so he could see it better. "I don't expect you to master how to fight with it overnight. I do expect you to respect the weapon—and me, which means taking orders without question. Got that?"

"Yeah, sure. Whatever." Everything came with a price whether or not he wanted to pay it.

Ranulf lowered the sword to his side and frowned. Sean recognized the look. He was skating pretty close to pissing off Ranulf big time.

He dropped his gaze in surrender. "Yes, sir, I got that."

After a quick nod of approval, Ranulf offered Sean the sword, pommel first. Sean held the weapon up and stared at it. "You still fight with swords?"

"Sometimes. Sandor and I both use firearms more often though, so we'll teach you how to shoot, too. But there's nothing like fighting with a sword to teach you control. And we both know you need that."

It was futile to hope the man hadn't sensed Sean's control slipping again. Still, learning how to swing a sword would be a whole lot more fun than endless reps with weights.

Ranulf picked up another sword, one that seriously dwarfed Sean's.

"Stand beside me and do what I do. Ask questions if you don't understand. I'd rather you learned it right the first time than have to break bad habits."

For the next hour, they lunged and retreated, gradually picking up speed. Sean thought his arms were going to fall off when Ranulf finally signaled that it was time to stop, but Sean couldn't stop grinning as he reluctantly surrendered the sword to Ranulf.

The Viking smiled back. "Liked that, did you?"

"Yes, sir, I did. Thank you." This time the respect came easily, especially because he felt better than he had in a long, long time.

Ranulf tossed him a towel. "I've taught a lot of recruits over the years, Sean. Most do all right with enough practice, but only a few show a real gift for it. I suspect you're one of the latter."

"Really?" Sean asked hopefully.

"Really," Ranulf echoed. "One thing, though. Your buddy Sandor really sucks at blades, so you'll have to work with me."

Sam didn't hesitate. "That would be totally sick!"

Another voice chimed in. "That means he likes the idea, Ranulf."

Neither of them had noticed Sandor come in. On second thought, considering Ranulf's snarky comment about Sandor's swordsmanship, the Viking had probably been well aware of Sandor coming down the stairs.

"Don't forget that modern English can be a bit of struggle for our ancient friend here." Sandor winked at Sean, and added, "Especially considering he was around when Middle English was all the latest rage."

"Go to hell, Sandor," Ranulf snarled as he cuffed Sean on the shoulder for snickering. "As for you, recruit, remember, I can make your training challenging or I can make it damn challenging. Got that?"

Sean rubbed his shoulder but couldn't help laughing. "Yes, sir! I got that, sir!"

"Smart ass."

"Yes, sir, I am." Sean danced back out of reach before Ranulf could smack him again. "Now, I'll get back to my weights."

Ranulf disappeared into the shower room while Sandor trailed after Sean. "I wanted to apologize again for missing our appointment."

"No sweat." This time Sean meant it.

"Good. For now, I need to borrow Ranulf. When

you're done with your routine, get showered and then find Kerry and get a hit of energy. You'll need it."

"Will do."

As Sean lifted weights, he noticed Sandor pacing while he waited for Ranulf. He also kept checking his watch and frowning. What had him on edge? Something to do with Lena? Sean hoped not. He liked her, and she obviously made Sandor happy.

Finally, Ranulf came out, back in his usual jeans and T-shirt. Sandor pulled him to the side and started talking fast and low. Sean couldn't make out what he was saying, but whatever it was had Ranulf frowning big time.

As they walked by, he thought he heard Sandor mention Grey Danby's name. What was going on with that guy that had Sandor so upset? Whatever it was must be big because Ranulf muttered a string of cusswords as he climbed the stairs two at a time.

Sean stared after the departing Talions. So he'd been right about Danby being a problem. Well, he'd keep an eye on the man from now on. Sean might not be a Talion warrior—not yet anyway—but he had street smarts. Whatever the guy was up to, he wasn't going to get away with it. These people had been good to Sean and his friends, giving them the first real home any of them known in years. He wasn't about to let some uptight jerk screw that up.

Grey's cell phone lit up and started vibrating. One glance at the number on the screen and he knew he wouldn't answer it. The last thing he needed right now was to listen to Harcourt's long list of demands. Grey had bigger problems right now than an aristocrat with aspirations to greatness.

The phone went silent for a grand total of ten seconds before starting up again. Obviously Harcourt was in no mood to leave a message, and he couldn't rant and rave nearly as well in an e-mail. Grey stuffed the phone in his top desk drawer and kept working.

He hadn't sent that damn e-mail no matter what the record showed. Sandor tried to act as if he'd believed Grey, but then he'd gone off looking for Ranulf. Grey had no idea what Sandor thought.

The real question, of course, was who *did* send the e-mail? And why to Piper Ryan? Was the threat directed at her? He pulled her file out of the drawer and started through it again, this time looking for any hint of trouble in her past.

There wasn't much to find. Maybe the gaps in her history *were* legitimate, but in light of the e-mail, Grey wasn't willing to take the chance. The missing bits and pieces might add up to a security risk for the Dame and her entire household.

Grey shot off an e-mail to an investigator he knew and asked him to dig into Piper's past with the biggest shovel he owned. Remembering the man's talent for ferreting out a person's deepest, darkest secrets, Grey knew he'd have his answers about Piper soon.

Damn, the phone was buzzing again. The drawer only muffled the sound, and Harcourt was self-centered enough to keep calling until Grey answered.

Might as well get it over with. Grey yanked the drawer open. Maybe he could get some real work down while the man ranted.

"Yes, Harcourt, what is it now?"

The man sputtered at Grey's response. "It's about time you answered, Danby. I'm still waiting for that report you promised me."

Grey closed his eyes and pinched the bridge of his nose. "Harcourt, I made no such promise. You *demanded* that I keep you informed. If, and only if, something comes up that affects you, I'll let you know. And I won't even do that much if it betrays my oath to Dame Kerry."

"She has no business being Dame."

Grey was tired of hearing the same old litany from the elitist bastard. "That doesn't change the facts, does it? Judith chose her to rule the Kyth and provided her with the knowledge to do so. You may not like it, but that doesn't make it any less true. Now leave me alone and let me get back to work."

"Yes, well, we'll see how long you manage to keep that job."

When the phone went blessedly silent, Grey hit the power button to turn it off. If anyone else wanted to talk to him, they could leave a message. He'd had enough for one day.

"Grey?"

He looked up from his laptop to see Kerry standing in the doorway. Crap, had she heard any of that? He hoped not, but she was good at hiding her thoughts. Force of habit made him rising to his feet, but he managed to stop short of bowing. Casual was definitely not his strong suit.

His Dame shook her head and sighed. "I don't mean to drive you crazy, Grey. I figure I'll get used to being bowed to about the time you get used to not doing it."

Her rueful smile matched his own. "It'll prove interesting to see which one of us wins that particular race."

Grey laughed. "That it will. Was there something you needed?"

"Not really. I just wanted to let you know that dinner is ready." She held up her hand before he could protest. "And yes, I know it's Hughes's job to announce it, but I wanted to see if anything came of that e-mail Piper got."

"No, no viruses."

"That's good. I'm glad you were here to handle it for us."

Grey followed her out the door, noting that she accepted his assessment at face value. He wondered if Sandor and Ranulf were as trusting. Well, there was nothing he could do about it now except wait to see what happened next.

The two of them were the last to arrive to dinner. Sandor and Lena were on the far side of the table with Sean beside them. Ranulf was at the foot of the table and Kerry took her place at the head, leaving Grey the one remaining seat next to Tara and Kenny.

Hughes must have been hovering in the other doorway because by the time they were all seated, he was already carrying the food to the table. As the various platters made their way around, Grey noticed that Sean was watching his every move. It was easy to sense the boy's hostility, but he wondered about the reason for it.

Grey waited until everyone else was listening to Lena talk about her plans to find a job and then met Sean's glare head on. Talions might wear a thin veneer of civilized behavior, but they were all predators at heart. And Grey wouldn't look away until the kid either blinked or backed off. It didn't take long.

Sean obviously didn't like it, not one bit. Too bad. The last thing Grey wanted was some punk challenging his authority. The only downside was that Sandor had picked up on the exchange. Damn it, now Sandor would think Grey was picking on his protégé, but the dinner table wasn't the place for explanations. It would have to wait.

Piper had hoped to beat Grey to work again, but his car was already parked in front of the house when the bus dropped her off. Despite her aggravation with him yesterday, she'd concentrated on studying enough to feel confident about her test. But once she no longer had that to keep her distracted, she kept returning to Grey's parting shot as she'd left his car.

How long had he been plotting that particular move? Probably since that first morning when he'd walked into the office and realized he was going to have share his space with her. If he'd asked her over lunch, she would've figured he was only making polite conversation. But no, he'd pounced when she'd least expected it, trying to startle her into revealing some mysterious deep, dark secret.

And he was right. She definitely had one.

Darn the man anyway. She'd just started to like Grey and now she didn't know how to act around him. Was he that suspicious of everyone, or was it just her? And if it *was* her, what had she done to set off alarms? She'd have to be more careful.

Inside, she went in search of Kerry, ostensibly to see if she had anything in particular for Piper to do. It was cowardly and Piper knew she was really just postponing the inevitable. She'd have to face Grey eventually.

Kerry was mumbling to herself and shuffling through a stack of files at her makeshift desk in the dining room. She looked up and smiled when Piper walked in. "Hey, there. Seriously, I cannot wait until our offices are done. Keeping track of stuff in this mess is almost impossible."

Piper understood her frustration. "Would it be better if I worked out here and you shared the office with Grey?"

"No, that's okay. I just misplaced something— again. So how did your test go?" It was just like Kerry to remember something Piper had only mentioned in passing the week before.

She held up her crossed fingers. "I'd say I aced it,

but I don't want to jinx anything. The teacher promised to have the grades posted by the end of the week, so I'll be on pins and needles until then."

"Any luck finding my husband mentioned anywhere?" Kerry asked in a low voice, her smile wicked.

"Not so far, but I'll keep looking," Piper whispered back.

"Too bad they didn't have cameras back when he was a young man. Thanks to Judith's memories, I know exactly what he looked like as a Viking warrior. It's enough to make a woman swoon." Kerry fanned herself with her hand, laughing the whole time.

The new Dame's ability to accept all the weirdness that had become part of her everyday life was one of things Piper liked most about her. After all, how many women had to deal with a husband who had a thousand years under his belt before they'd even met?

"I still think he should write a book. You know, something like *My Life in the Long Boats and Beyond.*"

Kerry added her own suggestion. "Better yet, *How to Pillage for Profit!*"

"Okay, you two." Ranulf appeared in the doorway, glaring at his unrepentant wife and then at Piper. Despite the frown, his eyes were twinkling.

"A word to the wise, Piper. I have enough trouble with Kerry wanting me to teach her Old Norse and sword fighting. I don't need you encouraging her."

"Yes, sir. Of course, sir." She couldn't resist tweaking him a little bit more. "So I guess that means interviewing you and posting it on Youtube is out of the question?"

He stared up at the ceiling as if seeking divine intervention. "I swear, sacking a village was less trouble than dealing with the two of you when you get together."

"Hey!" Piper said, holding her hand up in protest. "At least I wasn't the one who wanted to drag you on *Antiques Roadshow* to see what a thousand-year-old Viking was worth. That was your wife!"

Kerry feigned shock. "I just wanted to know how much to insure him for!"

"Very funny." Ranulf held out a hand to his wife. "It's time for our morning break. Hughes is bringing tea and scones to our quarters."

"You go ahead. I'll be there in a second." Kerry turned back to Piper. "Is there anything else or are we done here?"

Piper ran her finger down the list of notes Kerry had made earlier. "Yep, looks like everything is caught up for now."

"Great. Let me know if you run into any problems."

After Kerry disappeared down the hall, Piper picked up her files. When she turned to head for the office, Grey stood in the hallway. He was staring in the direction of the Thorsens' private quarters with an odd look on his face.

What was he thinking about so hard? Did he disapprove of the hired help teasing the Dame and her Consort? Or that Kerry and Ranulf took time out of their day to enjoy each other? Somehow, she didn't think that was it, at least not exactly. He looked almost . . . envious, as if he'd wanted to join in the banter but wasn't sure if he'd be welcome.

His expression changed so abruptly when he noticed her that she had to wonder if she'd read his mood correctly after all. Those blue eyes zeroed in on her, knocking all thoughts of Ranulf and Kerry out of her mind. His gaze was like a caress, brushing against her skin and leaving a burning awareness in its wake.

"I want to talk to you about what happened yesterday." Without waiting for her to respond, he turned the corner, presumably heading to their office.

She did *not* want to discuss why it was important for her to work for Kerry. She had her reasons, but it was nobody's business. And she'd tell Grey just that if he tried to force the issue. She could always ask Kerry if she could work at the other half of the dining room table, but that would only bring on more awkward questions. She didn't want to cause problems just because Grey was doing his job.

Taking a deep breath, she braced herself and walked into the office. She dropped her stuff on the desk and ignored him for a couple of minutes while she settled in. Finally, she ran out of excuses.

"So what's up?"

Grey closed whatever file he'd been reading before answering. "Sandor and I spent hours tracing down that e-mail you got yesterday. I wanted you to know that we'd both been in your files. It took a while, but Sandor finally managed to find it."

She'd all but forgotten that weird e-mail. It had been startling at the time, but her worry over Grey digging deeper into her background had shoved it to the back burner. Thank goodness she'd been so careful to keep only work files on the computer.

"And?" she pressed.

Grey's mouth settled into a deep frown. "From what he could tell, it was sent from my account."

"What? He didn't believe that, did he? You were as shocked as I was when you saw it!" It was nothing less than the truth. If he had sent the e-mail, there was no way he would have sicced Sandor on her computer to track it down. Grey looked slightly less grim when she told him so.

"Thank you. I can't vouch for what Sandor thinks, but I would hope that he'd realize I'm not that dense."

He leaned back in his chair and stretched his legs. "If you don't mind, I'd like to watch over your shoulder as you check your e-mail this morning. If our prankster has been at it again, I don't want to miss seeing the message and how the computer reacts to it."

Heck, no, she didn't want him that close! But she couldn't very well tell him that. "Fine, I'll get it booted up."

Her computer was top of the line and normally very fast, but with Grey hovering, it seemed as if her system was running on empty.

"Okay, I'm going online now."

She kept her eyes on the screen, ignoring the soft

sound of Grey breathing behind her. The warmth from his body heated the air between them, making her hyperaware of his proximity. There was no physical contact, but it was if he were pressed against her back. She shivered.

"Everything all right?" he asked, bending down so that his head hovered over her right shoulder.

Maybe he was asking about her, but she deliberately chose to act as if he was talking about her e-mail account.

"So far, so good."

She entered her password and waited for it to load. As usual, she had more than thirty e-mails waiting for her. She quickly scanned the list of addresses for anything out of the ordinary. There it was in the middle of the list.

She pointed at the unfamiliar sender. "I don't recognize that address."

"Is it the same as yesterday?" His breath tickled her neck as he leaned even closer to read the screen.

"I don't remember, but it's similar at least."

"Okay." He frowned. "Maybe we should have another pair of eyes to see this. Let me grab Sandor before you open it."

Grey disappeared down the hallway, returning a moment later with the other Talion. The two men bracketed Piper, hovering over her shoulders. She wished they were overreacting, but they weren't the kind of men to spook easily.

Grey rested his hand on her shoulder, giving it a

slight squeeze. "All right, then. Let's see what we've got."

She clicked on the email and waited for it to open. At first glance the e-mail looked normal. It even started off with "Hi, Piper." Then it got strange fast. "Please tell Grey hello for me. I bet he's standing right there."

She blinked, trying to make sure she was reading it correctly.

Grey's reaction was succinct. "Bloody hell!"

Sandor leaned in closer. "Son of a bitch, how could he know that?"

"Grey, how—" she started to ask, but then the screen blanked out again just as it had the day before.

She wove her fingers together into a tight fist as the screen slowly came back into focus. Small beads of light sparkled in random patterns. Despite their innocuous appearance her tension ratcheted up second by second as she waited for the other shoe to drop.

Then it did. The sound on her computer shot to full volume as the small bits of light exploded like fireworks on steroids. The sudden noise made her jump back and bump her chair into Grey. When the last burst of light zoomed across the screen, words appeared as if being written by hand.

"The reckoning draws closer. Watch for a little surprise to arrive, which should be any minute now. It's only a preview of what's to come, but I'm sure you'll find it entertaining. I'd be very careful if I were you."

A bell rang. At first she thought it was part of the e-mail, but then Piper realized it was someone buzzing at the gate, wanting in.

"Grey, someone just pulled up at the front gate."

"I'll handle it. You stay here. Sandor, warn Ranulf and Kerry."

He took off at a dead run with Sandor right on his heels. Ignoring his commands, Piper swept up her cell phone and followed them out.

Grey glared back at her. "Damn it, Piper. Follow orders. I told you to stay back."

"And I will. But, Grey, the bell rings in the kitchen, too, which means Hughes is probably already on his way out there." She immediately slowed down, heading for a window that would give her a clear view of the front yard.

Grey burst through the front door and sprinted across the lawn to where Hughes was already reaching out to accept a small box from the delivery man. Son of a bitch, he'd never get to them in time. He lengthened his stride, pumping his arms and leaning forward as if that extra inch or two would make all the difference.

As he reached the driveway, he bellowed, "Hughes! Both of you, freeze!"

His order went unheeded as Hughes stepped back through the gate and the driver put his truck in gear and drove off, his haste in doing so probably spurred on by Grey's crazed appearance. The butler gave Grey a puzzled look but stayed where he was.

With no time to waste on explanations, Grey jerked the box away from the butler and took off for the closest open area, the Dame's rose garden.

Once he was safely away from the house, he set the box down and studied it. Even though it was smaller than a shoe box, it could still hold enough explosives to take out the entire neighborhood. That wasn't going to happen, not on his watch.

It had been awhile since he'd last disarmed explosives, but he'd been trained by the best. He pulled out his pocketknife and knelt down. Easing the blade under the tape, he peeled back the plain brown wrapping. He wadded the paper up and stuck it in his jacket pocket. So far, so good.

Lifting the lid might trigger the bomb, if that's even what it was. Ignoring the pounding of his heart, he worked one corner up enough to get a peek inside. His blood ran hot and then ice cold. Dear god, the digital readout showed the countdown was almost over!

He was dimly away of Piper yelling. "Grey, get away from there. Now!"

He dropped the lid and back pedaled away from the package. Piper had been smart enough to keep her distance. As he retreated, he threw up his hands, using every scrap of energy he could muster to build a barrier around the bomb.

"Everybody, get to the other side of the house! That thing's going to blow!"

Before he could seal the barrier completely, thunder rolled and the earth rippled beneath his feet. The blast of air flung him upward, tossing him arse over teakettle across the yard.

He slammed into the corner of the house, the impact of the brick exterior rattling his bones and stealing his breath. His last thought as the darkness swallowed him was: *Bugger it, this is really going to hurt.*

Chapter 5

*P*iper's ears wouldn't stop ringing—or maybe it was all the sirens pouring into the neighborhood. Police officers swarmed through the gate and over the Dame's lawn and driveway. Either way, Piper's head hurt, and she had to shove her hands under her arms to control their shaking.

Ranulf stood nearby with his arms wrapped around Kerry, and the three kids were huddled together, looking a little lost and a whole lot scared. Poor Hughes was being seen to by one of the paramedics. Realizing how close he'd come to being blown to smithereens had understandably left him badly shaken.

After talking to Sean and the other two kids briefly, Sandor moved closer to Piper. He shifted his weight from one foot to the other, as if ready to leap into action if only someone could tell him what to do.

He glanced at her before turning back to watch

the police. Neither of them could stop looking at the blackened circle in the rose garden. A couple of bushes were damaged, but probably not enough to kill them. It was a stupid thing to be worried about, but thinking about the flowers helped to keep Piper's mind off of Greyhill Danby.

From where she stood, all she could see were his feet, and they weren't moving. At all. Paramedics hovered over him, talking in worried voices and performing first aid. He hadn't been killed by the explosion. That's all she knew, and she was terrified for him.

What kind of bastard shipped a bomb? If the delivery truck had been any slower arriving, it could have gone off in heavy traffic. Who knew how many people would have died as collateral damage? Or Hughes—what if he'd still been holding the box? God, she couldn't bear thinking about it, or how half the time *she* was the one who accepted deliveries. She wiped the tears streaming down her face with the back of her hand.

"Here." Sandor shoved his handkerchief into her hand. "Are you all right? You weren't hurt, were you?"

"No. Just rattled by the explosion. Grey warned us in time to avoid any fallout." She shivered. "I hope he's all right."

"We all do." Sandor settled his leather jacket around Piper's shoulders.

Then, after checking to see that no one was close by he leaned in close and whispered, "Talions are hard to kill, Piper. Once Kerry can get near him without all these outsiders around, she'll be able to jump-start the healing process."

Kerry's ability to heal was something Piper had only heard about. She wanted to believe that it would help Grey, but he had to stay alive for any kind of healing to take place. And he hadn't moved in a long, long time.

The clatter of metal on the asphalt jolted her from her thoughts. Two EMTs were making their way across the yard with a gurney. Either Grey was stable enough to transport or—no, she wasn't going to go there. With her heart in her throat, she watched the medics gently lift Grey onto the stretcher. It was difficult to read their expressions. Did they always look that grim when working over a patient?

As they started wheeling Grey back in her direction, she finally got a good look at him. The right side of his face was bruised and swollen, and he had a neck brace on. They had him on oxygen, too. Surely that meant he was breathing. Didn't it?

"Sandor, Grey shouldn't be alone. I'm going to the hospital with him."

"Have the police taken your statement yet?"

"No, and I'd rather not talk to them at all." But she'd have to. There'd be no getting around it.

Sandor pulled out his keys. "Take these and go out the back. My sedan is parked down the hill."

She handed him his jacket in exchange. "Thanks."

"Don't worry. The cops have more than enough to keep them busy, so they probably won't notice you're gone for a while. If they ask, I'll tell them why you left. I can always take you down to the station to make a formal statement later."

Once again he checked to make sure they wouldn't be overheard. "I'd rather go over things with you first anyway, just to get everyone's stories straight. Tell Grey somebody will be by to check on him when things get wrapped up here."

"I will. Thanks."

She made her way to the front door, trying not to draw any attention. Once inside, she picked up her pack and hurried out the back. Just as she slipped through the gate, she spied Lena Wilson getting out of a car and waited for her to cross the street.

The blonde headed right for her. "What's going on, Piper? Is everyone all right?"

She kept it short. "Someone sent a bomb to the house. Grey Danby was seriously hurt and has been taken to the hospital. Hughes was a bit shaken up, but everyone else is all right. Sandor and the kids were inside with Kerry and Ranulf when the explosion went off, and the house wasn't damaged."

Lena seemed to take it all in stride, although her relief that the kids and Sandor were all right was palpable. "Where are you off to now?"

"We thought someone should go to the hospital with Grey. Sandor loaned me his car so he could stay with Kerry and the kids."

Lena was already hurrying away. "Check in when you know something."

"Will do," she promised before running to the car.

• • •

Did he really want to open his eyes when he knew a world of pain was waiting for him? Where the hell was he anyway? The last thing he could remember was running . . . somewhere? But he couldn't remember being late for anything.

Grey was pretty damn sure that wherever he was smelled suspiciously like a hospital. Then there were all those annoying beeps.

Bracing himself for the worst, Grey gathered up his strength and attempted to open his eyes. He was right. This was definitely a hospital, and unfortunately he was the one hooked up to all those bloody beeping machines.

A feminine silhouette rose into view, blocking out the rest of the room. "Grey? Are you awake?"

He managed a small nod as he tried to focus on the face. Was she a nurse? Squinting, he could make out dark hair with streaks of pink and purple. Her eyes were dark, her expression worried, and her face familiar. Slowly the fog in his mind lifted. Ah, yes, he knew her. Not a nurse after all.

"Grey, it's me, Piper."

"I know. What the hell happened?" His words came out in a harsh whisper.

"First, let me tell the nurses you're awake. Once they've checked you over, I'll fill you in."

When she walked away, his wrist felt cold. Why had Piper been holding his hand? He missed the soothing warmth of her touch now as pain washed over him in cold waves. His eyes drifted closed again.

"Mr. Danby, can you hear me?"

A disturbingly young man with a stethoscope around his neck smiled down at him. "Glad you could join the party, Mr. Danby. I'm Dr. Gregory. Your friend here has been pretty worried about you."

Grey sought out Piper, who hovered in the far corner of the small room. He'd rather have her fussing over him than the cheerful but impersonal medical staff crowded around him. He wasn't up to ordering them to leave him alone, though. Besides, they'd never believe that he didn't need their help. As a Talion, he'd heal from anything short of a mortal wound, especially if Kerry lent a hand.

The doctor poked and prodded and generally made a pest of himself. He kept referring to Grey's chart with a puzzled look.

"Is something wrong, Doctor?" Piper asked.

The doctor flipped back and forth between a couple of pages in the chart before answering. "No, not at all. In fact, Mr. Danby here is in far better shape than I expected, especially considering the severity of his injuries."

His smile was meant to be reassuring. "You have a broken clavicle and a hairline fracture in your right humerus, not to mention some cracked ribs. The impact also cause multiple contusions and lacerations. Our main concern was the length of time you were unconscious, indicative of a pretty severe concussion. Bottom line, you're going to hurt for a while, but there's no permanent damage."

Then he frowned. "The bruising doesn't seem to be as extensive as the ER doc noted."

Grey wasn't thinking clearly enough yet to deflect this line of inquiry. Luckily Piper stepped in.

She maneuvered around the nurse and stood at the head of the bed. "Maybe they overestimated his injuries because he was covered with so much dirt and blood when they brought him in. That always makes things look worse."

Piper's dark eyes pooled up with tears. "You really scared me, Grey. I was so afraid I'd lose you."

She buried her face in her hands and gave a credible performance of a loved one collapsing now that the crisis was past. Dr. Gregory had no doubt seen family members and friends cry before, but when Piper looked up with those puppy dog eyes, the man melted. Or panicked. Either way, he retreated.

"Ah, well, um, since Mr. Danby here seems to be on the mend, we'll leave the two of you alone. He can have visitors now as long as they don't tire him out. Ring the nurse's station if you need anything." As he spoke, he backed toward the door, the nurse following close behind.

When they were alone again, Grey said, "Nice job, Piper."

He expected her to be grinning when she turned toward him, but her tears were all too real. Had she really been worried about him? The thought settled somewhere in his chest, warm and comforting, but he wasn't sure what to make of the sensation. Better to get back to the business at hand.

"So what happened?" he asked. "I remember your arrival this morning, but everything else is pretty

fuzzy at the moment. Start with when you sat down at
your desk."

Piper pulled a chair up to the side of his bed and
sat down. When she touched his arm briefly, most of
his pain subsided. How odd. If Piper felt anything,
she gave no sign of it.

"As soon as I got into the office, you asked me to
check my in-box to see if I'd received another strange
e-mail. Remember? You said Sandor traced the first
one back to your computer even though you hadn't
sent it."

The puzzle was starting to come together. "And
you did get another e-mail."

The fear in her eyes multiplied, making him wish
he wasn't tied to all these bloody machines so he
could hold her. He reached out to take her hand but
stopped himself. Where had that urge come from?
He wasn't sure he even *liked* her, and they were a
long way from trusting each other. Must be a reaction
to a near-death experience. Hopefully Piper hadn't
noticed.

"Yes," she answered. "And this one was even
stranger. The screen filled up with fireworks and a
message scrolled across saying we were getting a little
surprise. Then a delivery truck pulled up at the front
gate and rang the bell. Hughes got there before you
did, but you took the package and ran with it. It blew
up in the rose garden, flinging you against the corner
of the house."

More bits and pieces were coming back to him:
the noise, the blast, the sick feeling of being tossed

through the air like a rag doll, the bone-cracking impact of the house.

"Hughes? You?"

"Hughes is fine. No one in the house was hurt. You ordered me and the others to stand back, so we were out of range of the blast itself. My ears rang for a while afterward, but that was all."

"Good." It was too much to hope that the local authorities weren't involved now. "So what did the police have to say?"

She shrugged. "I slipped out the back while they were still poking around. One of the detectives stopped by a while ago, but left when the doctor told him you were unconscious. The nurses are supposed to call him when you're up to talking, so I'm sure he'll be back."

"How long have I been here?"

"About twelve hours. Which reminds me, I need to call Kerry and let her know you're awake. The last time I checked in, Ranulf said the cops were still hanging around. Sandor has been fending them off as much as possible, but there's no hiding what happened."

Damn it, Grey needed to be back at the mansion doing his job. "How soon can I leave?"

"The doctor hasn't said." She pulled out her phone. "I can't use my cell in here, but I'll be right back."

"Tell Kerry I'm on my way." He struggled to sit up. "Where are my clothes?"

Piper had almost reached the door, but she did an

about-face and charged right back. "Oh no you don't, mister. You're going to stay in that bed until the doctor says it's safe for you to be discharged. Besides, they threw away all of your clothes. What the bomb didn't shred, the emergency room nurses did."

He wanted to argue, but right now he wouldn't win a fight against a small child, much less a very determined woman. When he relaxed back against the pillow, Piper nodded.

"Look, Grey, I know how important it is for you to do your job, but it will be there waiting for you. Considering you're already looking much better than you did two hours ago, they won't keep you here long. And if Kerry can get here to do her thing, I bet you'll be discharged in the morning."

That would have to do. He noticed the dark circles under her eyes. "How about you? Have you had any rest?"

"Don't worry about me. I've been dozing in the chair. Now that you're being sensible, I'll go make that call."

Out in the hallway, Piper gave Kerry a quick update. "He looks so much better already. The idiot tried to sit up so he could get dressed and get out of here. I take that as a good sign."

She paused while Kerry repeated the news to Ranulf and the others. Although Piper couldn't make out what they were saying, there was no mistaking their relief. She understood just how they felt. Even now, her throat ached from the tension of watching the ER docs work on Grey, hoping and praying that he would live.

She'd had to lie about their relationship so she could stay with him when they transferred him to a room. Visitation was limited to immediate family only. After flashing the ring she normally wore on her right hand, she'd convinced the doctors that she was Grey's fiancée. They didn't so much believe her as they got tired of arguing with her.

Once he had settled in, she'd sat next to his bed, her hand on his arm, needing that physical touch to convince herself that he was alive and on the mend. She'd drawn comfort from that small connection. God knows she never wanted to see him look that ashen—that still—again.

"I'm going to stay here as long as they'll let me," Piper said when Kerry came back on the line. "I don't think he should be left alone."

Kerry immediately offered to come relieve her, but Piper refused. "He's already champing at the bit to get out of here, even if he falls flat on his face. But the doctor says he can have visitors now, so you could stop by long enough to give Grey one of your special gifts." Hint, hint. "Just tell them you're his sister or something."

Once again Kerry spoke quickly with her husband

before answering. "I'll be right down. Tell Grey—" Kerry's voice choked with emotion. "Tell him thank you."

Piper knew what Kerry meant. Without his quick thinking, Hughes would permanently maimed or dead. And if the package had actually made it into the house, there was no telling how bad it would've been.

"See you soon, Kerry. I don't want to leave Grey alone too long. He might try to escape again."

Piper snapped her cell phone shut, knowing she'd just lied to her boss. She needed to get back to make sure that no one potentially dangerous got near him. Granted, they didn't know for certain who had been the target of the explosion, but she wasn't going to take any chances.

The whack-job bomber had somehow known the workings of the Dame's household well enough to time the explosion so that Piper and Grey would be there. If the bastard didn't care who died, there would have been no reason to issue a warning. Just ship the package and wait to see who got caught in the blast.

She'd played out different scenarios, coming at the problem from every conceivable angle. It would seem that either she was the target or Grey was, since the arrival of the bomb had been timed for when they would be in the office. But again, why send a warning? And why to them? To make sure one of them ran out to intercept the package.

Back in Grey's room, she closed the blinds that the nurse had opened. As long as someone could see in, Piper felt like there was a big bull's-eye on painted on each of them. Maybe she was overreacting, but maybe not.

"Worried about him taking another run at us?"

Grey would see right through a lie. "Yes, I am. I have an awful feeling that this is just the beginning."

"I wish I could disagree, but I can't."

Grey's eyes followed her as she paced the small room. "What are you thinking, Piper?"

She reminded herself that Grey was still healing. It was no time for him to be thinking too hard. "We'll talk tomorrow. Why don't you try to get some sleep?"

For the first time since the explosion, his eyes flashed angrily, another sign he was on the mend. "I am not a complete invalid. If you know something about what happened or why, share it."

"No, I won't. You can bully me all you want tomorrow Greyhill Danby, but not now. Either get some sleep, or I'll go tell the nurse you need a shot of something. I might even slip her a twenty to use her biggest, dullest needle just for kicks."

"Fine," he snarled. "But tomorrow *will* be a different story, Ms. Ryan."

He must be tired to have given in so quickly. When his breathing slowed, Piper sank down in the chair by his bed and waited for Kerry.

Thank goodness for the Internet. Otherwise it would be impossible to get immediate feedback on how well the special present for the Dame and her lackeys had been received. The local newspapers and television stations had swarmed outside of the mansion for hours, hoping to talk to Kerry Thorsen or one of the others.

The reporters all asked the same question: Why had this average young woman and her friends been attacked? They'd stuck a microphone in the face of every neighbor but no one knew. All they could say was that the elderly woman who used to live in there had passed away, leaving the house to Kerry and her husband. Nice people. Quiet. Kept up their yard.

As if any of that was important. Kerry hadn't inherited the house—she'd stolen it. But evidently no one cared about that.

And no one was killed. Pity. The butler *should* have been injured, but, no. Instead, Greyhill Danby was being heralded as a hero. At least he'd been hurt badly enough to require hospitalization. Too bad that as a Talion, he wouldn't stay damaged for long. He'd soon be back to full strength and ready to be knocked down again. There was some satisfaction to be taken from that.

After all, he'd been sent to Seattle to gauge the interloper's weaknesses so they could topple Kerry Thorsen's fledgling dynasty. Instead, it was clear that he'd fallen under the woman's spell, swearing an oath of loyalty. Maybe a lesser man would've done so out of expediency, seeing it as a means to get close to the throne. Unfortunately, Greyhill Danby was that rarest of men—a true warrior whose oath meant something more than mere words. If he promised to serve the Dame, he would. It was that simple. His sense of honor would ensure he carried out his duty regardless of the cost.

Well, bully for him. That choice would cost him dearly.

Now Grey would be in the line of fire, just like Sandor and Ranulf. It was a shame that the three most powerful Talions would have to be eliminated, but their ties to Kerry Thorsen were too strong. They'd die protecting her, but they wouldn't be able to save her. One by one, the obstacles to the throne would fall, clearing the way for the real heir to take over.

Then things would change. First on the agenda would be to move the headquarters back to civilization. London would be best, but Paris or Stockholm would do—somewhere that tradition was understood and valued. There was no reason to decide that now. There were far more important plans to make now that the enemy had been engaged.

Rather than striking another blow immediately, it was time to fall back and let the silence build tension. That Ryan woman would wonder each morning if she would get another e-mail, and even the regular mail would be a potential threat. Grey would be spinning in circles, watching for the next attack. Sandor had a human woman sharing his bed now, and he'd dragged those three Kyth mutts into the royal mansion, so he'd be distracted.

But how stable was Ranulf these days? There was no way to know if his marriage to the Dame had hauled him back from the edge of insanity, but it was definitely a love match. And while the two of them were busy screwing themselves blind, their little empire would crumble to pieces.

So what next? What would stir the pot, leaving Grey on the outside looking in? Perhaps dropping a hint about the real reason Grey went to Seattle. With everything else going on, a few seeds of doubt would find fertile soil.

This was definitely turning out to be far more fun than she'd expected. Another couple of days for them to get complacent, and then she'd refuel the flames of fear. Perfect.

The darkness of sleep was washed away in a torrent of rainbow-colored power that soothed Grey's pain and eased his mind. He'd felt this way before, but this time the taste of the energy was both familiar and strange. Was he dreaming?

He fought the hold sleep had on him, blinking several times as he woke up. Once again Piper had her hand on his arm as she dozed in the bedside chair, and the warm connection was comforting. She'd pay the price later for that uncomfortable position, but he didn't disturb her. She'd insisted on staying with him, and in truth, he liked her being there.

"Hi, Grey."

He turned his head in the other direction to find Kerry standing beside the bed. He sensed her gentle fingers on his neck as his body soaked up her healing touch. That explained the mix of flavors in the energy: It had Kerry's own unique signature, but a strong hint of Judith's as well. Evidently the late Dame had bequeathed Kerry more than her memories at the time of her death. The rest came from Piper.

"Thank you, Kerry. That feels good."

For once, there was no need for formality. Perhaps it was because the small halo of light that surrounded his bed created a barrier between the three of them and the rest of the world.

"I'm glad to help, Grey. Sorry I couldn't get here sooner, but the police felt compelled to bring in federal agents, too. I didn't think they'd ever leave."

"Did they find anything to help trace the bomb?"

"Not so far. They were following up with the shipping company, but they weren't sure how much they'd be able to learn. They'll have questions for you, I'm sure. And Piper, as well."

"Yeah, she said a detective stopped by earlier when I was still out of it. I'm sure he'll track us down eventually."

"No doubt." Kerry gave him a puzzled look and let her hand drop away from his neck. "That's odd."

"Is something wrong?"

She shook her head. "No, not exactly. Keep in mind that I don't have as much experience healing injuries as I do simply sharing energy. I expected this to take a lot longer and leave me exhausted. But I feel fine, and you're already looking a whole lot better."

"How long were you feeding me energy before I woke up?"

"No more than two minutes, if that."

Huh. "I've only required extensive healing a couple of times, and it definitely took longer than this. You're right, though. I feel a whole lot better than I should so soon."

"Whatever the reason, I'm glad." Kerry stepped back. "Let's let that settle for a bit, and then tell me if you need more. I don't want to overload your system."

"That should be plenty for now. I'm hoping to get out of here tomorrow morning, mainly because it will raise questions if I heal too quickly. The doctor is already suspicious that my injuries aren't as severe as initially reported."

"At the rate you're healing, by morning the bruises will have faded almost completely." Kerry worried her lower lip with her teeth. "Maybe I should have waited until you came home to give you the high octane stuff."

"Nonetheless, I appreciate it." He pushed himself up higher in the bed. "Do you have enough left to share with Piper? I tried to send her home, but she wouldn't leave me."

Kerry immediately walked to the other side of the bed. She hesitated briefly, as if considering the best place to touch her assistant. She settled on Piper's hand, trying not to disturb her sleep.

The weary tension on Piper's pretty face immediately faded as Kerry fed her a quick boost of energy. Grey watched in silence. Kerry's strength was amazing, surpassing even Judith's ability to replenish her Talion warriors.

After a short time, Kerry eased away from Piper. He'd been about to suggest it was time for her to stop, knowing Kerry needed to keep enough energy to get home safely. Piper slept on, blissfully unaware of the Dame's visit.

Kerry brushed a lock of hair back off Piper's forehead. "Tell her I said to take tomorrow off. And that it's an order, not a suggestion. The next day, too, if she needs it. She's missed class today because of all of this and may need time to catch up."

Kerry turned her attention back to Grey. "Give me your hand."

He kept them firmly under the covers. "No, you've already given me enough."

Despite her diminutive size, the aura of power that surrounded her made her a force to be reckoned with. "Don't argue. That's only keeping me from my bed that much longer. Give me your hand."

"All right. But if you collapse, make sure that Ranulf knows I did this under protest." He smiled slightly to let her know he was teasing. Mostly, anyway.

She closed her eyes as infused him with another small dose of energy, then opened them again. "There, that should get you through the night."

Her dark eyes, alight with flames of gold, held his gaze. "Let me know when you're back at your hotel so I can come by to give you more. I need my Chief Talion in top fighting form as quickly as possible."

He knew why. Their enemy had yet to reveal himself, but his intentions were clear. The attacks would escalate until somebody died. Grey placed his hand over the brand on his chest, the one that tied him to the Dame and their people.

"Our enemy will be destroyed and our people kept safe. This I vow."

This time, Kerry bowed to him and then walked away.

Chapter 6

The next morning, Piper hurried through the front door of the hospital, hoping Grey was ready to be discharged. There was no way he could risk another day in the hospital. The longer he stayed, the more likely it was that someone would notice how fast he was healing.

How many patients were admitted near death one day and walked out the next? Not many, she bet. Somehow she doubted he'd want to play lab rat for the local medical school. If necessary, she'd grab him and run like hell. Although she had to admit the image of Gray running on one of those rodent wheels was pretty funny.

She'd snuck out just before dawn to pick up some clothes from Grey's hotel. After she showed the manager the article in the morning paper and explained that Grey was in the hospital, he had accompanied her into Grey's room so she could pick up his sweats and shaving kit.

The hospital's early morning routine was coming to life. Piper headed toward Grey's room, wending her way between food carts and flocks of doctors out on rounds. She stopped outside Grey's door to listen. He wasn't alone.

Rather than barge in, she called out, "Grey? Can I come in?"

"Please do." He didn't sound particularly happy, but then when did he?

Piper poked her head through the door to find him surrounded by a herd of doctors, most likely a specialist and his entourage of interns. The older man in the middle of the crowd was clearly in charge, and right now he looked none too happy with his patient. It appeared to be a standoff between two very stubborn men.

The Talion had his arms crossed over his chest, glaring at the doctor, who glared right back. This was going to get ugly fast. She sighed and did an end run around the lab coats, pushing her way to the head of the bed.

"Sorry I took so long, Grey. Is there a problem?" She set the bag of clothes down and put her hand on Grey's shoulder.

He continued to glower at the doctor, but surprised her by putting his hand on top of hers and giving it a quick squeeze.

"There wouldn't be a problem if Dr. Keane here would simply sign my discharge papers. You wouldn't think that would be difficult to do. Presumably if he graduated from medical school, he knows how to write his own name, even if no one can read it."

A couple of the younger interns tried not to snicker as the doctor in question flushed red.

He turned toward Piper. "It wouldn't *be* a problem if your fiancé here would be reasonable. According to the emergency room report, Mr. Danby was admitted with multiple contusions, a severe concussion, and various fractures. And now he's refusing to let me examine him, which makes it difficult to assess his condition."

"Oh, I assure you I'm more than ready to get the hell out of here, so just sign the bloody release." Grey used his snootiest British accent.

But before he had a chance to say more, Piper interceded. "Doctor, Grey and I both appreciate your concern. We've already scheduled a follow-up appointment for this morning with his regular physician. I promise to make sure he gets checked and then goes right home to rest."

The doctor looked only slightly mollified. "Very well, but I will be noting on his chart that the patient was uncooperative and is leaving against my advice."

"Thank you, Doctor." She gave him a sympathetic smile as she squeezed Grey's shoulder. "I don't know why it's so hard for some men to admit when they're hurting."

Grey quit staring at the doctors long enough to give her a look that promised retribution.

The doctor rolled his eyes, but at least he started

for the door. "I'll dictate your discharge orders, Mr. Danby. The nurses will be in shortly to go over them with you. I'll include a prescription for pain medication. Don't be an idiot about it. Take it before the pain gets too bad."

When the last intern had filed out of the room, Piper shut the door. "I picked up some of your things from the hotel. In case you're wondering, the manager was with me the whole time."

Grey threw back the covers, swung his legs over the side of the bed, and sat up. "I wouldn't have cared if he'd marched a parade through the bloody room if it got me out of here any faster."

She watched for signs that he was hurting more than he was letting on. "Have you been up out of bed yet?"

"The nurse helped me up after she disconnected me from all the machines. I can manage."

He slowly eased himself onto his feet. To Piper's eyes, he still looked a bit rickety. She carried his bag over to the bathroom and set it down inside. He walked slowly but surely across the room, more in control with each step. She remained within grabbing range anyway, trying desperately to ignore the way his hospital gown didn't quite close in the back.

Oh, yeah, like that was going to happen. No female with a pulse would have been able to resist at least a peek at that prime backside and well-sculpted back. Yum.

Too bad he caught her leering. "See something you like?"

She ignored both her blush and his question, asking one of her own instead. "Do you want to take a shower?"

He smirked as he shook his head. "I will, after you drop me off at the hotel. I'll want to change into more appropriate clothing before returning to the Dame's house."

Oh, brother. Would the man not cut himself any slack at all? "I doubt that Kerry expects you to work today, Grey."

"Maybe not, but I'll be there anyway. On the other hand, she told me to tell *you* to take the day off. Tomorrow, too, if you need the time to get caught up at school."

"If you're working, so am I. I wasn't the one who spent the night in the hospital."

Grey contradicted her. "Of course you did. At least I slept in an actual bed and not that nightmare of a chair. By the way, Kerry said it was an order."

Before he disappeared inside the bathroom, he looked back at her. "And on the way to the hotel, you can explain how we came to be engaged. The concussion must have wiped out all memory of our courtship. I assume it's a love match."

Smart-ass! He was jerking her chain, and they both knew it. She actually had been surprised when the hospital staff gave in to her lie. Of course, they really hadn't seen Piper and Grey in their usual attire.

She smiled at the image—she with her taste for funk and Grey in his tailored suit as they walked arm in arm. Would he see the humor in it? Probably not, but there was the occasional glimmer of amusement in those blue eyes that made her wonder. He was compelling enough when he was doing his job. If he ever let down his guard long enough to play, he'd be irresistible.

When the door handle turned, she stepped back to give him some space. When Grey appeared, her lungs stopped working. Oh, man, he looked far better in the navy sweats than he had in the gown, especially because he hadn't bothered to shave. Scruffy looked good on him.

Realizing she was staring again, she tried to put more distance between them. "I'll go see what's keeping the nurse."

"Thanks. I'd really like to get out of here before that detective shows up. We need to find out what Kerry and the others already told the cops."

She'd almost forgotten about having to talk to the police. Suddenly she wasn't in such a hurry to leave the relatively safe hospital. Back out in the real world, an attack could come from any direction at anytime. She reached out to the Chief Talion.

"Grey? I'm scared."

He didn't hesitate. He gathered Piper in his arms and tucked her in against his chest. The embrace was supposed to offer her comfort, but it felt pretty damn good to him too. No surprise there. After all, he'd come awfully close to being compost for the Dame's rose garden. Lovely image, that.

He'd wondered how long it would be before her brave face would start to crack. Last night, it had slipped some when that young doctor was in the room, but otherwise she'd been fiercely protective of Grey, her emotions locked down tight.

The small room, with its uncomfortable bed and noisy machines, had at least offered some respite from the very real danger outside the hospital walls. It was hard to fight a threat that had no name, no face, and no logic. Grey had his suspicions about who was behind the attacks but no proof. Yet. Once he found it, he'd go after the bastard and drain him dry.

Meanwhile, he held Piper as she quietly cried, small compensation for the way she'd been there for him. He still had a number of questions about her background and too few answers, but a lot could be learned from how someone handled a crisis. She'd shown herself to be resilient and resourceful. He liked that about her.

He also liked the way her body fit against his. And if he didn't put some space between them soon, she might discover the hard evidence of that. He was starting to like her. And he definitely wanted her. Moving slowly, he put a few inches of room between them.

He studied her face. It was blotchy and stained with black drips of mascara under her eyes. Using his thumbs to gently wipe her tears, he showed her the streaks of black. "Better wash your face before we leave."

She sniffled as she rubbed her face with the palms of her hands and gave him a shaky smile. "Sorry. I didn't mean to fall apart. It's just that yesterday you weren't moving and no one would tell me anything and it could have been me but you didn't let that happen." Her words came pouring out with not even a hint of breath between syllables.

The sheen of new tears made her eyes glisten as her smile melted away. "You almost died."

As she spoke, she touched his face, as if needing to verify that he was indeed alive. He closed his eyes and savored the powerful connection created when her fingertips brushed against his skin. He breathed deeply to draw in her scent, pulled her closer, and then captured her lips with his.

He'd almost died in the explosion, but that was nothing compared to the near total meltdown that kissing Piper Ryan started. Her lips were soft as they opened in invitation. There were probably a thousand reasons why this wasn't a good idea, but at the moment he couldn't think of a single one. He wanted this, wanted her, and had ever since he first saw her in his office.

Was there a lock on the hospital room door? Probably not, and it was a damn shame. Right now he craved nothing more than to strip them both down to the skin and see how far this kiss would take them. He wanted to bury himself deep in her slick heat, pushing them both until they raced screaming over the edge.

He didn't think she'd mind, not from the way her hands were wandering, testing the strength of his muscles as she murmured her approval and snuggled tightly against his rock hard cock. He cupped the curve of her ass, wishing they were someplace a lot more private.

Then all hell broke loose. "Hey, Grey, you ready to fly the coop? Oops! Sorry!"

Grey vaguely recognized Sandor Kearn's voice as the other Talion muttered something that sounded like an apology and said that he'd be out in the hall. Way, way out in the hall. Piper had heard him, too, because she instantly went from pliable to rigid, while Grey's body did the exact opposite.

Bloody hell.

He leaned his forehead against hers as he fought the very real urge to ignore the interruption. "Are you all right?"

Piper nodded. "I'll go wash my face while you talk to Sandor."

"Good idea," he said quietly, although he hated her washing away the moment they'd shared. Her cheeks were bright pink. It could be whisker burn, but more likely she was embarrassed at being caught out. Time to face the music.

He spotted Sandor standing a short distance down the hall.

Grey waved him in. "You can come back now, Kearn."

While he waited for the Talion, he checked the room one last time for any of his belongings. Good thing he did. His leather jacket had been stuffed into one of the drawers in the bedside table. Not that it mattered. No amount of mending would restore it to its original condition. He shoved it in his bag.

Sandor hesitated in the doorway. "Sorry, Grey. I hadn't realized Piper was still here."

Grey ignored both the comment and the unspoken question in Sandor's expression. "How is everything at the house?"

"Fine. Hughes feels guilty because you took the damage instead of him. Ranulf had a long talk with him about it, though, and reminded him what tough bastards we Talions are."

"Good. I'm not sure getting blown up is in any of our job descriptions, but it's definitely not in Hughes's usual list of duties."

The bathroom door opened and Piper stepped out into the room, looking far more in control of her emotions, thanks in part to a new application of mascara and lipstick.

"Hi, Sandor." She sounded a bit shy, not her usual confident self. "Is everyone all right?"

"I was just telling Grey that Hughes took it hard but he's okay physically. Kerry went to bed late, but she was up and about by the time I left to come here. They decided to keep all three kids home today, figuring we all need time to regroup. I wanted to make sure Grey had a way back to his hotel."

Grey couldn't help but notice that Piper kept her eyes firmly on Sandor and not on him as they spoke.

"I was going to drop him off on my way to return your car. Maybe it would better if he just drove himself though. That way he can pick up his car at Kerry's. In fact, I'll just take the bus."

She tossed Sandor the keys and was out the door before either Grey or Sandor could stop her.

What had she been thinking? Making out with Greyhill Danby had to be the dumbest thing she'd done since— no, she couldn't think of a single instance of greater stupidity in her life. And to get caught by Sandor was the icing on the cake. Did men gossip? If so, both Kerry and Ranulf would soon know all about it. Great.

There was nothing she could do about it now except pretend it hadn't happened. Oh, yeah, like that was going to work. Especially with those footsteps pounding down the hall behind her. The only question was if it was Grey or Sandor charging after her. At the moment, she wasn't particularly thrilled with the prospect of facing either one of them.

"Piper, wait!" Sandor.

She didn't want to, but he could outrun her despite her headstart. She stopped beside a vending machine and started digging for change, which, of course, she didn't have. Sandor, ever the gentleman, fished two dollars from his wallet and offered them to her. It would be churlish to refuse, so she didn't bother trying.

When the soda rolled out of the machine, she unscrewed the cap and took a healthy swig. It burned its way down her throat, and she forced herself to face her patient companion.

"Thanks. Was there something you wanted?"

"Just to give you these." He dangled the keys in

front of her face. "Did you really think we'd drive off and leave you waiting for the bus?"

She hadn't thought about it. "I'll be fine, Sandor. I take the bus all the time."

"I know you do, Piper. But Grey said he'd feel a lot better if you weren't standing out in the open at a bus stop today. I agree with him, so please take my car and keep it until we have a better handle on what's going on."

Before answering, she allowed herself a quick glance down the hall to see if Grey was watching. Yep, he was. Even from a distance, she could feel the impact of his icy blue gaze. When she allowed Sandor to drop the keys into her hand, Grey nodded once.

"Okay, thanks. I'll take good care of it."

"Don't sweat it." Sandor looked down the hall before adding, "Thanks for taking care of our boy last night. We all liked knowing you were by his side while we dealt with the police."

"It was nothing." Another lie. It was definitely something, but only time would tell what.

Sandor kept talking. "Kerry said for you to take the day off, but it's only a matter of time before someone wants your statement. We really should talk before that happens."

She thought for a moment. "Look, I'm going to head back to my place and zone out for a while. How about I stop by the house after my classes this afternoon?"

"Perfect. See you then." Then, in a surprise move, he gave her a quick hug before walking away.

Was Grey still watching? Yep, and he was looking

seriously ticked off about something. Surely it wasn't because of the brotherly embrace Sandor had given her. Judging by the way Grey was now glaring at the other Talion, though, maybe it was.

Cool.

Feeling much better, Piper headed for the nearest exit and stepped out into the bright sunshine. The day was definitely looking up.

Lawrence Harcourt was not a happy man. He was also swigging an expensive brandy like it was a pint from the local pub. He couldn't seem to help himself given how things were going at the moment.

His sources had verified that Grey Danby had spent the night in a Seattle hospital because of injuries received in an explosion outside of the Dame's house. So far, all that was known for sure was that the bomb was delivered by a shipping company.

No one had claimed responsibility for the incident, and the police were convinced it was a random act of violence. Of course, they had no way of knowing that the Kyth existed, much less that Kerry Thorsen was their current ruler. A nation of people scattered all over the world and owing homage to a young woman in jeans and a T-shirt wouldn't occur to the local police.

Hell, he could scarcely believe it himself.

How was Grey doing? he wondered. So far, there were no reports on his condition other than he'd been taken away by ambulance. If Kerry had given him her healing touch, he was probably already better, regardless of how bad the injuries had been. Hopefully the Talion would have the sense to disguise his ability to recuperate so quickly.

It wasn't Harcourt's problem, though. His concern was that Grey would now be out for blood. The man might have the pedigree of a stray dog, but he had the tenacity of a purebred bloodhound on the hunt. The Talion wouldn't rest until he tracked down the culprit. They all knew that a direct attack on the Dame, even if just a close call, meant the death penalty in their world.

Someone would die for this, and Harcourt really, really hoped it wouldn't be him. If Grey caught even a whiff of evidence that the trail led back to London, he'd be on the next plane. Ranulf Thorsen and Sandor Kearn would very likely be with him, a deadly trio if ever there was one.

Oh, yes, then someone would die, his or her life force scattered to the winds like dust. Harcourt had only witnessed one such execution, but he still had nightmares from it, especially lately. He was postponing going to bed for that very reason. There were nights when he could still hear the poor bastard's screams as the Dame's enforcer ripped his life force out by the roots.

Harcourt reached for the brandy. Maybe if he drank enough, he'd numb both the memories and the fear.

He sincerely hoped so.

• • •

Grey let himself into his hotel room. The staff downstairs had put on a good show of concern, wanting to know if there was anything they could to do. Hell, they might even have been sincere, but he needed to be alone more than he need the sympathy of strangers.

He tossed the bag on the bed and headed straight for the shower. A few minutes spent in the hot spray would have to do. As much as he'd like a good long soak in the tub, he couldn't afford the time. The bomber's trail was growing colder by the minute. The police had no doubt collected all the evidence they could, grinding what was left into the Dame's lawn in the process.

Grey's ability to trace evidence beyond the normal human senses would work best while the scene was fresh and relatively uncontaminated. Every minute the site was exposed to the elements—and to other people—diminished his chances of finding anything significant. He needed uninterrupted time to work the area and see what was left.

When Sandor had dropped Grey off at his car, there'd still been a few reporters lurking in the area. Must be a slow news day. He gunned the engine and tore off down the street. Hopefully some other headline would grab their attention soon because Talions worked best out of the spotlight.

And he'd learned to survive in the shadows early

in life, not that he spent much time thinking about his past. He'd made it a habit to never look back.

Although he had earlier today at in the hospital. Looked back, that is. He'd meant to return to his room as soon as he'd known for sure that Piper was going to take Sandor's car. But then those dark eyes of hers had met his, challenging him on every level. He'd acknowledged the unspoken question, that he had sent Sandor after her. Cowardly, perhaps, but she'd needed her space. So had he.

He cranked the shower up high and hot, wishing he could wash away the memory of how Piper had felt in his arms and tasted on his tongue. With a potential killer on the loose, he did not need the distraction.

And she was certainly that.

Right now he had more important things to consider. Like who that bomb had really been aimed at. Not Hughes, surely. The man was as inoffensive as they came. Piper wasn't a likely target either, although he'd be surprised if she hadn't pissed someone off somewhere along the line.

He found himself smiling. That woman definitely had a knack for stirring up his emotions. Rather than dwell on the possibilities that brought to mind, he shut off the water and reached for a towel. He'd get dressed and head back to Kerry's house to do his job.

After he had a chance to examine everything, he'd corner Ranulf and see if he'd picked up anything. Each Talion had his own unique set of abilities, and the Viking warrior was the best when it came to hunting. From what Grey had heard, Lena

Wilson had her own talent when it came to reading a crime scene too.

Since he'd be working outside, Grey put on jeans and a long-sleeved knit shirt. That reminded him—he'd take his damaged jacket with him to the scene as well. It was bound to have some residue from the explosion. He'd have Sandor send it to the local Kyth lab for testing.

Time to get going. He needed to check in with Kerry and then get started on his hunt. And if Piper happened to be there too, well, so much the better.

Chapter 7

Kerry and Lena met Grey out on the porch, both looking genuinely pleased to see him. Lena smiled and said, "Grey! I'm glad to see you're on the mend!"

Ranulf appeared beside his wife and gave him the once-over. "Yeah, you don't look nearly as much like a corpse as you did when they rolled you out of here yesterday."

"Ranulf!" Kerry gave her husband an elbow in the side. "That's not nice."

The Viking grinned. "Seriously, Grey, I'm glad you're okay."

"Thanks." Grey didn't mind Ranulf's rough humor. The man always said what he meant, a rarity in their world.

He turned his attention back to their Dame. "Kerry, I'd like to borrow your husband and Lena for a while."

"It's all right with me, as long as the doctor said

you could be out and about." She studied him for a few seconds and then held out her hand.

He appreciated the offer, but she'd done enough last night. "I'm fine. Really."

"I'll feel better if I find that out for myself."

A Talion didn't refuse a direct order from his Dame. Grey held out his hand, letting her take it both of hers. The whole process lasted only a few seconds, but the quick boost she gave him would last for hours. She'd have to feed again soon to maintain her own balance, but the powerful symbiotic relationship between the Dame and her Consort would soon replenish her reserves.

She gave Grey's hand one last squeeze before releasing him. "I'll sleep better knowing you've been restored, Grey. We owe you so much for what you did yesterday. I'm not sure how you did it, but you managed to contain most of the damage to the rose garden—well, and to yourself."

All of them felt the draw of the blackened circle of grass a short distance away. It could have been so much worse. He would work day and night to keep it from happening again.

"Thank you, Kerry. Now let's get started on finding the culprit behind this attack. Once we've read what's left of the scene, I'll go to work on Piper's computer again. Has anyone checked to see if she's gotten another e-mail today?"

Kerry moved closer to her husband. "Sandor looked earlier and didn't see anything out of the ordinary."

"Good." Grey backed down the steps. "We'll let you know if we find anything useful out here. Lena, would you care to join us?"

"Sure. You might want my help."

Ranulf kissed his wife and fell into step beside Grey. "I tried to get a reading out here yesterday, but couldn't get close enough. The police and bomb squad hung around until we were all ready to go ballistic. I doubt there's much left untainted."

"That's pretty much what I expected, but even a hint or two would be helpful."

Grey quickly looked up and down the street to make sure the reporters were gone before he knelt down at the edge of the burned area. He rested his hand over the damaged grass and opened himself up to the trace energy. A slight increase in the buzz told him Ranulf had joined in the hunt.

Grey let the rush of sensation flow through him unfettered. Gradually, he identified and then eliminated the various components: fertilizer, weed killer, the burned carbon scent of the grass, the distinct smell of the multiple humans who had worked the area.

Underlying it all was the sharp tang of the explosive, yet it was impossible to tell what kind it was. Perhaps Ranulf would know, but it didn't matter. Grey would recognize it if he were to ever smell it again.

When Ranulf finally broke his concentration, the Viking looked frustrated. "Nothing definitive. Just that something exploded and burned."

"It was worth trying. Lena, you want to give it a shot?"

"Okay, give me a minute." She stepped to the edge of the circle and closed her eyes for several seconds. When she opened them, she slowly walked around the damaged grass and then headed across the lawn to the gate.

What was she sensing? Grey shot Ranulf a questioning look, but the Viking just shrugged. Neither said a word, not wanting to disturb her process. Finally, she shuddered and reached out to the gate for support. They hurried to her side.

"Are you all right?"

She slowly nodded. "Sorry, it always takes me a minute to get back to normal."

After a long breath, she frowned. "I'm afraid I can't be of much help. My gift allows me to see bits and pieces of an event as if it's a movie playing out in real time. I saw Hughes and the vague impression of another man—possibly the delivery truck driver. Then I saw you running toward the rose garden, the bomb exploding, and you flying through the air."

She shuddered. "God, Grey, it's a miracle you're alive, but then we already knew that. Nothing on the bomber, though. I *can* tell you that there was a powerful mix of emotions built into the bomb. He'll strike again, and sooner rather than later."

"That's what I'm afraid of." Grey thought over what she'd said. "But you got a definite impression that the bomber is male?"

Lena nodded slowly. "Yeah, I did. I wish I could tell you more."

"So, we're back at square one." Ranulf sounded disgusted.

"Maybe not. We have one more thing to check out. The hospital staff threw out most of my clothes after the explosion, but they hung on to the leather jacket I was wearing. It should have some bomb residue on it."

He retrieved the bag from his car and pulled the jacket out. He unrolled it and offered it to Ranulf first, who held it up to his face and took a deep breath before handing it to Lena. After she checked it out, Grey followed suit, drawing in the mixed scents of smoke, hospital, and the explosive.

"I'd know it again, but right now I don't recognize this particular mix. How about you?"

Lena ran her fingers over the leather. "I only get more of what I already told you. A mix of hate and excitement. Maybe a sense he's trying to impress someone. I've mostly dealt with arsonists, and this feels much the same. Whoever he is, he gets off on playing with this stuff."

She closed her eyes and rubbed her forehead. "This always gives me such a headache."

Kerry must have been watching from the porch because she hurried across to take her friend's arm. "Lena, if you're done here, let's go inside. I have a pot of tea waiting for us."

"That sounds wonderful. Grey, let me know if I can do anything else."

"I will. Thanks." He and Ranulf watched as the two women disappeared into the house. Obviously Lena's gift took a lot out of her. He regretted having to put her through it, but they needed to use every resource at their disposal.

Fury glowed in Ranulf's eyes. Grey understood just how he felt. Talions knew they might face death in battle, but mailing a bomb was a coward's way to fight.

Both men instinctively reached for the symbol of their bond with their Dame and their people. Ranulf clasped the centuries old Thor's Hammer he wore at his throat while Grey placed his hand over the brand burned deep into the skin on his chest.

"This will end."

"This will end."

Two pairs of blue eyes met and held, each alight with the burning anger of a battle-ready warrior. "This we vow."

The moment passed. Time to get back to business. Grey considered the options.

"I want to have the jacket tested by our people, but technically speaking, we should offer it to the police on the case."

Ranulf studied the jacket. "There's no reason not to cover all the bases in case they pick up something our guys don't. The jacket is already in bad shape, so the police won't notice if another piece or two is missing."

"That's what I was thinking." Grey assessed the damage to the jacket. "Should be easy enough to remove a swatch without it being too obvious. I'll have Sandor see how much the lab will need before I turn the rest over to the authorities."

He folded up the jacket. "If possible, I'll do it when Piper and I give our statements. It will look like an act of good faith on our part. But if Sandor needs more time, I'll turn it over later and tell them that the jacket slipped my mind in all the confusion. The detective might not like it, but he won't be able to prove otherwise."

Ranulf nodded. "Speaking of which, Detective Byrne called again, wanting to talk to you and Piper today. We told him that we'd call with a time when you'd both be available."

Grey had been expecting it. "Piper's going to stop by after class. We can go over our stories and then call the detective. We need to agree on the major points, but not sound rehearsed. Nothing triggers suspicion faster than a group of witnesses singing the same chorus in perfect harmony."

"True enough."

Ranulf studied the blackened circle on the ground for a while before looking toward the house. The explosion had cracked a couple of windows, another indication of how close the bomber had come to the Dame herself. Ranulf's barely controlled rage was a mix of a Talion's warrior training and that of a man whose woman had been threatened.

Grey knew how he felt. At least Kerry had been safely behind thick walls. Piper had been standing out in the open, with only Grey between her and destruction. Energy burned under his skin, seeking a target to lash out against. That time would come, but not today.

He carefully banked the fire. He always hunted better when his emotions ran cold.

The detective spoke slowly, but it was impossible to miss the sharp intelligence in his dark eyes. Piper wondered if he knew how carefully this meeting had been staged. Ranulf sat in his wife's chair with Kerry perched on the arm beside him. Sandor and Lena had taken the three kids over to their house for the evening to give them privacy.

Detective Byrne had checked in with Hughes first to make sure he hadn't remembered anything else now that he'd had time to calm down. The butler had assured him that he hadn't and then retired to his quarters. That left only Piper and Grey to give their statements.

The detective had preferred to come to the house so they could walk through the events of the previous day.

"Miss Ryan, if you would go first. Why did you think there was something wrong with the package being delivered?"

Sandor and Grey had already decided that there was no getting around telling the authorities about the warning e-mail. However, they weren't going to bring up the first one unless they had no choice.

She chose her words carefully. "Grey and I share an

office, so he was there when I received a strange e-mail. We both read it the same way—as a threat. When the bell at the gate rang, Grey ran out to intercept the package in case we were right."

She swallowed hard. "Which we were."

Her voice quivered, but there was nothing she could do except lay it all out on the table for the detective. "Hughes had already gotten to the gate, but Grey took the package away from him and ran to the rose garden."

Her eyes sought out Grey, needing a reminder that he was okay. "Before he could get away from the box, it blew up. He'd warned me to get back, so all I ended up with was a ringing in my ears. But Grey hit the side of the house and was taken to the hospital. Luckily, it turned out that all he got was a few bruises and a slight concussion."

She avoided looking at Grey. It was hard to lie to the detective about the severity of Grey's injuries. He was sitting right there in the same room, yet even so, the memories of those moments when he wasn't moving were too fresh to be forgotten.

The detective asked a few more questions before moving on to Grey's version of the events. It was pretty much the same but varied a bit on the details. He described what the bomb had looked like, or at least what he could remember before being knocked unconscious. Then the detective patiently backed each of them up and went over it again and again, taking notes and asking questions when he wanted clarification.

It was exhausting work, and Piper was relieved when at last he stood up to leave.

"We'll be in touch." He pulled out several of his business cards. "Here's my number. Call if you think of something or if you get another one of those e-mails, Miss Ryan."

Kerry walked the detective out. As soon as the door shut behind him, Piper sagged back in the chair and closed her eyes.

"Piper, are you all right?" Kerry asked when she returned.

She nodded and mustered up a small smile for the Dame. "What is it about talking to the police that makes you feel guilty even when you're innocent? Like you should confess something—anything—just to make them quit looking at you like that."

Kerry stood beside her. "And don't they know it? But then their perspective is a bit skewed considering how many people lie to them day in and day out. We all have secrets."

Although she knew Kerry was talking about her role as Dame, it didn't keep Piper's stomach from knotting up. She didn't know about the rest of them, but she definitely had secrets she didn't want to get out.

It was time for her to leave. "Well, unless you need me for something else, I'm going to head on home. I'm pretty much wiped out."

She stood up and stretched, all too aware that Grey was watching her every move. The man had definitely perfected the skill of masking his thoughts.

Right now she'd give anything to know what was going on behind his stoic expression.

When she realized Kerry was talking to her, she tore her eyes away from Grey.

"I'm sorry you had to come in today after I told you could have the day off, Piper. Take tomorrow for sure. We could all use some downtime."

"I may take you up on that, Kerry, but I'll definitely be in on Friday."

Piper made it all the way to the porch only to remember that Sandor had taken the sedan because his other car was a two seater. He'd planned on returning it to her when he brought the kids back to the house.

"Now what?" she muttered to herself.

She really needed to get away from a certain individual, and the sooner the better. Between class and the detective, she hadn't had more than a handful of minutes to call her own since she'd bolted from Grey's hospital room. She needed to stop thinking about that kiss, but so far that wasn't happening.

"Is something wrong?"

She jumped about a foot. She'd been so intent on getting away from Grey that she hadn't noticed he'd followed her outside. She smacked him on the arm.

"Don't sneak up on me like that!"

By the gleam in his eye, she could tell he found her reaction amusing rather than painful.

"I didn't mean to scare you, but I wasn't exactly sneaking. I'm leaving, too. You're not the only one who is ready for . . . bed."

Light blue sparks flickered briefly in his gaze, making her suspect he wasn't talking about sleep. And now that he'd put that thought in her head, she wasn't either. She wanted to believe their kiss had been a reaction to the stress of the past twenty-four hours. But she'd be lying to herself if she thought that was all it was.

Back to the matter at hand. If he was leaving, she'd be all right waiting for Sandor to come back.

"I forgot Sandor took the sedan, so I'll have to wait for him to return."

"Let me take you home. I was going to drive by there anyway."

How did he know where she lived? What was he up to? He answered the question before she asked it.

"I assure you my motives for looking up your address were not sinister. After everything that's happened, I want to make sure you get home safely."

"I'm a big girl, Grey."

"It's my job to make sure our people are safe, nothing more."

She didn't know why that made her even madder. She stared up at the night sky, caught between the need to get away from Grey and the desire to get a whole lot closer. That would be absolute insanity; at the moment she was definitely feeling a bit on edge.

"What's it going to be? Are you going to let me take you home or are you going to keep Kerry and Ranulf up, not to mention me, while you wait for Sandor to show up?"

"Fine. Take me home." She clarified her comment. "I mean you can drop me at my apartment building."

"That was my plan."

He walked past her toward his car, leaving Piper to follow as she would. That was okay with her. Despite their earlier encounter at the hospital, it wasn't as if they really even knew each other at all. The moment had been born out of turmoil, not any real attraction between the two of them.

Of course, if that was true, then why was she so aware of how well those jeans fit him? He gave her a smug look as he opened the car door for her.

Okay, so she'd been caught ogling—again. Which just showed how far off her game she was. She had no business admiring anything about Greyhill Danby except maybe his work ethic.

She endured the ten-minute trip to her apartment in total silence. Grey seemed uninterested in carrying on any kind of conversation. Not that it mattered. She wasn't feeling like a font of sparkling repartee either. But the closer they got to her home, the worse she felt.

Whoever was behind the attacks had done it through her e-mail account and had timed that package to arrive while she was at work. A chill ran up her spine.

She was so lost in her thoughts that she didn't notice when they arrived at her building. And instead of stopping by the front door to let her out, Grey pulled up to the entrance of the underground parking lot and stopped. He kept his eyes forward and his expression serious.

"What's the code?"

Oh, no. He wasn't coming in. She couldn't let him cross that line.

"Let me out here, Grey. I appreciate the ride, but there's no need to see me inside." She reached for the door handle.

He hit a button on his side, taking control of the door lock away from her.

"Grey, let me out. Now." She gritted her teeth and added, "Please."

"I want to know you make to your door, Piper. I'll sleep better knowing you're safely in your apartment. Let me do this." He flipped the switch again, leaving the final decision to her.

"Because it's your job?" Her pulse surged fast and hard as she waited for his answer, not sure what she was really asking him.

"The code, Piper."

"Fine."

After rattling off the numbers, she leaned back in the seat, relieved he hadn't answered her. Of course it was his job. He'd signed on as Kerry's Chief Talion, responsible for the safety of her subjects. Well, she didn't really consider herself one of Kerry's subjects. Of course, if Piper admitted that, she'd have to explain exactly who she really was and why it had been so important for her to get the job working for Kerry. Maybe Grey would understand because he took his duties so seriously.

After all, a big sister's job was to protect her little sister.

• • •

What was going on inside that pretty head of hers? Grey steered his car into the parking spot with Piper's apartment number painted on the ground. She was out of the car and on her way to the elevator before he'd even set the emergency brake. Her rush should've been irritating, but instead he smiled. If she was that anxious to get away from him, it meant he made her nervous. Very nervous.

The only question was why? Was she remembering that incident in his hospital room or regretting it? Or was there something else behind her frown? He was probably reading too much into her reaction.

And if he didn't get moving, she'd be locked inside her apartment without him. Grey hustled after her, catching up just as the elevator door slid open.

"You really don't need to walk me to my apartment, Grey. This is a security building. No one can get inside without the codes."

While she talked, she punched the button for her floor and then stared at the digital display above the door as if actually interested in the numbers marking off their progress. He considered standing close enough for her to feel his body heat, but he didn't. Taking up position in the back corner accomplished two things. First, he could stare at her all he wanted, and second, it kept her from realizing his eyes were glowing again.

A soft *ping* announced their arrival on the fourth floor. Piper moved closer to the door as if those few inches would make a difference. Once she escaped the confines of the elevator, those long legs of hers carried her down the hall in purposeful strides. He walked beside her, letting her set the pace until they reached her door.

As she inserted her key in the lock, she tried one last time to send him on his way. "Okay, you've seen me door to door. Your job is done. Go home, and get some sleep."

"Not until I check to make sure there are no unpleasant surprises waiting for you inside." He'd changed the rules of the game on her.

She started to protest, but then resigned herself. She wouldn't get rid of him until he was sure she wasn't in danger. She opened the door, reached inside, and flipped on the light switch.

"Knock yourself out, sport. Don't forget to look in the fridge. I haven't cleaned it out lately, so there could be some rogue mold in there just waiting to pounce the next time I open the door."

"Cute."

She stayed in the doorway while he looked around. Ignoring her impatient toe tapping, he took his time checking each room. He'd known before he'd taken two steps that they were alone in the apartment, though. He would have sensed another heartbeat if there had been one.

He knew this might be his only chance to see where she lived. And there was much to be learned from someone's space. Piper obviously loved bright colors, which didn't surprise him. Her living room was awash with reds and greens, giving it a warm feel. The haphazard stacks of books around the said she was a reader, one with eclectic taste.

He moved on to the kitchen, where he peeked in the refrigerator. "Good news! You're safe from mold attacks."

"Very funny, Grey. Go home."

"I haven't checked the bedroom yet."

He gave her his most innocent look, although he had no doubt Piper saw right through it. She crossed her arms over her chest and waited him out.

If the living room decor had come as no surprise, her bedroom was a true shock. Knowing Piper's preference for black clothing, he'd expected her most intimate room to reflect some of that edge. Instead, the queen-sized bed was covered with a handmade quilt made in riot of colors. Heavy lace curtains reinforced the old-fashioned look, and her furniture appeared to be family hand-me-downs. While life had etched a few marks on the oak here and there, it was solid and would last for generations to come.

In the living room, Piper had her back to him. What was she up to now? She reached out to touch something on the small table on the far end of the couch. What had been there? Oh, yes, her telephone and answering machine.

Terror washed over him when he saw the rapidly blinking light. It shouldn't come as a shock that Piper might have friends who would leave perfectly innocent messages for her. But he was already hurrying across the room toward her when an eerie voice, neither male nor female, spoke. The mechanical sound, probably computer generated, was all the more frightening because of its placid monotone.

"Piper Ryan, I'm glad you're finally back. I was concerned when you didn't come home last night. I really wanted to know how you liked my little surprise. Oh, well. I'm sure you enjoyed it more than your friend Grey did. Tell me, should I have sent him flowers while he was in hospital? I wasn't sure. Maybe next time. Good night, Piper."

The machine beeped and went silent. Piper shuddered.

"Who the hell would do something like that?" She turned on Grey, her dark eyes wide and wild. "Is that some idiot's idea of a joke? Well, it's not funny, not at all."

He wanted to take her and run, drag her out of the apartment to someplace with thick walls and a stout lock. Right now. She'd fight him on it, but he wasn't about to leave Piper alone here.

"Go pack enough things to last you a couple of days."

She was already shaking her head. "If you think I'm going to be run out of my home by a phone call, you don't know me at all."

"I know stubborn when I see it."

She backed away from him, putting the width of the room between them. "I'm not being foolish, Grey. Whoever is doing this knows way too much about where we are and what we're doing. Running out the door won't change that. Heck, he could be waiting out there hoping that's exactly what we'll do."

Damn it, she was right, but that didn't mean he liked it. "I need to know you're safe."

"I know—it's your job."

"It's more than that, Piper. And you know it."

She ignored him. "I've got a locked door between me and the rest of the world. You've checked to make sure that no one is lurking under the bed. I promise I will stay inside for the rest of the night."

"And what about tomorrow?" He was losing the argument and knew it. "Will you stay home?"

"I've got classes in the afternoon." She edged closer to the door. "I can take care of myself, Grey. I always have. As long as I stay lost in the crowd at school, I'm sure I'll be fine."

"And if this stalker decides that killing a few extra people doesn't matter? What then, Piper? What if he follows you into that crowd?"

He was hitting her hard with ugly possibilities. She had to understand that pretending the crazy person they were dealing with had any limits was not only foolish, but also dangerous.

She was starting to crumble around the edges. Her eyes darted to the answering machine and then back to him.

"So what am I supposed to do, Grey? The detective wanted me to report anything else that happened. I'm assuming you don't want me to do that. So other than barricading myself in my apartment until you track the bastard down, what do you expect me to do?"

Good question. He had no answer—well, except

for one. He could stay here with her. The more he thought about it, the better he liked the idea. He'd have to come in through the back door, though, if he wanted to convince her to let him.

"Come back to my hotel with me. We'll both sleep better that way." He fought to control his expression, showing nothing but concern for her well-being.

Just as he expected, she wasn't buying it. "You forget, I've seen your room. One bed. No food. No deal."

"Okay, then I'll stay here."

Piper punched her pillow, wishing she had something far more satisfying to whale on. Or someone. She'd been in bed for over three hours and hadn't managed to sleep for more than twenty minutes at a stretch. Flopping over onto her back, she stared up at the ceiling.

Counting sheep hadn't worked. Neither had listing all the reasons she shouldn't have let Greyhill Danby camp out on her couch. But no matter how many negatives she'd managed to come up with, the one positive outweighed them all. The minute he'd announced his intention to stay, her stomach had unknotted and her pulse had slowed to somewhere around normal.

That phone message scared her far more than she wanted to admit, even to herself. And Grey had seen right through her bravado to the quivering mass of terror underneath.

The only question was why she still couldn't sleep,

even knowing Grey was out there on her sofa, ready to defend her from any threat. On second thought, she knew the answer. She couldn't sleep *because* Grey was right out there on her sofa.

She'd managed to dig up a new toothbrush for Grey and an extra pillow and blanket. Before she'd made it back to her bedroom, he'd already stripped off his shirt and was reaching for the fly of his jeans.

He'd taken a shower before turning in, while she'd stayed safely on her side of the bathroom door. Two inches of wood weren't enough to block her imagination though. She wondered how he looked in her shower, his skin slick with soap and hot water. In her next life, she wanted to come back as his washcloth or even his towel. Anything to get closer to all that masculine beauty.

Because, *man oh man*, he was seriously ripped. She'd be dreaming about him for months to come. Well, she would if she could get some sleep.

Maybe if she read for a while. Unfortunately, in her haste to put some space between her and Grey, she'd left her book out in the living room. She turned over onto her side and forced her eyes closed. It didn't help. Neither did envisioning the last Hugh Jackman movie, except with a heroine who had pink streaks in her dark hair.

Nope, nothing was working. She really needed that book.

Maybe if she tiptoed, she could make it out and back without disturbing her guest. The plan worked fine until she bent down to reach for her book. When she stood back up, the couch was empty.

"Looking for me?"

He startled her for the second time since she'd walked out of Kerry's house. The man had to be part cat to walk that softly. She turned to face him and saw that the feline analogy fit in another way. Grey looked ready to pounce—on her.

"No, I came out to get my book." She held it up. Her wayward mind pointed out that the bare-chested guy on the cover had nothing on Grey. That was not useful information at the moment. She needed to put some distance between herself and all that warm, muscular flesh in front of her.

"What's the matter, Piper? Can't sleep? Maybe I can help with that."

The combination of his sexy accent and deep voice brought all kinds of possibilities to mind. "I don't think that's a good idea, Grey. Thanks anyway."

"I meant a cup of warm milk." He grinned as he trailed his hand down her arm. "Unless you have a better idea."

Lots of them, but she was smarter than that. She knew this man came with all kinds of complications. It was time to retreat back to the sanctuary of her bedroom—alone—even if it killed her.

"I'm going back to bed."

She tried to walk away, she really did. But those wonderful hands touched her shoulders and began a slow massage.

Oh, yes, yes, yes, he was good.

He leaned in closer to purr in her ear, "I thought you might like this."

Had she said that out loud? Evidently she had, but right now she didn't care as long as he kept it up. She tipped her head forward, encouraging him to continue. His touch set off a slow burn, a deep-seated ache that would require a lot more than a shoulder rub to fix.

He knew it, too, because soon his lips followed the same path his hands had taken, teasing her with light kisses along the length of her neck and down her shoulders. His breath was warm, his movements gentle. She wanted more, much more.

She'd been clutching her book to her chest as if it were a shield, but at that moment, she didn't need protection. The paperback landed on the floor with a soft thud as she turned to face Grey.

Despite the obvious invitation, he kept his embrace light, letting her make the next move. She gave in to the temptation and touched his chest, testing his strength with the palms of her hands. The light dusting of hair tickled her skin as she followed its path to just short of where it narrowed and disappeared beneath the waistband of his boxers. She wasn't ready to take her exploration that far yet.

"Kiss me, Piper."

But rather than press her lips against his, she kissed his chin, followed by his throat, before travelling down to kiss the dark circles of his nipples. He groaned and cupped the back of her head, silently asking for more.

She loved nuzzling his chest, drawing in the rich, male scent of Grey Danby. For the moment, that was enough. But soon, very soon, she wouldn't be satisfied until she had something far more tangible deep inside her.

His hands were busy, too. She'd worn her favorite camisole and lace panties to bed, and neither provided much of a barrier when a determined male wanted to get skin-to-skin with her. Grey's hand was poised at the lowest point of her back, just above the curve of her bottom.

She shimmied a little, hoping to encourage his exploration, while at the same time finally offering him the kiss he'd demanded. The instant their lips touched, he wrested control from her, ruthlessly plundering her mouth, demanding everything she had to give.

As his tongue swept in and out, tasting her, teasing her, his hand finally made its move. His fingers slipped under the elastic of her panties to spread over her ass, pushing her forward against his erection. Impressive, but then she'd already known that.

Her arms wound around his neck and she rose just enough to settle her body against his. Their few bits of remaining clothing were still too much. And they would have so much more fun when they got horizontal.

She broke off the kiss, her lips already swollen and tender. "Take me to bed, Grey."

He swept her up in his arms.

"It would be my greatest pleasure."

Chapter 8

*L*iterally being swept off her feet was wildly romantic and erotic as heck. So was being pressed against the play and flex of Grey's muscles as he carried her to the bed. Then he slowly lowered her feet to the floor, allowing no more than the barest whisper of space between them. He rubbed his face against her hair, murmuring something about her shampoo.

Then his mouth found hers and all coherent thought ended.

She tasted so damned good. Who knew that tart tongue of hers would be so sweet? Her skin was silky smooth and pliant as he slid his hands under the scrap of fabric she wore. His fingers traced the curve of her elegant back, starting at the top and meandering down to where her waist narrowed and then flared out again at her hips.

He couldn't wait to take her, grab her backside with both hands and drive them both hard. But not yet. There were too many other delights to savor first. Resisting the temptation, he kept them vertical, hoping to maintain his sanity a little longer.

It didn't help that Piper, bright woman that she was, had discovered how much he liked it when she rocked the juncture of her thighs against his straining erection. It was like trying to contain a bottle rocket in his boxers, one that's fuse had never been designed to do a slow burn in the first place.

He closed his eyes and thought of Queen and country. No help there. Fast and furious would have to do.

He gave Piper a gentle shove, sending her tumbling back onto the bed. Oh, hell, she had a tattoo encircling her thigh. How had he missed that before? He reached down and traced the pattern of flowers and vines with his fingertip, vowing he'd follow the same path with his tongue.

The minx looked up at him and giggled. "In a bit of a hurry, are we?"

He didn't bother to deny it, especially when the evidence was so obvious when he stripped off his boxers. "It's all your fault, I'm afraid. I was prepared to take it slow, but that's not happening."

His eyes were flaming hot. So were his hands, and he knew the instant Piper noticed. Her dark eyes stared at the energy swirling across the skin of his fingertips. He touched her thighs with both hands, showing her that they wouldn't hurt her, that *he* wouldn't hurt her. When she didn't protest, he reached for the top of her panties, meaning to slowly peel them down the lovely length of her legs. But then, for the sake of efficiency, he simply ripped them apart.

He probably owed her an apology for the caveman tactics—or at least a new pair of panties—but all he could think about was how beautiful Piper was. She sat up long enough to pull her top off and toss it out of the way. Then she leaned back on her elbows, letting him look his fill.

Oh, yes, this was going to be so damned good. He smiled down at her.

"I'm glad I have a photographic memory, luv, because I'm never going to want forget this moment."

Her jaw dropped. "You say the sweetest things."

"I don't know about sweet, but it's the bloody truth."

He edged her knees apart and stood between her legs. Her scent filled his mind, driving him that much closer to taking her without so much as another kiss. Which meant he needed to attend to one little detail, now before things got out of hand.

"I've got to get something from my wallet."

Before he could step away, Piper wrapped her legs around his hips. "Check out the top drawer. Though you might have to dust them off," she admitted.

If she was going to share her truth, he could do no less. That she was special. That this whole night was special.

"Mine probably have cobwebs," he confessed as he pulled several packets from the bedside table.

She held out her hand. "Let me."

Before she took care of that little chore, she sat up on the edge of the bed. Keeping her eyes on his face, she indulged them both by running her hands all over his body—chest, back, thighs, stopping to pay special attention to his ass. When he flexed his muscles, she smiled her approval.

Then she visited a few more places with her lips and tongue. He closed his eyes as swirls of color clouded his vision. He needed her to stop, yet prayed that she wouldn't. How had she taken control so quickly?

Payback would be . . . amazing.

In a surprise move, he dropped to his knees, putting her lush breasts at exactly the right level to pay them the homage they deserved. He suckled one gently at first, then harder as he kneaded the other, bringing both nipples to full attention. Piper leaned into him, her fingers tangling in his hair to draw him closer as she whispered her approval.

Her skin tasted of temptation and late-night dances between the sheets. He kissed his way from one breast to the other and then down the valley between them to her belly button. He watched the ever-changing expressions on his lover's face, listened to her words of encouragement, and learned her desires as he continued down to the very core of her.

She bucked against the combined assault of his tongue and fingers. As he'd promised himself, payback was intensely satisfying. Almost immediately, his lover keened out in surrender as her body convulsed in ecstasy. Then Piper slid down off the side of the mattress and straddled his lap, dropping her head on his shoulder.

"Grey, there are no words—"

That was a damn fine start, but he wasn't finished with her, not by any means. He muscled them both up off the floor and onto the mattress. Taking his time to kiss her thoroughly, he once again revved them both up until his entire universe narrowed down to the driving desire to mate with this one woman.

"Grey, please!"

He settled into the cradle of her body, loving the way they fit together so perfectly. With one sharp thrust, he took her, seating himself firmly in the warm welcome of her slick heat. Piper urged him on as he poured the best of everything he had into making the moment last.

And as they crashed over the edge together, it felt like coming home after a long time in the wilderness.

As the morning light filtered into her bedroom, Piper tucked in tight next to Grey and rested her chin on his shoulder while her fingers toyed with his chest hair. The night had been long and eventful. Despite her lack of sleep, she felt nicely buzzed and ready to face the day. That is, if she could bring herself to leave the warm cocoon she and Grey had created here in her bed.

She smiled. "About last night—I hope it isn't tacky if I simply said 'Wow!'"

She studied her lover's face, waiting for a reaction. Grey lay on his back, his head resting on his arm. His eyes crinkled at the corners as his stern mouth softened into a slight smile.

"I would have to agree that was a fair assessment." He turned his head to look at her more directly.

She raised up to kiss him, gently at first, and then with more fire. His body fit hers so well, at once so new to her and yet so familiar after hours of touching and tasting, learning what he liked and what he liked even better.

Grey rolled into her arms, thrusting his knee between her legs as he took control of their kiss. "You certainly know the right way to start off the day."

Oh, yes, she was positively purring as his hands slid over her skin, reminding her of past pleasures and promising more.

Despite a few twinges from their enthusiastic lovemaking during the night, she wanted this. Wanted him. Wanted to be lost in the moment, shoving all of yesterday's fears and secrets to the back of her mind. There would be a reckoning, of that she was certain, because Grey wasn't the kind of man who would forgive deception. But if she confessed her secrets to him, this warm lover would be replaced by an ice-eyed Chief Talion.

Grey pulled back to study her face. "Is something wrong?"

Yes, but now wasn't the time to admit that. "No, I'm fine. Why?"

"For a minute there, you seemed to have left me." He brushed her hair back from her face.

She savored the tickle of his morning stubble against her fingertips. "I'm right here, Grey, for as long as you want me to be."

"Good, because I don't plan on letting you go anytime soon." And then he set about convincing her that he meant every word.

"Is that your phone or mine?"

Piper's heart was still pounding in her ears, making it hard to tell.

"I'll go check, although I'd rather tell the world to bugger off for the day." There was real regret in his voice as he threw back the covers. "But with everything that's been going on, I can't afford to be out of touch for long."

She propped herself up to enjoy the lovely view of Grey walking across the room, obviously at ease with being stark naked. When he disappeared into the living room she fell back and stared at the ceiling.

Piper could hear his muffled voice as he spoke. When he came back in, it was clear that their interlude was over. Sometimes reality sucked big time.

But now wasn't the time for whining. She sat up and stretched.

"You want the shower first? I'll make breakfast. I

can't promise much beyond cold cereal and coffee. Or tea, if you prefer."

He'd already gathered up his scattered clothing. "Sorry, luv, but I can't even stay that long. I need to stop by the hotel and change before heading to the office."

She stood up, wrapping herself in the sheet. "Did something else happen?"

"No, but Sandor and Ranulf want to meet up and decide what to do next."

She watched as he pulled on his clothes like armor, morphing quickly from lover to warrior. As he buttoned his shirt, he asked, "Will you please stay home today?"

She shook her head. "I can't miss class this close to the end of my last quarter."

His eyes flashed hot. "Damn it, Piper, nothing's changed. Whoever is behind the attacks is still out there. If you won't stay here, get dressed and come with me."

Okay, that sounded too much like an order and not enough like a suggestion. He was clearly trying to protect her, but she had to draw the line somewhere.

Not to mention that she was more worried about her sister than she was about herself. She didn't want him dividing his attention between the two of them. "Grey, I've got to go to school. Besides, isn't your job to protect *Kerry*?"

He jerked as if she'd hit him. Okay, that was mistake. Those blue sparks in his eyes had less to do with passion this time and everything to do with temper.

He closed the distance between them and stared down at her. A wave of heat shimmered between them.

"Don't *ever* question my ability to do my job, Piper. I know where my duty lies." His hand shot out to cup the back of her head. "I serve the Kyth and I serve the Dame. It is my job to keep her safe, as well as those who matter to her—and to me. That includes you."

His mouth crushed down on hers. In a heartbeat, he yanked the sheet loose, letting it pool at their feet as his hands swept over her skin. Once again he lifted her into his arms and dumped her on the bed. There was nothing romantic about the gesture this time. He snagged a condom from the bedside table, then yanked his pants down far enough to sheath himself.

Then he was on her, in her. It was all about staking a claim, possessing her so completely that she no longer knew where she left off and he began. The ride was hard and fast for both of them, transforming their anger into something just as hot but infinitely more wonderful.

"Piper! Now!" Grey shouted as his shuddering release triggered her own.

She closed her eyes and waited until she could string together a coherent sentence. "Okay, I probably owe you an apology, but at the moment I can't really say I'm sorry about how this particular discussion turned out."

Grey withdrew from her body and rolled to the side. "I need to know you're safe."

"I understand that, but you can't cover me in bubble wrap and put my life on hold until you find this guy." She traced his frown with her fingertips. "I promise I won't take any unnecessary risks. I'll go straight to class and then right back home. I can call you at each end of the trip if you'd like."

He kissed her fingers. "I'd like that, but don't forget. You don't want me to come charging to your rescue on campus with Ranulf in full Viking berserker mode right behind me."

She laughed as they both got out of bed. "I don't know, maybe my European history teacher will give me extra credit for bringing an authentic Viking to class. Think Ranulf would be interested?"

"I doubt it, but I'd love to be there when you ask him." Grey helped her put on her robe. "Now I'd better leave while I still have the strength to go."

He slipped his arm around her shoulders as they walked to the front door. Her eyes flicked toward the answering machine.

"What are we going to do about that message?"

Grey's tension ramped up. "I'll take the machine with me and work on it with Sandor. Then we can decide whether or not to report it to the authorities. In general, we police our own kind. However, I'm not too proud to call the locals when necessary. They have resources we don't. The tricky part is not letting them find out that we're doing our own investigation."

"Take it with you. I'd just as soon not come home to any more messages like that one."

She left Grey's side long enough to unplug the

thing. The whole situation made her furious, and she resented being scared in her own home. She shoved the machine in a grocery sack and then into Grey's waiting hands.

"No rush getting it back."

Grey cupped the side of her face and brushed a soft kiss across her lips. "Want to have dinner tonight? We could go out or I can pick something up and bring it here."

Suddenly the whole day was looking a whole lot brighter. "Take-out sounds really good to me."

She glanced back toward her bedroom door.

"I do like the way your mind works." He kissed her one last time. "Until later, then."

Her smile lasted all the way through her shower and the cab ride to school. Thanks to Grey, the day seemed warmer, the flowers were brighter, and even the pop quiz in accounting failed to dim her mood. That man's kisses really packed a punch.

By ignoring the speed limit and scooting through a couple of redlights, Grey would make it to the Dame's house almost on time. He even squeezed in a quick stop at the drive-thru of a fast food restaurant. He'd never been a fan of eating on the run, but he'd need to replenish his strength to get through the day ahead—and the night to follow.

He had to remind himself to stop smiling before he walked into Kerry's house. Nobody was used to seeing that particular look on his face, and the last thing he wanted to do was explain why he was in such a good mood. Memories of Piper flowed through his mind, like the way she made that certain sound as he took her over and over again. Or when she decided it was her turn to run the show, riding him hard until she collapsed on his chest.

What was even better was knowing that it hadn't been just a fluke born of proximity and fear. If he were honest about his feelings, he'd wanted to take Piper to bed from the day they'd met. Now all he wanted was to do it all over again as soon as possible.

He lowered the window and the wattage on his smile as he keyed in the security code at the gate. He'd never had trouble compartmentalizing his life, and this time would be no different. By the time he walked in the front door, he'd be all business, but he'd still be counting the minutes until he was back in Piper's bed.

Inside, Grey followed the sound of voices into the dining room. Just as he expected, the two Thorsens, Sandor, and Lena were gathered around the table. He was slightly more surprised to see Sean, Sandor's protégé, there as well.

Grey settled into one of the empty seats and waited for a break in conversation to update everyone on the message on Piper's answering machine. He hoped that between him and Sandor, they'd be able to learn something from the recording.

And if it led back to Harcourt, Grey would be on the next plane back to England to kill the bastard with his bare hands.

"You're looking pretty fierce there, Grey. Got something you want to share?" Sandor poured a cup of coffee and shoved it across the table. "And before I forget, thanks for taking Piper home. I forgot all about getting the car back to her."

Before answering, Grey debated on how much to share. Better to go with a limited truth.

"It was no problem. I was going to follow her to make sure she got home safely anyway."

He pulled the machine out of the bag and plugged it in. "I went inside with her to make sure everything was clear there, too. This is what we found."

The eerie voice filled the room. Afterward, everyone remained quiet for several seconds before exploding into a cacophony of questions and outrage. Grey held up his hand to silence them.

"I will be pursuing all possible leads today." He turned toward the Dame. "Piper has promised to check in with me so we know that she makes it to class and back home safely."

"This has gone too far." Kerry's face was grim. "I want this finished, Grey. Utilize whatever resources necessary."

Then she reached out to take her husband's hand. "Ranulf and I talked it over, and for the duration, I will agree to having guards posted twenty-four/seven. Grey, bring in enough additional Talions to make that happen."

"I will make the arrangements immediately." Packing up Piper's answering machine, he looked around the table. "If no one has anything else, I'd like to get to work. Sandor, I'd also like your help."

The other Talion stood up. "I'll be right there. I need to make a couple of calls to the lab about your jacket."

As he left the room, Grey noticed Sean glaring at him. Damn, that kid had attitude, and tons of it. Maybe that's why he reminded Grey of his younger self, right down to living on the streets and running wild. But he doubted Sean would believe that even if he told him.

"Sean, you're with me," Grey ordered.

He wasn't sure which of them was more surprised, him or the kid. According to Ranulf, Sean's potential as a Talion was sky high. But he had some serious catching up to do on his training.

It was also clear the kid had little or no use for Grey. Fine, but as Chief Talion, Grey was ultimately responsible for Sean's future within the Kyth. That made it mandatory to find a way to work together. And it would start with the kid losing the attitude and learning how to take orders.

"Yeah, sure, whatever." However grudging his acceptance sounded, there was no missing the surge of energy in Sean's eyes and flowing under his skin.

"Get us each a cold drink and then meet me in my office," Grey said. Then to Kerry and Ranulf, "If you'll excuse us."

As he logged onto his computer, Grey waited to see if Sean would actually show up. Several minutes passed before he heard the shuffle of footsteps in the hallway. Good. He wasn't going to have to drag the kid in by the scruff of his neck.

"Here." Sean set a can of pop on the edge of Grey's desk and then backed toward the door. "I'm out of here."

Grey was ready for the defiance. "No, you're not. You'll stay here until I say otherwise."

"Screw that. You're not my boss. You can't make me stay."

Okay, time to show the boy the error in his thinking.

"Actually, as Chief Talion, I am, and yes, I can."

Grey immediately shot a bolt of hot energy straight at the teenager. Sparkling bands of pure energy formed across Sean's chest and thighs, flattening him against the wall. Grey sat back and watched Sean try to claw himself free. Struggling only increased the strength of the hold, making it impossible for him to make a dent in the power that held him prisoner.

Sean cursed and kicked his feet, all to no avail. It took an impressive amount of time before the kid finally gave in. As soon the fight had drained out of him, Grey eased his hold on the teenager. Sean briefly sagged against the wall before jerking himself up and bracing for another attack. Resentment burned hot in his eyes as he glared at Grey.

Grey calmly studied his reluctant companion while he popped the top on his drink. "I hear you've impressed both Sandor and Ranulf with your training so far."

A shrug was Sean's only response, but his eyes were slightly calmer. It was an improvement, anyway.

"Which do you like better—blades or guns?"

A grunt this time. Maybe if Grey kept prodding, Sean would eventually string enough syllables together to speak in actual words. But right now, Grey didn't have the time or the patience to wait that long.

"I prefer guns myself, but blades definitely have their uses, especially when you want to make an impression."

With no warning he shot up out of his chair to shove Sean back against the wall again, pressing a knife to the boy's throat. Sean showed enough intelligence to freeze, although his face burned with a mix of fury and embarrassment. Grey pressed in close until they were almost nose to nose.

"You do *not* want to fuck with me, boy. Sandor may play nice with you, but he doesn't understand little wankers like you." He eased back on the blade a bit. "But I do, because you and I are two of a kind."

"Bullshit! We're nothing alike," Sean sputtered. "You've got money and that fancy car."

"Quit looking at my clothes, boy. Look deeper."

Grey froze while Sean read him using his fledgling Talion abilities. The attempt was clumsy and crude, but it gave Sean enough of the truth to make him listen.

When Grey spoke again, he let his upper-class accent slip, revealing his much more humble beginnings. "I'm pretty much self-taught with knives. It was learn or die out on the streets. Once I earned a reputation for cutting first and talking second, other predators mostly left me alone."

Sean's mouth dropped open in shock. Grey made the knife disappear just as quickly as it had appeared. He shoved Sean toward Piper's desk.

"Sit."

This time Sean did exactly as ordered. Grey took his own seat and kept talking.

"As a lad, I hung out in one of the worst parts of London. I did all right for myself. Didn't starve anyway. But one day I got cocky and was stupid enough to use my favorite switchblade to try to rob one of Dame Judith's strongest Talions. Not that I'd ever heard of such a thing."

Grey smiled. "Hell, I thought I was the toughest thing around, but Joseph Ivy showed me different in seconds. I was lucky he was in a good mood that day or he'd have done more than squash me against the alley wall without even laying a hand on me. The two of us had a similar discussion to the one you and I just had. Then he dragged me home with him."

He glanced over at Sean. "The bloody bastard actually made me bathe before he'd feed me. Evidently since I'd been living on the streets for months, he found me somewhat less than sanitary. Can you imagine that?"

"No way!" Sean said. But he could imagine it. It showed in his eyes that his memories of living out there were too recent to have faded. "What happened next?"

"He saved my life, just like Sandor did yours. He

worked with me until I had my Talion abilities under control and then convinced me to join the military for a while. I learned more about discipline there. By the time I got out, there wasn't much left of that street punk, which was all right with me. If I'd continued on the way I was, I would have been dead."

Grey took a long drink of his pop before speaking again. "Not many people know my real background, and I'd just as soon keep it that way."

From the look on his face, Sean was still not ready to accept Grey's story as gospel. "Are you bullshitting me?"

Grey ran his fingers down the lapel of his hand-tailored jacket. "No, I'm not. This jacket cost more than my old man made in a year. Of course, most of what he made got spent at the local pub. God knows, Mum and I never saw much of it. At least when he was out drinking, he wasn't beating me—or her."

Dusting off all the old memories was no fun, but at least they served as a reminder of how far he'd come. "After Mum passed on, living on the streets was a step up from living with the stench of old whiskey and flying fists."

He tossed the empty can into the recycle bin Piper had set up. "Believe me or don't. Your choice. But you're not the only one who needed a helping hand. I thought you'd like to know that."

Leaving Sean alone to mull it all over, Grey scrolled through his e-mail and saw nothing out of the ordinary. He turned his attention back to Sean.

"We'll stick to the training schedule Sandor set up.

You'll work with the three of us as time allows. Ranulf is the best with long blades. Sandor's a fair hand with martial arts and guns.

"My specialty is down-and-dirty street fighting. Knives, guns, as well as improvising with whatever's at hand." Grey let a little more of his former self shine through in his smile. "You'll be bruised and bloody at first, but I promise one day you'll thank me."

Grey held out his hand. "Have we got a deal?"

Sean hesitated only briefly before accepting the gesture. "Deal."

"Good. Now, since Piper's not here, I need to see what kind of mail she received this morning. Come closer so you can be my witness. The bastard who's been sending these e-mails has programmed them to disappear a few seconds after we read them."

The teenager immediately rolled his chair over next to Grey and watched as he logged on. "Why is this guy doing this stuff?"

"My first guess would be because he's not happy about Dame Judith's choice of successor. On the other hand, the attacks haven't been aimed directly at Kerry, although she would've been devastated if Hughes or Piper had been hurt by the bomb blast. And if either or both resigned as a result of the threats, it would make it that much harder for Kerry to carry out her duties as our ruler."

He found himself reluctant to click on Piper's in-box, so he kept talking. "You'd have to be crazy to do something like this, so we can't expect to follow his logic easily. The most we can do is use every avenue of investigation we can to catch him before his attacks escalate even more.

"Failure is not an option, because that means he'll have succeeded in hurting someone in this household. That's not acceptable. The bastard's already crossed the line. When I find him, he *will* die. Our job as Talions is to carry out the Dame's justice. The only question is if I will make it quick and easy, or if we'll have to pick up the pieces with a sponge."

He gave Sean a sideways glance. It hadn't been all that long ago that the teenager had been subject to a death sentence under Kyth law himself. Sean looked a bit pale, but he was nodding.

"Now, back to these e-mails."

Chapter 9

$\mathcal{B}$y now that Ryan woman should have found the message she'd left. It had been tempting to use her own voice to record it, but that would have revealed far too much. Grey Danby was no fool. He would have recognized her voice.

Besides, as long as he didn't know Adele was the one behind the attacks, he'd still be focusing on her father and his friends as possible culprits. It was always satisfying when plans came together so well. Harcourt deserved to take the fall for her. If he'd been doing his job, the old Dame would have kept Adele at her side to finish training her as ruler. Instead, she'd been too far from the center of the action, leaving the door wide open for that upstart American.

That was all right. Kerry Thorsen—she couldn't bear to think of the woman as Dame—wouldn't hold on to the throne for long. Adele would see to it personally. In fact, she'd already purchased her airline ticket. Soon she'd be off to the wilds of the Pacific Northwest. She wanted a front row seat when the walls came tumbling down.

Everyone in Seattle was running in circles trying to figure out who had sent that nasty little bomb to the imposter's house. Adele had really hoped for far more bloodshed, but that was all right. She could always have another special gift delivered whenever the mood hit.

Right now, though, she had to get to class. No telling what useful bit of information she'd pick up. So far all that advanced computer training had been most helpful. She had a real talent for it.

A worried-looking Sandor hustled into Grey's office. He stopped short as soon as he spotted Sean and Grey sitting shoulder-to-shoulder and staring at the computer. Clearly puzzled by the change in their relationship, Sandor parked himself on the edge of Piper's desk.

"What's up, guys?"

Grey nudged Sean's arm. The teenager looked over at his mentor. "We're going through Piper's e-mails looking for more of the weird shit she's been getting."

Grey added, "That woman gets more e-mails than any one person should have to wade through."

Grey was getting tired of reading them, too, and it was unlikely he'd pick up anything useful by going through all of the new ones. He logged off.

"Any luck with the jacket?"

Sandor nodded. "The lab guys say we just need to send them a small swatch. Then we can call Detective Byrne and turn the jacket over to him. Think he'll put up much of a fuss over the delay?"

"Don't know. Don't care. But I'll call him." The cop was lucky they were giving it to him at all.

"Good." Sandor looked as if he'd had a long night, too. He pushed himself to his feet. "Can we check the answering machine later? I forgot Ranulf was waiting to beat on us with his blades some more."

"Sure, no problem. Go ahead and go, Sean."

"That sounds like fun—*not*. See you later, Grey." The teenager was off and running, clearly excited about another chance to play with weapons.

Sandor stared after him before turning to Grey. "You two seem to have buried the hatchet. How'd that happen?"

"We found some common ground. Now get lost so I can get some work done."

"Okay, but you're welcome to join us. I'm always glad to have someone else for Ranulf to use as a target."

"I'll think about it."

When Sandor was gone, Grey pulled out the detective's card and punched the number into his cell phone. The call went to voicemail, so he left a message for Byrne to contact him as soon as possible.

The moment he disconnected, his phone rang. Without looking at the caller ID, he said, "Well, that was quick."

A familiar feminine voice answered him. "And

here I thought you'd rip into me for not calling sooner," Piper said with a giggle.

"It was next on my to-do list." Smiling, he leaned back in his chair and propped his feet up on the desk. "No mishaps?"

"Nope, but I barely got here before my first class started. I had to wait until it was over to call. I've only got ten minutes before the next one."

"I've got a lot on my agenda, too, but I can spare a couple of minutes. Let me tell you my plans for tonight."

Piper walked into her last class only to find the room empty and a message scrawled on the board that the professor had been called away on a family emergency. Class was cancelled. What a relief. She wouldn't have been able to concentrate anyway, not with Grey's voice still whispering in the back of her head about his plans for the night. His plans *for her*.

She had to give the man credit. He had quite an imagination. She wasn't sure some of what he had in mind was even physically possible, but she was willing to give it a shot.

Back out in the hall, she considered her options. She could go back to her apartment and—what? Stare at the door and wait for Grey? She sure wasn't in the mood for studying.

Since she had to take a cab anyway, she could just as easily check in at the office. There were a few things she'd let slide during the past couple of days that could use her attention.

Right. And the fact that Grey will be sitting only a few feet away the whole time is the icing on the cake, she told herself.

Her mind made up, she called a cab and went to the door to wait. And if she smiled all the way to the Dame's house, well, she had a good reason for it.

Unfortunately, Grey was nowhere to be found when Piper reached their office. His jacket and cell phone were thrown on his desk, so he was around somewhere. Odd, though, because the house felt empty. Kerry was likely in her private quarters, but the men were definitely MIA.

She settled at her desk and got to work. A few minutes later, Grey's phone rang. Should she answer it or let it go to voicemail? One peek at the caller ID made her decision for her. She had no desire to talk to Detective Byrne unless she absolutely had to. She picked up Grey's cell and went hunting for its owner. The phone finally went silent, but Grey could return the man's call when she found him.

There was no sign of anyone in the dining room or living room, so she headed for the kitchen hoping to find Hughes. He always knew what was going on.

The butler stopped what he was doing to answer her. "Dame Kerry is in her quarters doing a video conference with board members from the foundation in New York. Ms. Wilson took Tara and Kenny to run some errands. And I believe the gentlemen are in the basement gym."

"Thanks, Hughes."

She opened the door and listened to the sound of clanging metal and heavy breathing. What were they up to down there? Lifting weights? Maybe, but she didn't think so. She sidled down the stairs, moving quietly so as not to startle anyone.

When the stairs turned at the bottom, she couldn't believe her eyes. She sank down on the bottom step and drank in the sight. Sandor and Sean were banging blades in the far corner, but that wasn't what had her hormones taking notice.

Grey and Ranulf were both stripped down to sweatpants and nothing else. Both were barefoot, bare chested, and dripping sweat as they maneuvered around one another. They both charged, grinning like loons as they grappled and beat the stuffing out of each other. Grey wasn't nearly as big as Ranulf, but he made up for it in speed and just plain sneakiness.

When the Viking hit the mat with a teeth-jarring thud, Sean and Sandor quit sparring long enough to hoot and holler at the other two Talions. Piper couldn't resist joining in. Unfortunately, the sound of her voice distracted Grey long enough for Ranulf to get his revenge. Grey hit the floor, but came up fighting.

She was mesmorized by the two men moving with such grace and speed. Ranulf was a wonder to behold, but Grey stole her breath. He was all sleek muscle and power, bouncing on the balls of his feet, fists at the ready. The image was a far cry from his usual conservative appearance.

If they'd let her sell tickets to her female acquaintances, she'd make a ton of money. She couldn't wait to see the look on their faces when she suggested it.

Finally, Sandor called time and the two men broke off and shook hands. Sean tossed each of them a towel.

"Thanks, kid." Grey wiped down his face and chest on his way to join her by the steps. "Hey there. I wasn't expecting to see you here."

"My class was cancelled." She gestured toward the mats. "I'm glad, too, or I would have missed all the action."

"Liked that, did you?"

She wiggled her eyebrows at him in a playful leer. Careful to pitch her voice so that only Grey would hear her, she teased him a bit more. "I know a lot of women who'd pay good money to watch something that hot. If you didn't make a habit of hiding all that prime muscle behind those button down collars and silk ties, you'd be tripping over women whenever you set foot out in public. Mind you, I'd rather have you all to myself."

After a quick glance to see where his sparring partners were, he gave her a heated look. "I promise to show you a few moves I'd never use on these fellows."

"I'll hold you to that."

He nodded toward the phone in her hand. "Were you looking for me for a reason other than to watch me sweat?"

"Oh, yeah, I was." She held out the phone. "I was in the office when your phone rang. When I saw the call was from Detective Byrne, I thought it might be important."

"We need to give him my jacket. I'll go shower and then call him back."

She was hoping he'd kiss her, but he started to walk away. Okay, maybe their relationship was too new. She understood that. On the other hand, there was no time like the present.

"Hey, Grey, isn't there something you're forgetting?"

He turned back to face her. "What's that?"

"This."

She captured his lips with hers and gave him a kiss intended to boil his blood. God, he tasted so fine as he returned her kiss with hot enthusiasm. By the time they finally separated, both were having a hard time drawing a full breath.

Grey grinned at her. "My memory must be slipping. I don't know how I could have forgotten something that important. I'll certainly try to do better in the future."

"See that you do," she said with an impudent grin as she stepped back out of his way. "Now, if you'll excuse me, Mr. Danby, I've got places to go and people to see."

Her mood vastly improved, she headed back upstairs. Time to get some work done.

"Detective, come in." Piper held the door open. "If you'll follow me, I'll take you to Grey's office. He and Sandor are waiting for you there."

"Thank you, Miss Ryan." Byrne walked beside her. "I don't suppose you've remembered anything else from the other day."

"Sorry, no. It all happened so fast, and I told you everything I can." She stopped to let him go ahead. "I apologize about the crowded conditions. The Thorsens are remodeling, so I'm sharing Grey's office temporarily."

"Not a problem."

Piper sat down at her desk and did her best to ignore the three men. It wasn't easy, especially once the detective found out about Grey's jacket. She didn't understand what the big deal was. So what if Byrne got it a day or two late? He ought to cut Grey some slack considering the blast had landed the man in the hospital.

She gave up all pretense of working and turned to face the ongoing discussion. She could almost hear Grey's teeth grinding as he fought to contain his anger.

"As I said, Detective, the hospital threw away the rest of my clothes after they cut them off in the emergency room. If you have a problem with that, take it up with them. My jacket was shoved in a bag and stuffed in a drawer in my hospital room. Forgive me for having other things on my mind other than rushing over to your office to deliver it."

The detective had his own fair share of temper. "You had the jacket when I was here before. Why didn't you give it to me then?"

Piper held her breath, wondering what logical reason they'd come up with. They could hardly tell him the truth, that they were holding on to it to aid their own investigation into the bombing. The detective wouldn't have much use for civilians invading his territory.

Grey met Byrne glare for glare. "When Sandor brought me back to my hotel room from the hospital, he set the bag aside. It wasn't until earlier today that I pulled the jacket out of the bag, planning on throwing it away. But when it reeked of smoke and what I can only assume is the explosive, it occurred to me that it might be helpful to your investigation. I regret the delay, but it wasn't intentional."

Okay, that was a lie, but at least the detective looked mollified by Grey's explanation.

When he held the jacket out, the detective put on gloves before he took it. "Who all has touched the jacket?"

Grey looked to Piper for help. She held up her hand and ticked the names off on her fingers. "The EMTs, nurses in the ER, probably a doctor or two, Grey, Sandor, and me."

"Just great." He started roll the jacket up, but stopped half way. "What this?"

He reached into the pocket and pulled out a wadded up piece of brown paper. If Piper hadn't glanced at Grey at that moment, she would have missed seeing the quick flash of flames in his eyes before he looked down and away, clearly not wanting the detective to see what was happening.

When Grey looked up again, he was back in control. "I don't know. Let me see it."

She wasn't sure how she knew he was lying again, but he was. He'd recognized that paper instantly and didn't want the detective to see it. Then it hit her. She'd seen him peel it off the bomb right before it exploded. How had he and Sandor missed finding it before now?

Ignoring Grey's request, the detective put the jacket in an evidence bag and set it aside. Still wearing protective gloves, he carefully spread out the brown paper on top of Grey's desk. They all gathered closer, looking over the policeman's shoulder as he read the words written in black.

The label was printed out on a computer. To Piper's untrained eye, there was nothing special about the printing, but maybe a forensics lab would be able to tell more.

Byrne pointed at the address on the label. "Does all of the Thorsens' mail come to the street address or do they have a post office box?"

Piper thought it was an odd question, considering the package hadn't come through the regular mail. "The mail all comes here, but the mailman didn't bring that package."

"I know, Miss Ryan, but I wanted to know if receiving packages here at the house was the norm."

He leaned down to study the label again. When he straightened up to look at Grey, his eyes were definitely frosty. "I assume by your accent that you're not from here."

"No, sir. I already told you that I only recently moved here. I'm still looking for a permanent place to live, but my personal belongings have not arrived from London."

Sandor finally joined in. "Why are you asking, Detective?"

Byrne pointed at the label. "Because this return address is from London. Is it familiar to you?"

He stood back so that Grey could get a closer look. Grey blinked twice before answering.

"Bloody hell. It's mine."

Fifteen minutes later, Grey watched the detective drive off. Turning away from the window, he gave Sandor a rueful look. "Well, I'd say that went well, but that would be a lie. At least he didn't slap the cuffs on me when he found out the return address on the bomb was mine."

Sandor clapped him on the shoulder. "Hey, he knew you weren't stupid enough to mail yourself the bomb that damn near killed you."

"There is that. Now that he's gone, I'll drive our piece of leather over to the lab."

Sandor followed him back into the office. "Why don't you let me do that? It's not that far out of my way."

"If you're sure. I'd like to stick close by while Piper finishes up a few things in the other room that Kerry had asked her to look over."

"Not a problem. So unless you need me for something else, I'm out of here."

"Enjoy your weekend." Grey sat down at his desk, ready to deal with the paperwork that was piling up.

Sandor paused on his way out. "I'll be working from home, but don't hesitate to call if you need me. Lena and I can be here in under ten minutes."

Alone at last, Grey slammed his fist against the desk. Damn, he really wanted to punch something, or better yet, the bloody bastard who'd used Grey's address on that fucking bomb. It wasn't even logical. If he hadn't happened to peel off the paper and stick it in his pocket before the explosion, no one would have ever seen it.

Well, except for the shipping company. And certainly in the process of backtracking through the company's records, Detective Byrne would have seen where package had originated.

However, if Hughes or Piper had been injured— or worse—by the explosion, Grey was sure he'd be behind bars right now. But even an overly suspicious, hardheaded cop like Byrne had to admit that it was unlikely Grey would have shipped himself a bomb.

Kerry and Ranulf had left earlier for their mountain retreat for the weekend, taking the three teenagers and Hughes with them. The cabin was located in the Cascades, less than an hour-long drive from the house. Once there, Ranulf would set his wards in place, ones no humans and few Kyth could breach. Short of artillery, no one was going to lay a finger on Kerry or the kids. They'd return when Grey had more men on hand to guard the Dame's house. He'd issued orders transferring more Talions into the area, but they wouldn't arrive until Monday.

It would be a relief not to stand guard all weekend. Once Piper finished a few things, they would leave together, and the sooner the better. He reviewed his plans for their evening, the kind that had him horny and restless as he counted down the minutes until they could get naked together.

The king-sized bed in his room was perfect for what he had in mind, and he was betting Piper would enjoy the oversized tub with the jets running full blast. Room service was just an added bonus.

It was tempting to go hunt her down and see if he could hurry things along. Unfortunately, he had a handful of e-mails he needed to read before leaving for the weekend. He clicked on one from Rolf, a Talion who he wanted to transfer to Seattle permanently. Good, he'd arrive by Sunday night. The next two were updates on ongoing investigations across the globe, neither one anything major, just annoying.

And the last one was from the firm he'd hired to do a more in-depth background check on one Piper Ryan. The short message was a status report, revealing nothing that hadn't already been in Sandor's notes. The investigator said the full report should be completed within the next few days, after he heard back from a couple more sources.

As Grey scanned the message, he heard Piper coming down the hall and closed the file. Vetting employees was part of his job, and even though they'd taken their relationship to a different level, he still had to do his job. Yet it felt strange to be investigating someone he was sleeping with. It was definitely a first.

Piper walked in just as his phone rang. He was too busy savoring the hot look she shot him to pay attention to who was calling him. Damn it all, it was Harcourt.

The arrogant bastard got right to the point. "I'm still waiting, Danby. Do I need to call the Dame myself and tell her that you're ignoring calls from her subjects?"

Grey fought to keep his voice calm, uncomfortably aware that Piper could hear him. "You're bluffing."

"Rest assured that I'm not." Then Harcourt paused for a few seconds. "I hear that you've had a bit of a mishap. Something about a package."

"All you need to know is that I'm investigating the situation. When I manage to track the shipment back to its origins, there will be hell to pay. No one threatens the Dame or her people and lives to tell about it."

He didn't want to listen to the sputtering coming from the other end of the line, so he hung up.

"Sorry you had to hear that."

She gave him a worried look. "Is whoever that was a suspect in the bombing?"

"Not really. He's more of an interfering jerk." Another lie, but he wouldn't point the finger at Harcourt before he could prove anything.

"You ready to go?"

She swung her pack over her shoulder. "What kind of food do you want to pick up?"

He pulled her in for a quick kiss. "I thought we'd go to my hotel and have something delivered."

"Hmmm . . . let me think about it." Her eyes were

laughing as she hooked one of her long legs around his, pulling him tightly against her.

He groaned. "Keep that up, and we'll find out how comfortable the top of your desk is."

She reached behind her to run her hand over the desk's surface. "Not too bad. What do you say?"

"I say we get moving while we still can."

He grabbed her hand as he stepped back and all but dragged her down the hallway and out the front door. When he gunned the engine and peeled out, Piper laughed.

"In a hurry?"

He smiled. "Do you have a problem with that? I've been waiting all day to get you alone—just you, me, and a bottle of wine."

Piper settled back in her seat. "I love a man with a plan."

"Any more of that fried rice left?"

Pleasantly exhausted, Piper nudged the box in Grey's direction. They were both sitting on the floor by the coffee table, boxes of Chinese food spread out between them.

She was wearing a thick terrycloth robe, compliments of the hotel, just like the one Grey had on. Neither of them had felt like getting dressed for dinner, not when they had every intention of picking up where they had left off when hunger had driven them from the bed. Piper studied her companion, trying to decide where she wanted to start.

He had been concentrating on his dinner, but looked up as she bit her lip while she stared. His hands froze halfway from the box to his mouth.

"What's the matter? Did I spill on my robe?"

"No, I was just thinking how much I'm going to enjoy having my wicked, wicked way with you again. And again."

"Really?"

"Oh, yes, really." She ran her tongue over her lower lip.

His eyes tracked every movement she made, but he remained right where he was. "Can I finish my dinner first?"

"If you really want to." She set her chopsticks and food aside. Making sure she had his complete attention, she tugged her belt loose and let the robe fall open.

He took one last bite of broccoli before setting his food aside. "Come and get me if you want me."

Her robe slipped down her shoulders as she crawled over to where he sat. She knelt in front of him, freeing up her hands to get past the terrycloth to all that warm and wonderful skin underneath. Grey didn't stop her, but he didn't seem in a big hurry to help her out.

Fine. Two could play that game. She ran a hand up his leg, starting at his ankle and working her way up until she found what she was looking for. A stroke, a gentle squeeze, and a soft caress was all it took to have those sparks of blue fire dancing in her lover's eyes.

She loved the little catch in his breath when she repeated the process from his other ankle. This time, she wrapped her hand around his cock and briefly dipped her head down toward his lap. She immediately straightened back up.

"Your robe seems to be in the way of my plans. Do you want to fix that little problem?"

He looked mildly insulted as he shrugged out of his robe. "I'll have you know, there's nothing little about my problem."

Looking down at the hard evidence, she had to agree. "You have a point. I suppose I could make it up to you somehow. Any suggestions?"

He leaned back on his elbows and shifted his legs so that she was sitting between them. "You were headed in the right direction when my robe got in the way."

"Well, I aim to please."

And she did.

Harcourt's voice sounded tinny and worried as he pleaded with her to answer. "Adele, please, where are you?"

She counted off the seconds, waiting for her father to speak again. It didn't take long.

"I've been trying to reach you for two days, Adele. I know you're busy with classes, but it's imperative that I speak with you. There seems to be a problem with your credit card. Someone bought an airline ticket with it."

Yes, someone had. She had, in fact, but how was that any of his business? Granted, he paid her bills, but that was a father's duty. If the credit card company had questions about her spending habits, they should have contacted her.

She sighed. What would he do if she continued to ignore him? Cause her more problems, no doubt. If the nitwit got it in his head that someone had stolen her identity, he might just cancel her cards altogether. That simply wouldn't do. Why couldn't the stupid wanker just leave her alone?

She smiled. Her father would totally lose it if he heard her use such language. A lady wasn't supposed to use street language or even know what it meant. Sometimes she wondered how her father managed to remain so out of touch with the real world.

He probably thought she was still a virgin. If he only knew.

But for right now, she still needed to play the game, to be his pure and innocent daughter. She hit his number on speed dial and waited for him to pick up. As much as she prefered to leave a voicemail rather than actually speak to him, it would only delay the inevitable. But luck wasn't with her—or perhaps it was. Either way, she'd leave him a message and get on with her plans.

"Father, I'm so sorry I missed your calls. Silly me, I forgot to recharge my phone, so I just got them all now."

She paused, trying to decide what to do about the charges. "I'm sorry about the mix-up on the credit card, but I took care of it. No reason for you to be concerned. They promised it would be straightened out on the next statement."

By the time he found out she was lying, she'd be on the other side of the world. Once she passed through Customs in the States, she'd start using the cash she'd saved for just this purpose. It should slow him down considerably when he tried to track her down.

"I'm in the midst of my exams. I'll be busy with studying for a while, so don't worry if you don't hear from me."

When she disconnected, she shut the phone off in case he tried to call her back again. She simply did not need the distraction.

Two more days of exams and then she'd be on a nonstop flight to San Francisco. There, she'd rent a car and drive up the coast to Seattle. She couldn't wait. For the first time in her life, she was going to be on her own, free of the constraints her father and Kyth society had placed on her from day one.

There was a lot about being Dame that she wasn't excited about, but having power over life and death was a serious rush.

It was rather ironic that her father was worried that someone had stolen her identity to charge a few measly purchases on a credit card. The one who had really robbed her of her birthright was Kerry Thorsen. Since no one had raised an uproar or rushed to Adele's defense, she would eliminate that problem herself. So far, she'd used an intermediary to launch the opening salvos. She savored the knowledge that she—and she alone—controlled the fate of people halfway around the world. Little did they know that soon, very soon, she'd take a much more hands-on approach.

But right now, she had exams to study for. After all, the future Dame of the Kyth couldn't risk failure of any kind.

Chapter 10

*P*iper took her time walking from the bus stop to Kerry's house, thinking about her fledgling relationship with Grey. They had talked all weekend—well, not *all* weekend. It would be more accurate to say they'd squeezed in a few conversations between other activities.

She'd been unable to think about much else since Grey had dropped her off at home last night. Once again he'd insisted on seeing her to the door—and inside.

The man was nothing if not thorough. There wasn't a square inch of her apartment—or her—that he'd overlooked. She hoped he'd gotten some rest after he'd left. Her head had hit the pillow right after she kissed him good-bye, and she'd slept straight through until her alarm went off.

Her past was the one thing they hadn't touched on. They'd discussed everything from sports to books to music without once mentioning their lives before Seattle. For her, it had been a deliberate, if difficult, choice. But now that she thought about it, Grey hadn't exactly poured out his childhood memories either.

Maybe he, too, had secrets he wasn't in a hurry to share. She thought about her own. It had only been a few months ago that she'd learned the truth about her father, and therefore her connection with the Kyth. In some ways, finding out that he'd died while she was just a toddler had eased the hurt she'd felt her entire life.

But that she had a *sister,* well, that was the real shocker. She still didn't know what to do about that. Going from having no family to being related to royalty was a lot to absorb.

She let herself in the front door of the Dame's house and paused for a few seconds. She could hear the rumble of Ranulf's voice coming from somewhere toward the back of the house. From the sound of it, he was talking to Sean and Kenny.

Keeping to her normal routine, she stopped in the dining room to pick up her folder from Kerry. It was heavier than usual because of several upcoming foundation events. Good. She'd rather be busy than bored anytime. Not that she'd find sitting only a few feet from Grey boring. Nerve-wracking, maybe, but certainly not boring.

So finding their office empty was disappointing. She set her file next to her computer and unpacked her things, including the extra scone she'd picked up for Grey on the way to the bus.

As soon as she sat down at the computer, though, her good mood disappeared. She'd had fun with Grey over the weekend but the events that had brought them together had never been far from her mind. She logged on and sat back to eat as the computer did its thing.

Should she check her e-mail or wait for Grey? There was no telling how long it would be before he showed up. Especially if he was out on Talion business. The Dame's correspondence couldn't wait all day, but for now she'd start processing the bills that had been piling up. Most were routine, but the last one came from what she guessed was a law office. Though not the one the Dame used. Piper studied the envelope.

Maybe the firm had a website. It was worth a try anyway. She did a Google search and found it. When she looked at the homepage she realized Horn and Burns, Inc., wasn't a law office after all. They did private investigations, specializing in background checks.

With a trembling hand, she opened the envelope and skimmed the bill, her eyes zeroing in on the project name—Piper Ryan. She forced herself to set the bill back down on the desk rather than give into her urge to run it through the shredder.

Damn Grey! He had no right poking around in her life. Okay, maybe he did, but what if the investigator had gone far beyond her work history?

She was running out of time in more ways than one. She needed to leave for class soon, but she was worried about the PI report. Feeling sick, she processed the invoice, wondering if she was issuing payment for her own doom. She had to talk to Grey, and soon.

After shoving her things into her backpack, she gathered up the documents that needed Kerry's attention and carried them out to the dining room. Her hopes that she could just drop them and run died instantly.

Kerry looked up with a smile. "Hey, Piper. I was just going to come looking for you. I hope your weekend was as relaxing as ours. There's nothing like a couple of days up in the mountains."

Okay, what should she say? Less information was better. "It was great to have some downtime after the week we had."

She handed the folder to Kerry. "Do you want to take a quick peek through that in case you have any questions?"

"That's all right. I'll read it this afternoon. Any problems can wait until tomorrow." Kerry leaned back and stretched. "Have you heard from Grey this morning? I knew he was going to be running late, but I expected him before now."

It wasn't like him to not check in with Kerry. "Do you want me to track him down for you?"

"No, he'll show up eventually. Ranulf's here, and Sandor is on his way, so I'm not alone." Then Kerry frowned. "Maybe you should wait until Sandor gets here, though, so he can run you over to school."

"No, I'll be fine."

Kerry looked hesitant. "Okay, if you're sure. But

call when you get there and when you get home. We worry."

Piper had to laugh. "Have you always been this much of a mother hen or did special training come with the job?"

"Hey, now. Show some respect! I'm royalty, you know. Queen Elizabeth and I are like this."

Kerry held up her crossed fingers and tipped her head back in an effort to look down her nose at Piper. Even if she'd been standing up, it wouldn't have worked with their height difference. At least she had a good sense of humor.

Piper tilted her head to the side and made a slow study of Kerry. "I somehow doubt the good queen would be caught dead wearing ripped jeans, flip-flops, and a football jersey."

"Well, she did grow up in Buckingham Palace." Kerry sipped her coffee and added, "Trust me, I didn't."

The Dame rarely mentioned her background. Piper had so many questions, but now wasn't the time.

To keep the mood light, she bowed as she backed away.

"I'm out of here, your royal highness. Don't forget to leave your crown on my desk. It's time to polish it again. Wouldn't want you to look tarnished next time you royal folks get together to toss back a couple of cold ones."

She and Kerry were too busy joking to notice they were no longer alone. Piper backed right into Grey, startling herself. He caught her around the waist to keep her from falling. Her body recognized his touch well before her brain did and wanted to go into cuddle mode. Then she remembered she wasn't all that happy with the man and jerked free of his grasp.

"Sorry, Grey. I didn't mean to run you down." She slipped past him. "Bye, Kerry."

She made it all the way to the door before Grey caught up with her. "The Dame suggested I drive you."

"Suggested or ordered?"

He gave her a puzzled look. Smart man, he was clearly picking up on her temper. "Does it matter?"

Being alone with him in that fancy car of his was the last thing she needed or wanted. "I already told her I'd take the bus."

"Don't be stubborn, Piper, unless there's a reason you don't want to be alone with me."

He planted himself in front of her, frowning. She didn't want to see the hurt in those blue eyes. This wasn't her fault. Yeah, sure, he was in charge of security and investigated anyone who worked for the Dame. Yes, she was being unreasonable, but he could have told her. If it was routine, why not say something? He'd had plenty of time over the past few days. It was killing her to not know if he'd even read the report yet.

Her intuition said he hadn't. There's no way he would have seen her file and not come after her demanding answers. Better to start putting some space between them right now.

"Listen, I don't mean to be a pain." She ran her

fingers through her hair, pushing it away from her face. "I'm not used to having people hover so much. But for the sake of maintaining the peace, if you've got time, I'd appreciate a ride."

"I'll make the time."

They walked to the car, neither of them making any move to pick up where they'd left off last night. It was surprising how much it hurt, but now wasn't the time for a long discussion.

The short drive to school passed in silence. Grey concentrated on driving, and she fiddled with the straps on her backpack. It was a huge relief when he pulled over to let her out.

"Thanks."

But before she could make her escape, Grey was out of the car and heading for her. Breaking and running was the coward's way out. She held her ground and let him come to her.

Grey didn't hesitate. Piper was pissed about something. Fine. He got that. But damned if he had a clue what he'd done. At first he'd thought she was just trying to play it cool in front of Kerry. He didn't blame her for not wanting to be the subject of office gossip.

But she'd kept it up even after they were out of sight. He certainly didn't appreciate being treated like some nameless chauffeur. She'd better explain herself or he was going haul her delectable ass back to his place. He could bloody well guarantee she wouldn't enjoy the direction the discussion would take after that.

She slammed the car door, drawing the interest of passersby. All right, if she wanted to make a spectacle of herself, he'd gladly to help her with that.

He stalked toward her, taking petty pleasure when she stumbled one step backward and then another. At least she had enough sense to read his mood. He kept his hands at his sides but pressed close enough to feel her pulse racing.

"Care to tell me what's going on in that head of yours?" He shifted his hands to his back pockets because he couldn't be this close to her without wanting to touch.

"Grey, get out of my way."

He'd never been one for public confrontations, but he wasn't about to back down now. Inching a little closer, he did his best to make his demand sound reasonable. "Answer my question, Piper, and I'm out of here. Or tell me to fuck off, if that's really what you want."

She flinched at that last one. "Grey, not now. I really do need to go."

"Fine, but you're just postponing this discussion." He checked his watch. "I'll be waiting right here to pick you up after class. Don't make me hunt you down."

She got right up in his face. "Yes, and we all know how good you are at hunting, don't we? We'll have that talk, Greyhill Danby—but I won't be the only one doing some explaining."

She poked him in the chest with her forefinger for emphasis. He captured her finger with one hand and the back of her head with the other, yanking her into kissing range. It wasn't clear who closed that last little gap.

Right now her temper was a definite match for his, as was her passion—hot, spicy, and one hell of a turn-on. The envious whistles from a couple of frat boys reminded them that they were in public. With great effort, he broke off the kiss and took a step back. Both of them were breathing hard.

He pointed at her. "I'll pick you up. Right here."

Her chin lifted. "Fine. You do that."

He stared into her eyes for another few seconds, drinking in all that heat. "I'm leaving now."

"Good. While I'm in class, you can do what you do best."

"And what would that be?"

"Screw with people's private business."

All right. So much for waiting until later for all of this. "What's that supposed to mean?"

"People have secrets for a reason, Grey."

Then she was gone, leaving him staring after her and wondering what kind of secrets had made those pretty brown eyes so damn sad.

It wasn't until he sat down at his computer and logged on that he figured out the answer to his own question. The PI's report had come in. The only question was how would Piper know about it? Any correspondence should've come directly to Grey.

There was only one way to find out what had happened. He checked his e-mail. Sure enough, the investigator had sent him an update. Rather than open it, he checked Piper's e-mail next. Her in-box was full of new messages, but nothing suspicious. Then he spotted an envelope with the firm's letterhead tossed in the recycling bin. Obviously the bill had landed on Piper's desk instead of his, which explained her temper.

As Chief Talion it was his job to know everything about those who surrounded the Dame. That he was even hesitating to delve into the report was a clear indication of how much Piper had come to mean to him. What the hell was he supposed to do? His duty to his Dame or to the woman he . . . liked a whole lot?

Damn it all, he didn't need complications like this when they still had a bomber on the loose.

He logged out of Piper's e-mail account and returned to his own desk. He'd pick her up at school and take her someplace private. His hotel or her apartment, it didn't matter which. Then he'd give her the chance to explain herself before he read the report. He was putting them both in a difficult position, but he very much wanted her to trust him with her secrets.

Satisfied he had a solid plan in place, he called Sandor to see if he'd heard back from the lab on the explosive. It would probably be another dead end, but they had to start somewhere.

"Adele, this is your father calling"—Harcourt paused for effect—"again. Now quit avoiding me and return my call. Your exams are over, so you can't use that excuse any longer. Also, don't bother lying about the airline ticket. I verified that you did in fact purchase it."

The phone cut him off for talking too long. He hit the redial button and paced the length of the parlor while he waited to finish leaving his message.

"I want to know why you're making a trip to the States. If you want to take a trip to celebrate your graduation, there are many more appropriate destinations."

He drew a ragged breath. "Please, sweetheart, don't cut me out of your life like this. Whatever you have planned, we can work on it together."

Rather than hang up, he held on to the phone, his knuckles white and aching, until the final beep told him he'd run out of time.

He worried that he was out of time with far more than just the phone call. Now he had to fall back and regroup before the silly twit ruined everything. His decision made, he called the airline and booked a ticket to Seattle.

He was sure her final destination would be the Dame's house, so he'd be waiting for her when she got there. Then he'd remind her of something she'd obviously forgotten: When it came to plotting their future, he was at the helm.

Piper walked outside, her eyes immediately seeking out Grey's in the crowd. She started down the steps toward him and the knot of tension he'd had all afternoon eased. He'd wanted to believe that she would honor their agreement to meet after class. He *had* believed it, for the most part, but it was relief to know for sure.

He waited at the bottom of the steps, wishing he could read her thoughts without forcing the issue. All Talions, especially the more powerful ones, had the ability to control weaker minds, change memories, read the truth behind the lies, and even bend ordinary Kyth and humans to their will.

That wasn't going to work with Piper. The woman had a forceful personality, one that would make it difficult to get through the outer layers of her mind without doing some serious damage. He wasn't about to risk it, if for no other reason than she mattered to Kerry.

But he preferred to face hard truths head-on. The real reason he wouldn't fuck with her head was that she meant too much to him. After decades of holding himself aloof from others of his kind, it was a shock how quickly this one woman had managed to sneak into his life. He had no idea where their relationship was going, but he wasn't about to let a few bumps get in the way.

She stopped on the last step, giving her the height advantage. He couldn't fault her understanding of power plays. That was all right—women with attitude had always appealed to him. He could also play the game. He joined her on the step long enough to press a chaste kiss on her frowning mouth. Then he immediately backed down onto the sidewalk, willing to give her all the space she needed, as long as she stayed with him.

"How was class?"

"Fine. Finals are coming up, so my profs are cramming in all they can before we run out of time. I'll be glad when it's over."

She stepped down beside him. "Sometimes it feels like I'll never finish my degree. Once I graduate, I'm not sure what I'll do with all my free time."

"I'm sure you'll adjust." He led her toward the car. "I hope you're hungry. Sandor and I worked through lunch, so I thought maybe we could pick up a couple of sandwiches and eat down by the water."

During the time they'd been apart, he'd decided the best way to deal with the investigator's report was to talk about it in neutral territory. If she didn't go for that, then he'd let her choose the location. The only option he wouldn't accept was to not talk at all.

Piper waited until they were in the car to answer. "Look, Grey. I'm not sure this is a good idea."

She waved her hand in the air as if searching for the right words. "This weekend was fun. Great, in fact. But how much of it was because you almost died?"

Okay, he hadn't seen that one coming. "So you think the best sex I've had in . . . in fact, the best sex I've *ever* had, is solely in response to a near-death experience?"

Damned if she didn't nod and smile, as if proud of a slow student finally getting the answer right. "I'm not complaining, Grey, or pointing fingers. It was good for me, too, but I'm not sure we have any kind of basis for a real relationship."

He flexed his fingers on the steering wheel, his hands flickering with streams of angry energy. "Other than the scorching hot sex, you mean?"

"Well, yes. Don't get me wrong, I had a nice time with you, but I think maybe you should just take me home."

"Nice?" he asked, echoing her description. "You're saying it was *nice*?"

She stared out the windshield. "Didn't you think so?"

What could he say to that? He shifted into first gear and jerked the car out into traffic, forcing the guy behind him to slam on his breaks. Grey responded to the blare of the horn with a casual flip of his middle finger. He almost hoped it would push the driver too far. A brawl might help take the edge off.

Piper settled back into her seat and stared at her lap. As he approached the intersection ahead, he debated which way to turn. The water was a bad idea, he decided spontaneously. So right to Piper's apartment or left to his hotel? No contest. Left it was. He wasn't about to give her a home field advantage.

Judging from the white-knuckled grip she had on her backpack, Piper wasn't as calm as she was acting. Good. He didn't want to be the only one tied up in knots. She'd yet to notice that they weren't headed toward the water, which was fine with him. Far better if they had already pulled into the hotel's underground parking before she exploded.

They almost made it.

All of sudden Piper sat up straighter and whipped her head around as she took measure of their direction. "Grey, where are you taking me?"

"Home." His smile held a great deal of satisfaction.

"I meant *my* home."

"You should have been more specific."

He whipped the car into an empty parking spot. She was still sputtering in protest when he yanked her door open.

She stayed where she was, giving him a narrow-eyed stare. "What are you doing?"

"I'm waiting for you to get out of the car."

"And if I don't?"

He almost wished she wouldn't. "I'll toss you over my shoulder and carry you up to my room. Your choice."

Evidently she correctly judged his mood because she got out of the car on her own, looking much put upon. She trailed along beside him, but her eyes kept judging the distance to the nearest exit.

"I wouldn't, Piper. Chasing you down wouldn't help my mood at all." He kept walking as he spoke. "But if you need to test my resolve, go for it."

"Fine. But I'm not staying long."

"Don't worry. I'm not planning on holding you prisoner indefinitely."

When he hit the elevator button, the doors immediately slid open. He stood back and motioned for her to go first. Nothing like good manners to impress a lady—even if he really did it to keep her from bolting.

She knew it, too. "So you do have a plan."

"Yes, as a matter of fact, I do."

"Care to clue me in?"

"As I recall, you said having sex with me was—what was the word? Oh, yes, *nice.*" He shot her an innocent look. "That's right, isn't it, Piper? That it was *nice.*"

She backed up a step as she nodded. "I didn't mean it as an insult, Grey."

"Yes, well, it was. But not to worry." He clasped his hands behind his back.

"Why not?"

"Because once we get to my room, we'll order in a meal and have that talk I promised you. And then—"

He flashed her a wolfish smile, letting his gaze travel from her face down to her toes and back. He lingered on his favorite places.

Piper's eyes widened, her breathing shallow in the confines of the elevator. "And then?"

He leaned in close enough to let his breath brush against her skin. "And then, my dear Piper, I plan on showing you just how *nice* I can be."

Chapter 11

This *so* wasn't working out the way Piper had expected. She should have known that a Talion warrior wouldn't behave like the human males she'd dated in the past. Her gentle slight had turned into a direct challenge to Grey's ego. She would've called him on it, but she realized she'd been hoping he'd call her bluff.

He wasn't the sort of man to make idle threats. If she hadn't gotten out of the car when she did, he would have hauled her off like some Neanderthal hunting for a mate. His hotel room might be far more luxurious than the average cave, but the principle was the same.

What was freaking her out, though, was that she liked Grey's primitive attitude. A lot. Instead of making her furious, his bullheaded behavior was making her hot and achy, to the point that if he'd wanted to make "nice" in the elevator, she'd have been all for it.

But one of them needed to maintain control. At least for now. After they talked, he probably wouldn't be interested in being nice anymore. It was surprising how much that thought hurt.

He unlocked the door to his room, once again letting her enter ahead of him. The man definitely had trust issues, but then he wasn't the only one. She tossed her bag on the floor and walked to the window overlooking the Seattle skyline.

Grey ducked into the bathroom and reappeared after only a few seconds. When she glanced back at him, he was unbuttoning his shirt.

She tried to look away, but her eyes were riveted on his powerful hands and on each bare inch of his chest as the buttons slipped free. The shirt hit the floor as he kicked off his shoes and reached for his belt buckle.

"Uh, I'll wait out on the balcony while you . . . um, change."

Except she didn't move. It was all she could do to *breathe*. Grey tossed his belt over the back of a chair and then very deliberately unfastened the snap above his fly. The slow rasp of the zipper seemed to echo throughout the room even after he'd stepped out of his pants. The navy boxers he wore did nothing to disguise how much he wanted her.

The afternoon sun streamed in through the sliding door, outlining his face. Grey was a hard man, one determined to win every battle he faced. He would never hurt her, but he had every intention of conquering her. If she ended up in his bed, there would be no quarter given.

"Come here, Piper."

Not a good idea. They both knew where this was headed. She held her ground. Her pride demanded it, even as part of her very much wanted to give in. The sex between them had been amazing, but this felt different, a claiming perhaps. If she . . . if they . . . well, she very much feared that nothing would ever be the same.

This would be no gentle wooing. It was there in the determined set of his mouth and the blue flames in his eyes. Grey would take her fast and hard with everything he had. On the floor. On the bed. Maybe even against the wall. All of which sounded just fine to her. She threw her shoulders back, ready to make a few demands of her own.

Her breasts already felt heavy, craving his rough yet gentle touch. Her clothing trapped her, and she wanted it gone.

Grey didn't ask a second time. He simply held out his hand and waited for her to take it. To do so, she'd have to concede the distance she'd put between them, to surrender to his masculine strength.

She kicked off her shoes and pulled off her shirt, then shimmied out of her jeans. Smiling, she slowly raised her hands up to cup her own breasts, taking satisfaction in the greedy hunger in Grey's expression as he followed her every move. With a quick flick of her fingers, she released the front clasp on her bra and shrugged it off.

It required every ounce of courage she could muster to take that first step forward, and then a second, her hand reaching out. When her fingertips brushed his, she felt them tremble. She settled her palm over his, savoring the desire arcing between them. He wrapped his hand around hers, but continued to hold her at arm's length.

"Honey, please tell me you want this, too."

"Yeah, Grey, I do."

He jerked his head down in a quick nod and dropped her hand. Okay. Now what? Then she knew. She hooked her fingers in the top of her panties and slowly slid them down her legs. After kicking them aside, she put her hands on her hips and silently invited Grey to look his fill.

"Your turn."

When he dropped his boxers, she realized why he'd been in the bathroom. He was already sheathed and ready for her. How resourceful—and single-minded.

"What if I'd said no?"

"I was pretty sure that wasn't going to happen."

The time to play coy was long past. "Then what are you waiting for?"

He might have picked up a shiny veneer of manners and civilized behavior somewhere along the way, but now Grey shed it without hesitation. Piper was a strong woman who could handle whatever he dished out. He loved how she shivered when he nibbled on her shoulder and wrapped her in his arms, pulling her back against the length of his body.

It felt like heaven to have her lush backside up against his erection. She liked it, too, judging from the way she leaned into him and tugged his hands up to cover her pretty breasts. They fit his hands perfectly as he plumped them with not quite gentle squeezes.

"Grey! Please."

Clearly both of them were already reaching the boiling point. The only question was where—the bed or the couch?

The bed was closer. Two heartbeats later they were tangled together. He took his time kissing her, starting with that smart mouth and working his way down to the juncture of her lovely legs. God, she tasted so damned sweet. If he didn't have this burning need to take her fast and hard, he would spend hours driving them both crazy with nothing but his tongue.

He couldn't wait any longer. As he surged back up her body, she wrapped her ankles around his hips, locking him into the cradle of her body. With one powerful thrust, he was deep inside her sweet heat. They fit together as if the gods had crafted them as mirror images, neither complete without the other.

He tried to slow down, to give her time to adjust, to give himself time to savor the moment, but it wasn't happening. Not this time. The vestiges of his temper mixed with the perfume of her skin and the amazing taste of her kiss and quickly became too volatile to hold back. They exploded in a frenzy of give and take. Piper held on to him with all her strength, digging her nails into his back as an intense climax rolled over and through her, and then him.

Piper cried out, he groaned, and the world around them exploded into flames.

An hour later, Piper looked in the mirror as she finger combed her damp hair. Grey had let her shower alone. Part of her was disappointed, but the rest knew she'd needed those few minutes to piece herself back together. To remember where she began and Grey left off. After the mind-shattering experience in his bed, she wasn't sure if she'd ever be able to draw that line clearly again.

Grey stepped out of the bathroom. This time, he was buttoning his shirt up. *Good.* They would need all the layers between them that they could find just to get through their talk.

"I'm going to order sandwiches. Any preference?"

"Whatever you're having is fine."

While he dialed room service, she opened the sliding door and stepped out onto the small balcony, pleased to see that Mt. Rainier was clearly visible. One of her favorite things about Seattle was how the mountain was right there, looming over the city one day, and nowhere to be seen the next. The whole thing was a puzzle, much like the man who had just joined her outside.

"The food will be up shortly."

Even though Grey stood on the other side of the balcony, he still managed to crowd her, making her ache for his touch, for his kiss. God, she had it bad.

At first he seemed content to stare out at the mountain, too, but then he turned to face her. Resting his elbows on the railing, he slouched back. To anyone who wasn't paying close attention, Grey looked relaxed, as if enjoying the warm evening. But all it took was one glance at those ice-cold eyes to know that he'd only banked the coals of his anger. All that fury still lurked near the surface, ready to erupt at the slightest provocation.

And how convenient. She was in exactly the mood to do a little provoking.

"So, you had me investigated." She wished she didn't sound quite so wounded by that fact.

He nodded. "I wondered if that was what set off this snit fit."

Okay, so he was in the mood for a little poking and prodding himself. "This is no snit fit, Danby. Watch it, or this will become a full-blown nuclear meltdown!"

She stood her ground, ready to counter his next move. Then the big jerk surprised her.

"I could apologize, Piper, but I won't. It's my job to defend Dame Kerry, which includes making damn sure that any employees are exactly who they say they are. The previous report left too many gaps and too many questions unanswered. I ordered the investigation right after I returned from London. At that point, we hadn't exchanged more than a few dozen words."

He slowly edged closer to her. "In my opinion, Sandor should never have allowed Kerry to hire you until a thorough search had been done."

He was right. They both knew it, just like they both knew she was overreacting. He came closer yet, finally reaching out to wrap his arm around her shoulders. She let him tuck her in close to his side. Considering his volatile mood only a few minutes before, his gentle approach surprised her.

He pressed a kiss to her temple. "For the record, I haven't read the report."

Maybe there was some merit in that old adage about confession being good for the soul. Her mood had improved considerably since he started talking, even if it hadn't really changed anything.

"Why?"

He stared out toward the mountain, but somehow she doubted he was even aware of what he was seeing.

"Because I've learned over the years that most people have something to hide, something they would rather their employer—or even their friends—not know."

He turned so that they were facing each other. "As the Dame's Chief Talion, those are exactly the details I'm supposed to dig for. I need to make sure that none of those dark little secrets are a threat."

He traced the curve of her cheek with his fingers. "But you're more than just another employee, Piper. I don't want to know your secrets unless you're ready to share them."

"But—" she protested.

He pressed a finger to her lips. "No buts. All I ask is that you promise me nothing in that report could hurt the Dame, her Consort, or any members of their household."

There was a knock the door. "I'll be right back." Grey gave her a quick kiss and went inside to deal with room service.

Piper was uncomfortably aware that she hadn't actually answered him. What kind of promise could she make? She meant no harm to any of them. But Kerry might be devastated when the truth came out. That is, *if* the truth came out. She still hadn't decided what path to take, and time was running out.

All she'd wanted to do was approach the Dame, identify herself as Kyth, and then hang around the fringes to see what kind of person her sister had turned out to be. She hadn't expected to like Kerry so much. And she'd originally been hired to work as Kerry's assistant only for the duration of the school year. With graduation looming on the horizon, she'd soon have to do something. The longer she lived the lie, the harder it would be to confess the truth.

Grey spread the food out on the small table. "How much time do you need to study tonight?"

"An hour, two at the most." The abrupt change of subject was jarring. "I have to read about thirty pages and go over my notes. Why?"

"Because I promised to show you how nice I can be. Part of that is making sure I don't make you fail your exam."

"And the other part?" she asked as she sat down across from him.

He looked past her to the wreckage of his bed with a fond smile. "I thought I'd done a thorough job of demonstrating that particular definition of *nice* when we first got here. However, after we've eaten, I'll be glad to review."

Piper picked up her sandwich. "Normally, I'm a quick study, but in this case, I think you'll need to go slow and use a lot of visual aids."

While she talked, she reached out with her foot and ran her toes along the inside of Grey's leg. "I promise to pay close attention."

"I see."

Grey captured her foot briefly with his hand, running his thumb along her arch several times, his eyes smoldering. "Well, rest assured that I'm definitely up for a hands-on demonstration."

"I bet you are." Damn, it felt good to laugh. She held up her pop in a toast. "Eat your dinner, big guy. You're going need all the strength you can get."

Adele cranked up the radio and sang along as her car's big engine ate up the miles. Driving on the right side of the road had proven to be more of a challenge than she'd expected. But once she'd left the big city behind and had nothing but highway stretched out in front of her, she'd been able to relax and enjoy the ride. Too bad her old geology professor wasn't with her. He would have enjoyed cruising up the West Coast and counting off the volcanoes along the way.

Maybe she'd send the old man a postcard. Or not. It had been with great relief and absolutely no regret that she'd walked away from school after exams. Now she could turn her complete attention to her future. Plans that didn't include any more kowtowing to Kerry Thorsen and her entourage.

Ready to achieve her goal of becoming Dame, Adele planned to enjoy her last days of freedom. Thanks to her father's ambitious plans, she'd rarely had more than a day or two at a time free of obligations. Looking back, she supposed she should be grateful for his efforts to prepare her for her future, but it hadn't been much fun.

But now, it was up to her whether to stop in the next town for the night or drive straight through to Seattle, whether to eat a greasy hamburger and fries or a steak, rare and bloody. Truly, sometimes the little decisions were the most fun. Speaking of which, it was time to start looking for a place to stop for the night.

There was plenty of daylight left, so she wasn't in a great hurry. However, it was time to check in with her talented accomplice. She'd been dating Wes for the past year, enjoying his skills both in bed and out. Hopefully, he had everything on schedule, because she'd ordered another little surprise to stir things up a bit. Playing around with everyone's e-mail had been fun, but it was more of a sideline.

Maybe she'd even give her darling father a call. He should be frantic by now. He had probably figured out what she was up to. He might be a conservative prig, but he wasn't a fool. Well, except for trusting Grey Danby. After all, if her father and his cohorts hadn't treated the Talion as a superior servant instead of as an equal, Grey might not have betrayed them all by taking the Thorsen woman's side.

Grey was a commoner who had only a nodding acquaintance with true culture. Born and bred on the streets of the Docklands, being a Talion was the man's only claim to fame. Poor fellow. It was obvious that he wouldn't jeopardize that for the likes of her father, who had nothing to offer Grey except his disdain. Her father had been a fool to trust him.

Adele could have put Grey's talents to good use—all of them. If he hadn't sided with the great pretender, she would've offered him the same job he now held, but with some benefits he definitely wasn't getting from Kerry. Too late now.

She'd always suspected Grey was spectacular in bed, not that he'd ever looked at her twice—or even once. When she took over the throne of their people, he would see her differently, as a Dame in need of a powerful Consort. But meanwhile he'd thrown the dice and gambled on Kerry remaining ruler of their kind. *Hmmm. Would it be too tacky to take him for a ride or two before having him killed? Probably, but then who would care?*

Of course, Kerry had to die, along with her Consort and those trashy brats she'd let Sandor drag out of the gutter. Sandor and his human lover would meet with an unfortunate end as well. Adele tapped the steering wheel in time to the music as she reviewed her potential victims.

It was really quite an impressive lineup, if she did say so herself. Once they got past the necessary bloodshed, she would share her world vision for the Kyth with her new subjects. If they didn't like it, she'd keep Wes around for a while longer to help reinforce her ideas.

She spotted a sign for a hotel promising clean rooms and free Internet access at the upcoming exit. Perfect. Once she was settled in for the night, she'd call Wes with the throw-away phone she'd purchased in San Francisco. It was time to step up the action again, and she had some wonderfully creative ideas.

When the fireworks went off next time, maybe she'd watch all the fun. Not from too close, though. It wouldn't do to get caught in the fallout. She hit the turn signal and moved over to the right lane. With luck, she'd soon be settled into a room.

It was a shame Wes wouldn't be around to share more than a phone call or an e-mail. The man definitely had a talent for more than computer hacking and explosions. Maybe it was the edge of danger he wore as comfortably as his faded jeans while teaching her all he knew about bomb making. Her father hadn't approved of Wes, but that was part of the attraction.

She pulled up to the motel and sneered as she studied the exterior. For all practical purposes, it was identical to the one she'd stayed in by the airport the night before. The Americans had a lot going for them, but good taste wasn't part of it.

This was hardly a place a woman of her breeding would frequent, which made it perfect for her purposes. She'd be just another traveler in the anonymous crowd of people streaming up and down the highway. Come morning, she'd be on her way and her presence would be forgotten.

In truth, she was rather proud of herself. So far, her plan was playing out smoothly. Her father was no doubt panicked by now, but not quite frightened enough to warn the Dame's Talions. He'd want to rein her in himself first.

And she was only one day away from Seattle. Since Wes had already rented a house, she could remain under the radar until she announced her presence in a loud and spectacular way.

With her suitcase in hand and a satisfied smile on her face, she headed inside to check in.

The guy working behind the desk was about her age, and rather cute. He looked up as she walked through the door, his automatic smile warming up several degrees as their eyes met. Randy—according to his name tag—definitely checked her out, top to bottom and back again.

"Hi, welcome to our hotel. How can I help you?"

She smiled back as she handed him her identification. "I need a room for the night, and I prefer to pay cash. That isn't a problem, is it?"

"Not at all." After typing in her information, he studied the computer screen for several seconds. "I've put you in our best room, Miss Harcourt. It's on the second floor and has a king-size bed and a Jacuzzi.

"Let me know if there's anything else I can do for you." He dropped his voice. "Personally, that is."

She raised up on her toes to check him out more carefully. Yummy. "You know, I think there is. I'm all by myself, and it gets lonely."

"I get off at seven," he whispered. Then, at a more normal volume, he added, "Thank you for choosing our hotel."

"I hope to see much more of you while I'm here." She deliberately trailed her fingers over his hand before accepting her room key.

He grinned and shifted his stance, no doubt in response to the sudden strain on his zipper. An impressive strain, she noted happily.

"Call me if you have any problems. I want to make sure you enjoy your stay, Miss Harcourt."

"It's Adele, and I'm sure you will, Randy. I'm looking forward to everything you and your hotel have to offer."

The poor boy was almost tripping over his tongue, but at least she could count on the evening being far less boring than she'd feared. Slutty of her, yes, but Wes was all the way in Seattle, and the road was a lonely place after all.

"Okay, Grey, wherever you are. We didn't decide whether to downplay our relationship around the others."

Piper punched in Grey's number, hoping to catch him before she reached the office. The call went right to voicemail, so he either hadn't turned his phone on yet, which seemed unlikely, or he was talking to someone. She'd have to play it by ear. No biggie.

As she turned the corner toward the house, she noticed a young man loitering down the street. Normally, she wouldn't have given him more than a momentary glance, but something about him was off.

For one thing, he was standing directly across the street from Kerry's and staring at the house with an intensity she could sense from a block away. For another, he was almost vibrating with energy, making her wonder if he was high on something. The instant he realized she was watching, he closed his notebook and started toward her.

Keeping a wary eye on him as he approached, she let the strap of her backpack slide down off her shoulder to her hand. If the guy made any kind of suspicious move, her textbooks would make a good weapon.

When he stopped a few feet away, she aimed for friendly, but cautious. "Hi, were you looking for someone?"

Up close, he didn't look high, but he sure had the jitters. "No, I was checking out the architecture in the neighborhood for a project. I'm a new student at the university."

He held up his spiral notebook as if it were proof. But she wasn't buying what he was selling.

"Well, I'm late for work, so I'd better get going. Good luck with your project."

"Thanks." His eyes kept straying toward Kerry's house. "I'll need all the luck I can get to pull this one off."

"I hear you."

Piper forced a smile as she walked away. When she looked back, he'd moved down the street, apparently to "study" another house. His excuse might be plausible, but it didn't ring true. Unless he was a procrastinator of epic proportions, it was far too late in the quarter to be starting a major project.

She'd mention him to Grey when she got inside. She didn't want to cause trouble, but it was better to err on the side of caution. As she waited for the gate to open, she looked back one last time.

He'd disappeared completely, which was more disturbing than if he'd still been lurking around. Maybe she should have asked his name, but then there was no guarantee he'd have told her his real one. She was probably blowing everything out of proportion, but having the solid iron gate between them now felt darn good.

Inside the house, she could hear deep voices coming from her office. Good. She could tell them about the guy outside.

The small office was overflowing with testosterone. Grey was at his computer, his expression fierce as his fingers flew over the keyboard. Sandor was hovering near Grey's shoulder, pointing at the screen, while Ranulf leaned against the corner of her desk and watched them.

To her surprise, Sean was there, too. He was focused

on cleaning his nails with the point of a nasty-looking knife. But from the tilt of his head, she suspected his attention was really on the three adult Talions.

"Morning, Piper." Ranulf nodded at her as he pushed up off her desk and moved closer to Grey.

"Good morning. Looks busy in here." She sat down in her chair and booted up her own computer.

As soon as she spoke, Grey stopped typing long enough to smile at her. "Sorry about the crowd. We're trying to track down our hacker. He's a slippery bastard."

"Him? You know it's a guy?"

Sandor answered without looking up. "Not necessarily, but it would match up with the bombing. It's always possible the bomber is a woman, but most of the time that's not the case."

Which reminded her. "When I was coming in a few minutes ago, a guy was standing across the street watching the house."

Suddenly, she had four pairs of glowing Talion eyes intensely focused on her every word. She cleared her throat uncomfortably and kept talking.

"He wasn't sneaking around or anything. In fact, when he saw me coming, he came up to me. He said he was studying the architecture in this part of town for a class project."

"That sounds likely enough." Sandor had clearly lost interest, turning his attention back to the computer.

But Grey was still listening. "Something about him bothered you?"

She nodded. "The quarter ends next week. If he's just starting his project, the timing is all wrong. I looked back a couple of times as I walked away. First he checked out another house down the street, but when I was waiting for the gate to open, I looked one more time and he'd left. I don't know if he took off running or if he ducked into someone's yard."

Grey started to get up. "I'll go check him out."

But Sean was already pushing through the crowded office toward the door. Ranulf blocked his way. "Where do you think you're going?"

Sean didn't back down. Oddly, he sought out Grey's approval. "Let me be the one to go. Any of you would stand out too much. He won't even notice me, so I'm less likely to spook him. I can trail him for a while to see where he goes."

Sean turned to Piper. "What's he look like?"

Grey gave her a slow nod.

"He's about five-ten. Dark blond hair, cut long in the front, shorter in the back. He was wearing cargo pants with a dark blue T-shirt that had some logo on it."

"Got it. I'll be back."

Sandor reached out to stop him. "Sean, wait. Do you have your cell?"

The boy rolled his eyes. Of course he had it. No one his age would be caught dead without one.

"I'll check in when I've got something to report."

Ranulf pegged the kid with a hard look. "Don't do anything stupid. Right now we don't know that this guy is anything other than what he says he is. Check in often. Call for help if you need it. If he spots you, haul ass back here, but don't lead him to our front door unless you have to. Got it?"

Sean grinned at the Viking. "Yes, mother."

Then he took off before Ranulf could do more than sputter. Piper managed to keep a straight face, but neither Grey nor Sandor tried to hide their amusement.

Sandor looked pleased. "Sean's going to make Kerry one hell of a Talion. God knows he's got enough attitude for it."

Ranulf wasn't ready to be placated. "If he lives long enough. If he keeps smarting off like that, it's doubtful he will."

It was fun to pick on the Viking, but Piper was worried about Sean out on the streets. "Will he be okay out there?"

Sandor poured himself a cup of coffee. "Don't let Sean's age fool you. He's been on his own for years and knows the streets of Seattle like the back of his hand. Even with all our experience in tracking down rogues, Sean managed to evade Ranulf and me for an embarrassing length of time."

Grey concurred with him. "The kid's a street rat, and smart to boot. I'd tell you not to worry, but you will anyway."

She wondered if either of the other two men noticed the knowing smile Grey gave her. Even if it hadn't given them away, her blush probably would. She turned back to her computer.

"Any weird e-mails today?" she asked.

"Not for any of us. We hadn't gotten around to checking yours yet."

She quickly logged on to the system. As soon as her in-box appeared on the screen, her good mood did a serious nosedive. Again. Dear God, the entire first page showed the same sender, "1xploshun," with "Future Pyrotechnics" in the subject line.

"Grey?"

Before she had time to point at the screen, he was beside her, one arm around her shoulders and his other hand holding hers. Energy was running hot under his skin and the same was probably true for Ranulf and Sandor.

"Are you going to open it or not?" Sandor sounded far calmer than Piper felt.

She deferred the decision to Grey. "I don't know. What do you think?"

"We don't have a choice. If we had ignored the second one, Hughes would be dead." Grey's jaw twitched as he gritted his teeth. "Make sure you both can see the screen. This bastard makes his handiwork disappear after he delivers the message."

"We're ready."

Despite the air conditioning, the room was stifling with all the heat pouring off the three Talions in full warrior mode. Piper braced herself for whatever the hacker had planned and clicked on the first e-mail.

Her screen lit up with a picture of an all too familiar sight: Ranulf's pristine 1940 Packard convertible. Then the car silently exploded into a million pieces as a single word appeared at the bottom of the screen:

"BOOM!"

Chapter 12

"*W*hat the fuck?"

Stunned by the explosion playing over and over on the computer screen, Piper wasn't sure which Tailon had spoken. Not that it mattered. No doubt they all had the same reaction. There was enough anger in the room to temper steel.

Grey asked the one important question. "Where's your car, Ranulf?"

When the Viking didn't immediately answer, Piper dragged her attention from the fragmenting picture to him. It was difficult to tell if he was actually processing anything. She reached out to touch his hand.

"Ranulf. Where's the car right now?"

If he didn't answer, she'd go look out the front window herself to check. But he blinked a couple of times and shook his head.

"I left it up on the mountain. We drove the SUV

back." He stood up straighter. "If the bastard got past my protections, then we're dealing with a major power. Although, if someone *was* messing with my wards, I'd feel it even from here. In all the years I've lived up there, the only one who got past them without being tied up in knots was Kerry."

Sandor leaned in closer. "Can you tell where the picture was taken? Your house and garage can't be seen from the road. Besides, you've buried the title to that property so deep only someone with a lot of time and a big shovel would be able to trace the ownership back to you."

Piper hit the "Print" button, hoping the catch the image intact before it disappeared. Luck was with her. She handed a copy to Grey and another to Ranulf.

"It was taken out in the driveway. The bastard snapped the picture through the front gate. The top's down, so most likely it was right before Kerry and I left for the weekend."

Ranulf crushed the paper in his hand and threw it in the wastebasket. "What if he followed us up to the mountain?"

"Don't worry, Ranulf." Grey's stone-hard expression matched Ranulf's. "We'll get him."

"Easy for you to say, Danby. Your wife isn't the one who likes to drive that car. What if he planted a bomb in it while Kerry was out with the kids? As much as we'd like to, we can't protect them from everything."

Grey straightened up to his full height. "We will

keep our Dame and her people safe, Ranulf. This rogue will die. This I vow."

Grey laid his hand over his heart, covering the brand just above it. Sandor repeated the words, his hand on his bicep, while Ranulf clasped the Thor's Hammer around his neck. As soon as they were done, Grey pulled a gun out of his desk drawer and clipped it to his belt.

He held out another one just like it. "I've got a spare if either of you need one."

"Thanks," Sandor said, looking awfully proficient as he checked it out.

Ranulf shook his head. "I'll get mine out of the gun safe when we're done in here."

Ranulf stepped back, giving Piper more space. "No one goes unescorted until this is resolved. I hope your men get here fast, Grey."

"More are on their way. I'll have someone posted around the clock by tonight."

"Good."

"I'm thinking we may need to close ranks." Grey glanced at Piper. "At least Sandor and Lena. Me and Piper, too. Otherwise we'd be spread too thin to be effective, especially while we're out tracking down leads. I don't want any of us out there alone."

"Sounds good," Ranulf agreed. "I'll let Hughes know to expect company so he can get rooms ready."

Grey nodded. "Good. Once everyone's tucked in safe, we'll do some patrolling. Maybe we'll get lucky and catch the bastard sniffing around the area. Which reminds me, Sean hasn't checked in. Give him another ten minutes and then yank his chain."

It was Piper's first experience seeing the Dame's Talions prepare to . . . to what? The answer to that question was terrifying in its simplicity: They were going to hunt the bomber down and kill him.

"Isn't it Detective Byrne's job to bring whoever is behind this to justice?"

She knew the minute the words left her mouth that she'd asked the wrong question. Three warriors stared down at her with nearly identical looks of incredulity.

"Hell, no!" That came from Ranulf.

Sandor joined in. "It's not his job."

Grey finished. "Byrne might dispute that point, but too damn bad. We will track down the renegade, and when we do, we'll suck the life out of him, leaving nothing but dust."

The imagery was too much. "Okay, I'm out of here. You're scaring me."

They all were, but she directed the comment at Grey. When he made a move to stop her, she feinted to the side and darted past him into the hall. He went to grab her, but jerked his hands back when she dodged him again.

She kept her distance. "Keep your hands to yourself."

"Fine, I will." He shoved his hands in his pockets as a sign of good faith. "I was just trying to make sure you weren't going to leave the house alone."

"I was going to see if Kerry needed any help."

"Good idea."

Even though she was trying to escape, he followed right behind her. She wheeled around to face him, prepared to do battle. It was hard to keep her voice low, but she did her best.

"You know, I *can* actually make it all the way to the dining room on my own. I've done it hundreds of times. Ask anybody."

He snuck around to block her way. "Why are you running from me?"

"It isn't just you I'm running from." She pointed past him toward the office. "E-mails about bombs and exploding cars are bad enough. But do you guys have to go all Three Musketeers on me? Because, really, all you needed were plumed hats and swords to make the whole picture complete."

When Grey didn't budge, she threw her hands up in the air. "Don't you get it? You even sent Sean out on the streets to play D'Artagnan. This might come as a shock to you, but I signed on to assist Kerry, not to hang out with the Kyth's answer to the Special Forces."

"Damn it, Piper, this is my job. Most of the time we do let the local police handle things, but they're not equipped to handle a renegade on a rampage." He stepped closer. "And don't go all us-versus-them on me. You're Kyth, too. You know this is how it has to be."

"I get that. And you're right." Not that she liked to admit it. She brushed her hair out of her face. "This is all new to me, and the thought of you three dusting some guy scares me."

Grey's hands were seething with dark swirls of energy but he was gentle when he touched her face. "Damn it, Piper, that bastard tried to kill you and Hughes. He's threatening our Dame."

He pointed down the hall to where the other two Talions were surely hanging on their every word. "Ask Ranulf and Sandor what happens when a renegade goes unchecked. How many people have to die before you think we should be let off our leashes to do the job?"

It was all too much. As a Talion warrior, Grey was clearly capable of great violence. But in truth, she was more afraid *for* Grey than *of* him.

What could she say? "I just want all of this to go away."

"I'm not a magician, Piper. But you have my word that I will keep you safe, and this *will* end."

Grey flinched at the powerful emotions Piper was throwing at him. He would never read her thoughts without her permission, but right now he didn't need to. Her feelings were loud and clear. It didn't surprise him that she'd been horrified by her first experience with Talion warriors preparing for battle.

Maybe she would have been able to process it all better if she wasn't emotionally involved with one of them—him.

"Go talk to Kerry. She's been where you are right now, and recently. See what helped her deal."

He held out his arms, hoping Piper would at least accept that much comfort from him. She barely hesitated before she slammed up against his chest.

"I don't mean to be a total wuss, Grey." She sniffled a little, and then let out what sounded like a giggle.

He leaned his head back to get a look at her. Sure enough, her mouth was twitching as she held back her laughter.

"Care to share?"

"When I came in this morning, my biggest worry was whether or not you wanted anyone to know that you and I were . . . well, you know."

Yes, he did know, and now, thanks to the Talion's sensitive hearing, so did Sandor and Ranulf. "I'm guessing it's a bit too late to worry about that."

She nodded. "Hope you don't mind."

"That a beautiful woman has outed me as her lover? I'd have to be four kinds of crazy to mind that."

And while they were on the subject, he needed to kiss her right then and there. When she melted into his arms, the fear that she'd been about to walk out of his life rather than just his office disappeared.

He held her close and rested his chin against her head. "We'll figure this out, Piper. Go have some tea, talk to Kerry, and leave this mess to me."

Grey pulled back and looked her in the eye. "I'm really good at my job. I know you worry, but no more than I do when you're out there on street waiting for the bus. We can't let fear rule us, not if we're going to have any kind of future together."

Piper gave him a solemn nod. "All right, then. We agree it's okay to worry, but not to let it ruin what we have."

"Exactly."

They kissed again to seal the pact. Damn, he wished they were back at his hotel or her apartment. Anywhere but here with two Talions and his ruler just down the hall.

His phone vibrated in his pocket. He grabbed it without letting Piper go. After a quick glance at the screen, he answered.

"Damn it, kid, it's about time you called in."

As he listened to Sean, Piper slipped out of his embrace and disappeared down the hall. He was being pulled apart by his need to keep everyone safe and to keep Piper with him at all times.

He knew his duty even if he didn't like it.

"You did good, kid. Come back and we'll figure out our next move."

Grey braced himself to face the two men waiting in his office. The silence from their direction was oppressive. They were bound to have questions about his relationship with Piper. So did he, for that matter. He wished he had some answers.

When Grey walked back into the room, Sandor pretended to be mesmerized by the exploding car. Ranulf, on the other hand, sat on Grey's desk, his arms crossed over his chest. Okay, so the two of them had decided to let the Viking be the point man. Great.

Grey tried to avoid the conversation. "Sean called. It took him a while to spot the guy, but he found the kid a block over right behind the house. He was standing on a rock at the edge of the yard, snapping pictures with his cell phone.

"Our boy Sean's got definite potential as a Talion. He managed to trail his quarry all the way to the guy's car and even thought to get the license plate number. There was no way to track him once he drove off, so Sean's on his way back."

Sandor looked like a proud papa. He was entitled to, especially considering he'd been the one to give Sean a new chance at life. Even Ranulf looked impressed, but then his eyes flared as he focused back on Grey.

Okay. Fine. Let's get down to it.

"Get it out of your system, Viking."

"You and Piper?"

Grey picked up a piece of paper and ran a finger along the edge, leaving small flames burning in its wake. He watched with satisfaction as the paper curled up and blackened. As a show of strength it wasn't much, but it was a damn fine indicator of his current mood.

"Yes, me and Piper." He tossed the flaming paper into an empty wastebasket. "Got a problem with that?"

Sandor spun around to face him. "You haven't known her long. How far has this gone?"

Grey's temper hit the flashpoint. "What the hell is this? The bloody Spanish Inquisition?"

"Damn straight it is," Sandor snarled right back at him. "We like Piper."

What the hell was that supposed to mean? "So do I. Or is this because you don't like me? Well, too fucking bad."

"That's not what I meant, Grey, and you know it." Sandor was sparking a few flames himself. "She's only been aware of her Kyth heritage a short time. You saw how she reacted to our plan."

Ranulf reentered the fray. "She needs time to adjust to what she is without adding complications like—"

Okay, this was going to get ugly. "Like what, you bloody berserker? From what I've heard, you two wankers were both sniffing around Kerry from day one. How much time did you give her to adjust before you added those very same complications to *her* life?"

"Watch it, Danby. That's my wife you're talking about, not to mention your Dame." Ranulf's hands were at his sides, tightly fisted and ready to fight.

Grey didn't give a damn. "And what about you, Sandor? We're supposed to keep our identities secret from humans like Lena. How long after you met her did you 'complicate' her?"

Sandor jumped to his feet. "Hey, now!"

Facing off against two pissed off Talions might be suicidal, but Grey planned on giving as good as he got. That didn't mean he really wanted to start trading punches with these two, especially with Kerry and Piper around. The two women would not appreciate their men acting like idiots.

He forced his anger down a couple of notches.

"I will be careful with Piper. That's all you need to know. Now, can we get back to business?"

Ranulf was already nodding. "Fine. But Piper has no family to stand up for her, so I'm the one you'll answer to if you get careless with her feelings."

"Right. But the bottom line is that this is between me and her. Nobody else."

They all froze when Sean appeared in the doorway. He hesitated to cross the threshold, no doubt sensing the tension in the room.

"Come on in, Sean. Tell us everything."

"Adele, I thought you'd be here by now. I've been waiting to set the final timetable."

She winced, hating the possessiveness in Wes's voice. There was a lot about the guy she enjoyed very much, but she'd had enough of being treated like a prized possession by her father. She wasn't about to put up with it from anyone else. On the other hand, she still needed Wes's services—all of them.

"I'm sorry it's taking so long, but I'll be in Seattle tonight. Thanks for texting me the directions. I shouldn't have any trouble finding you."

She dropped her voice low and gravelly, just the way he liked it. A whisper near his ear was all it usually took to get him hard and ready to ride. "You don't know how much I've missed you. I've had nothing to think about on this long drive but how I want to please you, and I know just how to go about it."

Especially because she'd tried a few ideas out

with the highly talented Randy last night. Her compliments to his parents; they'd certainly named him appropriately.

Wes's reaction was predictable. "Hope you're prepared for a long night then. I've been saving all my energy for you."

What a shame she couldn't say the same, but she wisely kept that little tidbit to herself. Instead, she began, "Here's what I've been thinking . . ."

To entertain both of them, she described in great detail what she had in mind for the evening. Wes made a few suggestions that had her clenching her knees. He was inventive; she'd give him that.

She pressed down on the gas pedal, wanting to get to Seattle as fast as possible. She glanced at the mileage sign up ahead. "I'm about ten miles south of Olympia. I'll see you soon, lover. I can't wait to see how our plans are coming along."

She let him ramble on about e-mails and his plans to blow up an antique car. It all sounded good, but traffic was getting too heavy for her attention to be split. "Sorry, Wes, but I've got to go."

He was still talking when she closed her phone.

The Seattle airport was busier than Harcourt remembered, but at least his flight had been on time. He shuffled along in line to clear customs and retrieve his luggage. Normally, he would have found the whole process tedious, but he needed time to figure out his next step. He'd been eating antacids by the handful since this mess had started. Between the burning in his stomach and his inability to sleep, he was a disaster.

If Adele were with him, he'd be sorely tempted to choke the life out of her and be done with it. Nothing—not even seeing his daughter ascend to the throne of their people—was worth this misery. If he didn't put a stop to whatever madness she was up to, the Talions would kill her for him. Maybe that was inevitable, but that didn't mean he wanted to die with her.

The stupid bitch! Why couldn't she have inherited her late mother's compliant nature? All he'd wanted was for her to be the face of the Kyth while he ruled their world from behind the throne. No chance of that happening now. The most they could hope for was to skulk back to London without anyone knowing.

It certainly didn't help that Adele continued to ignore his phone calls and e-mails. He was convinced she was heading straight for Seattle, if not already parked in front of the Dame's home with a detonator in her hands. Did she really think he wouldn't piece it all together?

He'd always suspected that her superior intellect was going to cause them both problems. Yes, she'd always done everything he'd asked of her: excelling in school, making friends in all the right circles, being stylish without being ostentatious. The perfect daughter. The perfect candidate for Grand Dame of the Kyth.

And yet, there'd been clues all along if he'd only

paid attention to them. Her taste in music was appalling. She'd also alienated more than one of her professors with her sharp intellect and even sharper tongue. Granted, he didn't suffer fools well either, but occasionally one had to deal with them. Insults and shrewish behavior did not make things any easier.

Finally, there was Wes. He'd had the boy investigated when Adele first started seeing him. Despite his dreadful origins, Wes had used his freakish genius to worm his way into the same university as Adele. The school prided itself on its scholarship program. Fine. He supposed that was necessary in today's PC culture.

That didn't mean Harcourt appreciated them allowing—even encouraging—such beings to associate with their betters. He wished he knew if Adele was using Wes as a way to rebel or for some other, darker reason. Wes had taken a degree in chemistry with high honors. And the investigator Harcourt had hired found magazines on weapons and explosives in the boy's apartment when he'd searched it.

Harcourt had searched Adele's room himself, looking for clues about her current whereabouts. When he found her stash of birth control pills, he'd almost become ill. Did she need to risk ruining her entire life by tarnishing her reputation with the likes of that boy?

Obviously she didn't care what anyone—especially her father—thought. At least her mother hadn't lived to see Adele treading such a dangerous path.

"May I see your papers, sir?"

The question startled him. He'd been so lost in thought that he hadn't noticed the line ahead of him had finally disappeared.

"I'm sorry." He held out his passport. "I'm afraid the long trip has left me a bit foggy."

In short order, Harcourt had his passport tucked safely in his pocket and his luggage in hand. Ordinarily, he would have contacted the Dame's butler to arrange for a car, but not this time. Sneaking into town uninvited and unannounced, he would have to find his own way to a suitable hotel.

Once he was settled in, he'd hunt for his daughter. If he could find Adele and derail her plans for destruction, they'd be on the next plane to London. With luck, their brief presence here in Seattle would go unnoticed. If the Talions needed a target, he could throw Wes their way.

And if Adele wouldn't listen—or worse yet, if he was already too late—he would return to the UK alone and disavow any knowledge of her affairs. He'd grieve for her passing as any good father should, but he wouldn't die for her.

That was simply too much to ask.

He stepped outside and headed for the long line of waiting taxis. One driver was already opening the trunk for Harcourt's luggage. He surrendered it with great relief.

It was the first thing that had gone right in days. As he climbed into the backseat of the cab, he prayed it wouldn't be the last.

Chapter 13

"*L*et's take a walk."

Kerry was already heading for the door, leaving Piper no choice but to follow the Dame out to the rose garden. Both women paused to stare up at the bright blue of the Seattle sky. Nothing like soaking up a little sunshine to soothe the soul, especially in a city known for its gray days.

Kerry took the lead as they wandered through the garden. Piper drew in a deep breath, inhaling the intoxicating scent of a dark red rose. Both of them carefully skirted the blackened circle where the bomb had exploded. It was hard to ignore the spot completely, festooned as it was with strips of yellow crime scene tape. But eventually the damage to the garden would fade.

The memories wouldn't. Not completely.

Despite Grey's resilient Talion physiology, he had almost died when he'd been bashed into the wall by the explosion. Piper could still see him flying through the air, out of control, until he bounced off the brick wall and landed unmoving on the ground. He'd healed, but it had been a close call. Too close.

"He's fine, Piper."

Kerry stood beside her, looking at the clumps of charred grass. Had she read Piper's thoughts? Kerry had that ability, but as far as Piper knew, she'd never used it on her. Kerry glanced up at her and shook her head.

"No, I'm not reading your thoughts. Given the expression on your face, it wasn't hard to guess what you were thinking about." Kerry wrapped her arms around herself, looking chilled despite the warm weather.

Piper picked up a piece of burned grass. "I keep seeing it over and over again in my head. I have to remind myself that he's all right. Or at least he is for now."

Kerry made a wide turn around the crime scene. "Let's go try out the new swing. I had it installed in memory of Dame Judith. I looked at all kinds of fancy benches, but as soon as I saw this swing, I knew it was perfect."

They sat down, and Piper used her longer legs to set the swing in motion. It was surprising how soothing she found the gentle sway. For several minutes, they sat in silence, enjoying the heady combination of roses and sunshine.

Finally, Kerry spoke. "So tell me, what do you think of my new Chief Talion?"

Piper's jaw dropped. Before she could come up with an appropriate answer, Kerry giggled.

"What?" Piper asked, trying not to sound defensive.

Kerry quickly erased most of her grin. "I should say that I wanted to know what you thought of him in his professional capacity—but that would be a lie."

She turned and leaned against the arm of the swing, then crossed her legs on the seat. "Come on, Piper. Dish."

"Are you asking as my employer or as my— friend?"

God, she'd come so close to letting the word "sister" slip out. Now was not the time for any more great revelations. That she and Grey were lovers was enough of a bombshell for one day.

"Definitely as your friend."

"It's all happened so quickly," Piper began. "From that first day, he's been impossible to ignore. There's just something about those blue eyes and solemn expression. I kept wanting to find ways to mess with that solid control he has on his emotions."

She tipped her head back to stare up at a passing cloud. "Maybe we would have ended up involved anyway, but seeing him almost die made the attraction even stronger. I feel everything more intensely when he's around. Safer for sure, but it's like all of my emotions are running on high."

She risked a look at Kerry. "Am I making any sense?"

"You sound like me not that long ago." Kerry looked toward the house. "It was as if I got dumped in the deep end of the pool with no swimming lessons. You've heard about the night of the fire. Ranulf was there, helping me get people out, although I didn't actually meet him until later. It was Sandor who first approached me. He was supposed to ease me into the world of the Kyth."

"I take it that things didn't work out as planned."

"It depends on whose plans you're talking about." Kerry picked at a hole in her jeans. "Sandor was supposed to finesse me, and Ranulf was to protect me. At least that's what the two of them thought. However, Dame Judith suspected from the beginning that I shared her talents. She decided to throw both of her strongest Talions at me in hopes one of them would end up my Consort."

Piper had already heard some of the story. For a short time, the two men had been in fierce competition for Kerry's attention. "Well, it obviously worked. Was Judith surprised that you'd pick a Viking barbarian over a Cary Grant?"

"No more than Ranulf was." Kerry's expression quickly turned pensive. "Yes, it worked out, but at a cost. We lost Judith way too soon. Sandor was almost consumed with the need to protect me not just from the rogue, but from Ranulf as well. Sandor thought him too unstable to be trusted. Having to kill another Talion hurt both of them in ways we'll never understand."

"They seem to be doing all right now."

Kerry kicked at the dirt. "Better anyway. Finding Lena and then the kids has made a world of difference for Sandor. Actually, for all of us. None of us have any blood family left, and the kids have helped fill that gap. From what Ranulf tells me, training Sean has proven as much fun for the three men as it is for Sean. They'll eventually add Kenny to the mix, too."

Piper winced at the comment about blood kin. Maybe she'd been wrong, and now *was* the time to tell Kerry. The longer she waited, the harder it would be to admit the truth or explain why she hid it. Before she could decide, Kerry reached over and put her hand on Piper's wrist.

"Okay, what's up? As handsome as my Chief Talion is, I don't think he's responsible for the sudden panic on your face. Your pulse is going a mile a minute, and your hands are shaking."

Before Piper could come up with an answer, the man in question stepped out of the house. He hesitated briefly to give Kerry—or maybe Piper herself—time to wave him over. Piper drank in the sight of him. What was it about the man that called to her so strongly?

She suspected much of it was the calm façade he showed to the world. Her childhood had been tumultuous because her mother had never found the fairytale happiness that she'd been searching for. The least little disappointment, and the two of them would be off to some new place to start over.

Grey had a temper but kept it under ruthless control, at least most of the time. She flushed with the memory of when she'd pushed him past his limits. He'd been angry, sure, but the war they'd waged had become a seduction that she wouldn't forget.

"Piper, you're drooling." Kerry winked at her before turning her attention back to Grey.

Piper was actually raising her hand to wipe her mouth when she realized what she was doing and stopped. *Please, God, don't let Grey have heard what Kerry said.* No such luck. There was a definite smirk on his face as he tossed her a neatly folded handkerchief.

"Jerk!"

Damn the man, even his chuckle was sexy. But his gesture, silly as it was, gave her the courage to take the first step. She rose to her feet, needing to be closer to him when she dropped her own little bombshell on them. "Look, there's something you both need to hear, something I should've told you before now."

Grey obviously sensed her growing distress. All the humor drained from his expression.

"What's wrong, Piper?"

"Nothing's wrong. Not exactly." She braced herself and forced the words out. "Okay, here goes. Grey ordered a complete background check on me, but I want you to hear the truth from me, not some stranger."

Kerry gave Grey a puzzled look. "Is that true, Grey? Why would you have Piper investigated again? I know Sandor did a check on her when she was hired."

"Yes, he did, but there were too many gaps in the report." He edged closer to Piper, but kept his eyes focused on Kerry. "Piper works directly with you, so I ordered the PI to dig deeper."

Piper presented no threat to Kerry, but he'd had no way to know that for certain. While she didn't appreciate strangers rooting around in her past, she couldn't fault Grey for doing his job. From the way the Dame was frowning, Kerry didn't agree.

"Kerry, Grey was just protecting you, not attacking me." She managed a small smile. "That wasn't my initial reaction, but it's the truth."

Now Kerry's frown was aimed at her. "So I'm guessing that what the report will reveal has you all tied up in knots."

Piper took a deep breath. "Earlier, you said that none of you have any blood relatives. Well, that isn't exactly true. Not for you anyway. You have a sister—a half sister, to be more accurate."

"What? There's no record of my having a sister." Kerry jumped to her feet, looking around as if she expected someone to pop out from behind the bushes.

Piper wished she could take it all back. No, that was a lie. One way or another, Kerry needed to hear this as much as Piper needed to say it.

"Let me explain, Kerry. Please." She waited for permission before starting again.

When Kerry didn't respond, Grey took control of the situation. "Okay, both of you look like hell right now. Sit down."

He pushed enough authority into his voice that they both obeyed without question. He was right, though. She was pretty shaky and Kerry was probably feeling the same. They settled on opposite ends of the swing.

Grey positioned himself directly in front of them, making sure neither one tried to escape. "Now talk."

Bless him, that man loved to give orders. Right now she appreciated his take-charge attitude. She leaned her head against the back of the swing, grateful for its support—and Grey's.

"After my mom died, I was going through her things and came across a locked box I'd never seen before. Inside, she left me a letter about my father. Explaining what he was, what I am."

She pinned her gaze on Grey's hands, which were alight with swirls of energy. Despite his stoic expression, his emotions were definitely running high. "He left right after I was born, so I don't remember him at all. From what I now know about our people, I would guess he was at least half Kyth, probably more. Whether he knew what he was, I'll never know.

"Anyway, according to Mom, she got scared when he started developing these weird powers. One night, he lost his temper and set the couch on fire with just a touch. She thought he was a danger to us, not to mention himself. That was the last direct contact she had with him."

Kerry spoke for the first time. "You were their only child?"

Piper nodded. "Yes. As soon as the divorce was final, Mom took me and ran. We moved around a lot when I was young. She was always searching for the gold at the end of the rainbow. But looking back, I suspect she also worried that my father might want to establish a relationship with me, not that he ever did."

She sat in silence for a few seconds, feeling the pain that still lingered. Slowly, she gathered her wits and her courage, and continued. "I guess I took after Mom, but then I'm probably only a quarter Kyth. She left me instructions that if I ever noticed myself developing any of those same weird powers, I should find my father. She said he'd remarried and had another child, but I have no idea how she even knew that much."

Piper looked up, trying to gauge Grey's reaction. He gave her a brief nod of encouragement, urging her to lay it all out on the table. "If I couldn't find him or didn't want to, I was to contact the Grand Dame of the Kyth and ask for help."

Grey jerked as if she'd shoved him. "But if she was human, how did she know about the Grand Dame and her people?"

"I have no idea. I also don't know why she never told me any of this herself. Maybe she couldn't deal with the guilt of hiding me from my father. She was probably crossing her fingers that I didn't inherit any of his abilities."

She wrapped her arms around her body, feeling cold and alone. "Anyway, I decided, powers or not, that I wanted to track down my father. I used part of my inheritance and hired someone to search for him."

She tried to smile at Grey but wasn't sure how successful she was. "It will be interesting to see if your guy was any more successful than mine."

Grey nodded. "He didn't find your father?"

"He couldn't. My father and his second wife died

under mysterious circumstances about twenty-five years ago. With no other known family, my sister was put up for adoption. It took him a while to get a lead on what happened to her because the adoption was handled privately, maybe even illegally. No court records, no nothing. Even the law firm's records were destroyed in a fire."

Kerry finally spoke. "All of that fits with what Sandor dug up about my past. But how did you manage to trace me if all the records were gone?"

"Luck, pure and simple. The investigator found a paralegal who had worked for the law firm. Turns out she'd secretly kept copies of the shady adoptions her bosses had handled. Too much money exchanged hands for them to all be legit. When the offices were burned to the ground and the partners died within weeks of each other, she stashed the files in a safety deposit box and laid low."

"My guy guilted her into giving him the name of your adoptive parents. From there, it was just a matter of time before he traced you here to Seattle. Imagine my surprise when he gave me your phone number and it was the same one I had for the Grand Dame."

For a few minutes there was nothing but strained silence in the garden. Even the street traffic was muted. It felt as if her story had whisked them of out of the real world and into another dimension that held just three people who had no idea how they'd gotten there and no idea of what to say.

Finally, Piper couldn't stand it anymore. "Look, I know this is a lot to take in. Grey, I'm sure you'll want to compare what I've told you to your investigator's report."

Now it was time to make herself scarce. Rising to her feet, Piper looked at her sister. "I have to leave for school in a few minutes. I understand if you'd like me to clean out my desk before I go."

The tears streaming down Kerry's face matched her own. Maybe she should have kept her mouth shut and just quietly disappeared. "I'm sorry to have hurt you, Kerry. I wanted to get to know you first, to decide whether you had room in your life for a sister you'd never even heard of. You've already had so many changes in the past year."

She headed toward the house. Before she'd gone more than a handful of steps, she crashed into a barrier that stopped her cold. Instinctively, she struggled to break free before finally surrendering to her invisible prison. She'd heard about Kerry's ability to immobilize those around her, but she'd never expected to experience it herself.

Kerry's voice rang out over the garden. "I did not give you leave to depart, Miss Ryan."

Damn, Kerry could really sound as imperious as a Grand Dame ought to. Bracing herself, Piper backed up a couple of a steps before finally turning to face her ruler. But it was her sister who stood there, her dark eyes sparking with flames and what looked like happiness.

"I should have told you sooner." Piper whispered.

"You could have told me sooner." Kerry said at exactly the same time.

Piper didn't hesitate. She ran straight into Kerry's outstretched arms.

Grey stood back and watched the two women blast past those first awkward moments and collide in a messy explosion of hugs. Toss in a distressing number of tears and giggles, and a wise man knew to stand back and let them muddle through their reunion without interference.

He'd imagined all kinds of possible secrets Piper might have had, but being Kerry's long-lost sister hadn't been one of them. But now that he knew, it amazed him that he hadn't seen the similarities before now. Yeah, Piper was a head taller than her younger sibling, but they had the same dark eyes, sharp intelligence, and fearless nature.

He watched as they retreated back to the swing to talk. They both had to know that Piper's startling revelation could have serious repercussions among their people, but all of that could be dealt with later. For now, he'd stand guard while his Dame and his woman adjusted to the sudden change in their relationship.

Unfortunately, their time alone didn't last long. He should've known that Ranulf would sense his wife's distress and charge to the rescue. Nor was it any surprise that Sandor was hot on his heels. Grey placed himself directly in the Viking's path and did his best to head him off.

Ranulf pulled up short. "What the hell is going on out here? Get out of my way, Danby."

"No."

Ranulf tried to get around him, but Grey blocked him again. Frustrated, he grabbed Grey by the front of his shirt. "Damn it, do you want to die? Kerry's upset, and I want to know why."

Grey dug in his heels. "If you'll give me a second, I'll explain."

"Fine, but if you're the one who's making her cry—" Ranulf emphasized the threat with a shove.

"It bloody hell wasn't me. It was Piper, and as you can see, the two of them are still as thick as thieves."

Ranulf gave the women a considering look and then stood down. Sandor took his cue from Ranulf, but neither man showed any sign of retreating to the house.

"Come with me." Grey led them a short distance away. "On top of everything else that's happened today, it seems that the initial investigation into Piper's background left out the fact that she's Kerry's half sister."

Both men stared at him as if he were spouting gibberish. He repeated himself, speaking more slowly. "Piper just broke the news that she's Kerry's half sister. They have the same father."

"That's crazy!" Ranulf clearly wasn't happy about the whole mess. "If that were true, why didn't she say something before? Why now?"

"I don't know why she kept it secret this long, but I will find out. Piper found out I'd ordered a deeper investigation into her past and wanted Kerry to hear the truth from her. That's all I can tell you."

Sandor looked sick. "How did I miss something that important? I've been digging into Kerry's past for months and getting nowhere and your guy hits pay dirt?"

"I don't know that he did, but Piper wasn't taking any chances." He wished like hell she'd trusted him enough to tell him sooner, but he could only play the hand she'd dealt him.

Ranulf ran his fingers through his hair in frustration as he watched his wife and new sister-in-law talking. "I've got nothing against Piper, but this is the last thing we need right now when we're already under attack."

He wasn't saying anything Grey hadn't already known. "If this gets out it could make Piper both a target and a weapon to be used against Kerry."

"Exactly."

The three men stood in silence, trying to come to terms with the ripple effect of Piper's unexpected confession. They all knew their primary duty was to Kerry. She'd been protective of Piper before, and this would only strengthen that bond.

As he watched, it was clear that the two women had reached an accord over the change in their relationship. Piper said something that made Kerry laugh, but then she stood up and walked away. Where the hell was she going? He checked the time. School.

"Gentlemen, if you'll excuse me."

Piper was relieved to find her office was devoid of Talion warriors. With her great revelation and the earlier confrontation with Grey, it was no wonder she was exhausted. She felt as if she'd been running a marathon in cement boots. The quiet allowed her to center herself, calming the cacophony of emotions that had her stomach tied in knots upon knots.

It might actually be a relief to lose herself in a long afternoon of lectures and review sessions. She grabbed her backpack and walked out the front door. Outside, a familiar figure was waiting by the gate. No use in denying that she was glad to see him. She got in Grey's car and buckled in.

"Thanks for the ride."

"You're welcome."

"I would say that taking the bus would have been fine, but I hate to lie." She leaned her head back and closed her eyes. "God, what a day. Promise me you won't ask me any more about my past until tonight."

"Agreed. We'll have plenty to talk about, too. Like why you didn't warn me or say something when I asked you if there could be anything in that report that might hurt Kerry or—"

"Grey! This is not later."

He sighed. "Okay, later it is, but we *will* talk."

"Fine." She turned to study his profile. "But back to what happened earlier. How do you live with this tension all the time? My stomach hurts from worrying about you and the others going after these crazies. I can barely stand to let you out of my sight for fear something will happen to you."

Okay, that was more than she meant to reveal, but sometimes the truth had to be told.

His hand settled on her thigh, and he gave it a soft squeeze. "I'm sorry you got dragged into this, Piper, but I promise to keep you safe."

She ignored the waves of heat that his touch sent coursing through her. "You can promise to try, Grey, but that's all. You can't be with me round the clock. Even if you could, that wouldn't prevent some crazy from coming at us out of left field. Besides, your job is to keep my sister—your Dame—safe."

He clenched his jaw, wanting to deny it. They were all vulnerable to attack no matter how vigilant they were. But then, accidents happened, too. There were no guarantees.

"I'll pick you up after class. If I can't make it for some reason, I'll send Sandor or Ranulf to bring you back to Kerry's until I'm done for the day."

He entwined his hand with hers. "The plan was for all of us to stay at Kerry's, but I'm thinking you might want a little more privacy. If so, I'll change hotels to throw whoever is behind this off track. Your choice— Kerry's or a hotel. But either way, you're with me."

If he was expecting her to argue, he was going to be disappointed. She'd already considered her options and knew that she had none. No matter what the future held for the two of them, she'd be a fool to waste a single chance to be with him.

"I'll be waiting." Then to lighten the mood, she added, "And I expect you to be extra *nice* to me when we get to the hotel."

She loved the way his eyes sparkled when he replied, "It will be my pleasure."

• • •

Adele stretched languidly, trying to decide what to do next. Traffic had been cooperative, so she'd reached Wes's earlier than expected. He'd been waiting outside in the driveway when she pulled in. Freed from the constraints of all the spying eyes back at school, she'd shown him exactly how great it was to see him. She'd run straight into his waiting arms, wrapping her legs around his waist and plunging her tongue into his mouth.

By the time they'd reached the porch, she already had his pants unzipped. They'd barely shut the door before he took her, slamming her up against the closest wall. That had been the start of a long, energetic evening.

Oh, yes, it was definitely nice to be missed. The man had stamina, but right now they were both down for the count. Come morning, they'd get back to the business of claiming her throne. For the time being, she'd doze for a while before coaxing Wes into an encore.

He'd already sent the warning about that old car Ranulf Thorsen was so bloody proud of. When they were finished with it, the Packard would be nothing but scrap metal. Hmmm. Would blood stains lessen the value at the recyclers?

With that happy thought, she cuddled in closer to her lover and drifted off to sleep.

• • •

Even with Sandor sitting beside him at the computer, the office felt empty without Piper across the room. He'd dropped her off two hours ago, and he swore he could still breathe in her scent. The first time he'd drawn in a long breath of air Sandor had shot him an odd look. The second time he'd grinned but hadn't said a word. But judging by the way he'd clamped his lips together, he'd been tempted.

Finding out that Piper was Kerry's sister was one helluva complication. Grey had enough on his plate as he and Sandor tried to trace the e-mails. He'd made it his business to learn some serious computer skills, both through formal schooling and from some talented hackers he'd met along the way. Sandor was no slouch either. Eventually they'd track the bastard down, but so far, they had no leads. Frustrated, Grey leaned back in his chair and closed his eyes. Not that it mattered—the computer screen was burned on the inside of his eyelids.

They'd made so damn little progress, and he couldn't shake the feeling that time was running out. Slamming his hand down on the desk, he stared at the screen, but nothing registered with him.

"There has to be something else we could be doing. Some avenue we haven't explored."

Sandor looked as close to the edge as Grey felt. "I agree, but what?"

"Let's take a harder look at that file you'd started on Kyth who had reacted adversely to Judith's choice of a successor."

"Why? There were a few disgruntled e-mails and a couple of calls, but nothing that crossed the line. After a thousand years with a single ruler, there was bound to be some unrest with the change," Sandor said.

"What can it hurt to look at it?"

Sandor quickly pulled the file up on the screen and moved out of the way so Grey could scan through it. He paused to make note of a couple of names before continuing. Toward the bottom of the list, one person stood out. He let loose a string of curses.

"Who are you looking at?"

Grey jabbed a finger at a name. "Lawrence Harcourt and his daughter, Adele."

"What about them?"

"Judith had assigned me to the London area, ostensibly because a fair number of Kyth live there." He linked his hands behind his head, hoping to hide the burn of tension running through him.

"But the real reason?"

"Until Kerry came along, Adele Harcourt was the heir apparent to Judith's throne. The Dame stationed me in London because she wanted one of her stronger Talions to quietly keep an eye on the girl. Though the Dame never made any official announcement about Adele's status, Harcourt apparently believed it to be true. The greedy bastard is as ambitious as they come and invested a lot of time and energy, not to mention money, in preparing his daughter to rule."

Sandor was nodding. "You know, the two of them

used to come to Seattle every year to visit his cousin, Reginald Harcourt. The two of them were very close. But Harcourt also made of point of having Adele spend time with Dame Judith once the girl was old enough to exhibit her strong gifts. As I recall, she can manipulate energy and influence minds but lacks the talent for healing."

Grey leaned back in his chair. "That's right. I suspect that lack was why Judith hesitated over publicly declaring Adele her heir. We'd heard rumors that the Dame's health was failing for some time; it was the manner of Judith's death that hit us all so hard. Knowing how power hungry Harcourt is, I'm betting he had his bags packed and ready to go long before Judith's passing."

The more Grey thought about it, the more the pieces fit together. Even if it wasn't Harcourt behind the attacks, it had to be someone with a similar axe to grind. Who else would profit from Kerry's death? He handed his short list to Sandor.

"Harcourt is why I came to Seattle when I did. He wanted me to spy for him and his friends, and to report back on any weakness I saw. I'm sure he figured if they compiled enough evidence that Kerry wasn't capable of ruling the Kyth, he and his elitist buddies would be able to replace her with someone they deemed more suitable."

Sandor ran a finger along the list, scorching the paper in the process. "We figured as much. Ranulf was all for shoving you back on the plane."

Grey laughed. "Or under it, knowing him. In

truth, I used Harcourt's greed as an excuse to get away from those jackasses he surrounds himself with. His one real claim to fame was Judith favoring Adele. When that went away, he was just another Kyth with more pedigree than good sense. There's no telling what he'd be willing to do to get that back."

"He has to know that if something happens to Kerry the Talions will be out for blood."

Sandor's left hand was rubbing up and down his right arm over his brand. Grey recognized the gesture for what it meant because his own hand had just settled over his chest. Both men were feeling the heavy weight of their office as guardians of the Grand Dame. It wouldn't surprise him if Ranulf showed up at the door at any second. The Viking might now serve their people as Consort rather than as the Dame's enforcer, but he would still feel a connection to Talions gearing up to defend his wife.

"We can't assume that it's Harcourt, though. We'll need to check out that whole list, starting with any locals. See what they're up to, if they're doing anything that sets off alarms."

Ranulf appeared in the doorway. "What list?"

Grey motioned to Ranulf to come in. "We're going to investigate any Kyth who questioned Kerry's qualifications to take over as Dame. There may be more who felt the same way, at least at first, but the ones on this list were stupid enough to put it in writing."

He hit the "print" button and handed a copy of the list to each of the men. After Ranulf read over the names, Grey said, "It will save time if we each take a third of the list. Look for unusual travel patterns. Check phone records, both cell- and land-lines. It won't help if they're smart enough to use throwaway phones, but maybe we'll get lucky."

"Do you want me to take Harcourt, since the two of you have a past?" Sandor asked.

"Oh, no, he's mine." Grey checked the time. "If I leave right now, I'll have time to pay a call on Harcourt's cousin before I pick up Piper. I'll call you if I learn anything interesting. We won't be coming back here until morning. I'll work through the rest of my list tonight, and you two do the same. By tomorrow, we'll have some answers. Call my cell if you find anything or have any questions."

Ranulf blocked his way. "Don't forget that Kerry is your first priority, even if Piper is her sister, Danby. We all know you've got feelings for the woman and that's your business. But know this: if you're thinking with the wrong part of your body and my wife suffers for it, I will kill you myself. So tell me now, is your head in the game? And I'm not talking about the one in your pants."

Grey chest-butted the Consort, forcing him to back up. Considering Ranulf was a tank, it was quite an accomplishment.

"I am the Chief Talion, Consort. I take that very seriously and know exactly where my duty lies. I have guards stationed here on the grounds and extras patrolling the neighborhood. Sandor has already brought Lena here, and he'll be in charge of security tonight. I'll relieve him at first light."

Grey eased back, giving them both more breathing room. "Look, I know you're worried. We all are. But don't presume to tell me what to do. The Dame has no reason to doubt my abilities or loyalty, so I will do my job as I see fit."

After a few seconds, Ranulf nodded. "I'll let you know what I find out about the people on my list."

"Good. Now, if you two will excuse me, if I don't get a move on, I might be late picking up Piper. She's stubborn enough to take the bus if I'm not waiting at the curb."

Sandor looked up from his computer screen. "Doesn't take orders well, does she?"

"No more than Kerry or Lena from what I've heard."

Ranulf actually laughed and clapped him on the shoulder. "I don't know whether to congratulate you or offer my sympathies."

Grey resisted the urge to rub the spot Ranulf had hit. The man didn't know his own strength—or then again, maybe he did. Talion tempers didn't cool off quickly.

"I'll settle for a little of both. I've a feeling I'm going need it."

Sandor and Ranulf's laughter followed him down the hall.

Grey pulled up in front of a stately brick home, the kind of place that spoke of old money and an upper-class pedigree. He studied the exterior for a couple of minutes. The place was well tended. It didn't tell Grey much about the man. If Reginald had the same kind of money his cousin Lawrence did, he probably paid other people to take care of the place for him.

As Grey got out of the car, an older man came around the corner of the house pushing a wheelbarrow. He wore grass-stained jeans and a faded work shirt. As soon as the guy spotted Grey, he stopped and waited for him make his approach.

Looking curious rather than worried, he asked, "Hi, can I help you?"

Grey nodded. "I'm hear to talk the owner, Reginald Harcourt. Do you know if he's in?"

"No, actually he's out—here, that is. I'm Reggie," he said with a smile as he stripped off his work gloves and tossed them down in the wheelbarrow. "And you are?"

"Greyhill Danby. I am here on a matter of great urgency on behalf of the Grand Dame of our people."

"I see." Reggie's smile dimmed considerably. "Why don't we take this conversation inside?"

Without waiting for Grey to respond, Reggie headed for the front door. Inside, he kicked of his shoes. "I'll make a fresh pot of coffee while you tell me what brought you to my doorstep."

Grey followed him into the kitchen and took a seat at the table. He watched with interest while Reggie started the coffee. Either the man had no idea why the Chief Talion was paying a call on him or else he had nerves of steel.

"I'm going to get out of these dirty clothes. I'll be gone just a minute."

"No need to do that on my behalf, Mr. Harcourt."

"If you're sure." Reggie joined Grey at the table after setting out coffee cups along with cream and sugar. "I've heard of you, Mr. Danby, but I wasn't aware that you were here in Seattle."

"It was a recent move, Mr. Harcourt. Grand Dame Thorsen offered me the position of Chief Talion, and I'm here in that capacity. Someone has been threatening our Dame and the people who work for her."

"Is she all right? I've only met her once when I attended her wedding, but she seemed like a nice young woman."

"She's fine, but the Talions are investigating the situation. Such attacks constitute high treason according to Kyth law."

"I'm sure, but what does that have to do with me?" Reggie avoided looking Grey in the eyes, instead staring at the steady drip, drip, drip of the coffeepot. The bastard knew something. The question was what.

"We have a list of people who questioned Kerry's right to assume the throne when Dame Judith died." Grey pushed enough energy to ensure that his eyes were flaming. "You and your cousin Lawrence were right at the top."

All pretense of good humor disappeared from Reggie's expression. "Damn it, I knew he'd go too far."

"Who would?"

Reggie looked thoroughly disgusted. "Lawrence, of course. He and I used to be close. But ever since he got it in his head that Adele was the anointed one, he's been impossible. Putting on airs, acting like it was only a matter of time before he took control of our world. Since Judith died and Dame Kerry took over, he's gotten worse and worse."

Reggie got up to fetch the coffee. "He asked me to send a letter expressing my concern over a relative newcomer to our culture wielding so much power. I still feel that way, but that's all it was—concern, nothing more."

"But your cousin feels differently." It wasn't a question.

"Yes. But when he started talking about a bunch of us forcing the new Dame to abdicate, I backed away quickly. I want nothing to do with that kind of talk. As I already said, Dame Kerry is a nice young woman. Who knows, I trusted Judith's judgment in everything else." He shrugged. "Maybe she knew what she was doing when she chose Kerry as her heir."

"When's the last time you heard from your cousin?"

Once again Reggie's eyes flicked to the side. "Last time I saw him was when I took a trip to London earlier this year."

Okay, now he was definitely dancing around the truth. "Reggie, that's not what I asked. When did you last hear from him?" Grey injected a compulsion into his question, determined to get a straight answer.

Reggie fought him briefly, but then slumped back like a deflated balloon. "Last night. He called wanting to know if I'd seen his daughter lately, you know, here in Seattle. I told him no. I haven't seen nor heard from Adele."

"Is there anything else you haven't told me?"

Reggie wrapped his hands around his coffee mug, probably to hide their shaking. "I'm not part of this, Mr. Danby. Whatever it is you think Lawrence is involved in. I swear."

Grey believed him. "If you hear from Lawrence or Adele, I expect a call. Should I learn that you've been less than forthcoming, I will be back. Trust me, Harcourt, you do not want that to happen.

"Thank you for the coffee." He stood up and held his hand out to Harcourt, mostly to make sure the man saw the surges of energy burning under his skin. "I can see myself out."

Just before he reached the end of the hallway, he glanced back at his host. Reggie was leaning forward, elbows on the table, supporting his head with his hands. Grey's gut feeling said Reggie would throw his cousin overboard if it would keep the Talions off his back. He might even warn others before they threw in their lot with Lawrence.

Mission accomplished.

Time to pick up Piper.

"So should I try calling her again or not?" Harcourt asked himself, wishing he had a more satisfactory answer to offer than, "What else can I do?"

He could call Grey Danby. He even considered it

for all of ten seconds before rejecting the idea. That would be tantamount to signing his daughter's death warrant and quite possibly his own. Right now, he'd let them have Adele in a heartbeat if it meant saving his own skin. If that made him a bad father, well, he could live with it.

Literally.

All right, he would call her one more time. If she didn't answer, he'd have no choice left but to sacrifice her for the greater good and save himself. As he reached for the phone, it started vibrating. Could the silly twit finally be showing some common sense and returning his call? A glance at the name and number displayed on the small screen quickly disavowed him of that notion.

His blood ran cold.

What did Greyhill Danby want with him now? It was a bit late for that fool to suddenly decide to clue Harcourt in on his activities since returning to Seattle. In fact, the Talion had made it clear that he had no intention of betraying Dame Kerry.

Before answering, Harcourt swallowed hard in a vain attempt to dislodge the bitter lump of fear clogging his throat. "Danby, what do you want? It's the middle of the night in London."

"You don't sound as if I got you out of bed. Are you having trouble sleeping for some reason?" A nasty laugh echoed in his ear. "Besides, that's not very friendly, Harcourt, but no offense taken."

That was a lie. Cold fury dripped from every word the man spoke.

Harcourt tried to bluff. "I repeat, *what do you want?* I have more important things to do than talk to you."

"No, actually, you don't. As Chief Talion, I'm officially putting you on notice."

There was a definite predatory growl underlying his words that had Harcourt's knees shaking. It was so very tempting to simply hang up, but that would leave him wondering what kind of threat Grey posed to him and Adele.

"About what?"

"Someone is playing games with us, Harcourt. Dangerous games. If I manage to trace any of this back to you—and I suspect I will—the consequences will be terminal. I can't wait to check your credit card records. What little surprises will I find?"

Dear God, this was a bloody disaster. Had Grey stumbled across something that could possibly link Adele to some attack on the Dame? Or was the Talion casting his line in hopes of startling Harcourt into confessing something? How best to play this?

He aimed for righteous indignation. "Danby, you have no right to make such threats against me. The new Dame may think you're worthy of serving her, but we both know the truth. You're nothing but a guttersnipe playing dress up to mimic your betters."

"The thing about guttersnipes, Harcourt, is that we know our way around shadows and back alleys. You'll never see me coming." Then the bastard laughed. "Take care, Harcourt, and give my regards to your daughter."

• • •

Grey disconnected the call just as he saw Piper coming out of the building. Perfect timing. Later he'd have to think long and hard about Harcourt's response to his call. Had that really been a faint note of panic he'd heard in Harcourt's voice? Maybe. It definitely put the man at the top of Grey's list. He'd tried the same surprise calls on two others before dialing Harcourt's number and had definitely gotten them out of bed. Somehow, their anger had felt more genuine, although that didn't let them off the hook, either.

But right now, he planned to concentrate all his attention on the woman who'd just spotted him and waved.

As Piper made her way down the steps, a couple of college punks watched her walk by. As she moved, he caught a glimpse of that tat on her thigh. God, how had he missed how short that skirt was when he'd dropped her off? If he was the jealous sort, he'd tell them to keep their effing lechery to themselves.

Considering he was now out of the car and heading straight for the little pricks, he guessed he was that sort. Lucky for them, Piper walked straight into his arms and allowed him to give her the kind of kiss that staked a very public claim. When he was sure the point had been made, he gave her a second kiss, meant for her alone.

She gave him a considering look. "Somehow I think there was more to that kiss than that you were glad to see me."

He didn't bother to deny it. "But I *am* glad to see you."

She fell into step beside him and caught his hand in hers. "Good. Let's go home. I want a hot bath, some greasy food, and some quiet while I study. How does that sound?"

"Fine, as long as I get to scrub your back." He lifted her hand up to kiss it. "I also have work to do tonight, so I think we're set. What kind of grease do you want for dinner? Pizza? Burgers?"

"How about fish and chips? I know a great little place closeby."

"Perfect. It will remind me of home."

Piper sat curled up on the couch studying for her history exam. Every few minutes, though, her eyes were drawn to the man sitting at the table across their hotel room. She'd soak up a few seconds of his compelling presence and then drag herself back to her book. Each time, a variety of expressions paraded across Grey's face as he stared at his computer screen.

Right now he was looking decidedly grim, as if what he'd been reading had given him a bitch of a headache. She could help with that. After marking her place, she set the book aside.

As soon as she touched his shoulders, Grey reached up to pat her hand without taking his eyes off the laptop. She began to knead the tight muscles across his shoulders.

Grey sighed as he tipped his head forward, offering her easier access to the back of his neck. "That feels like heaven. Do you think you might have a touch of the healing gift?"

"I've never been tested, but anything's possible." She moved on to gently rub his temples. "You looked as if you might have a headache coming on."

"More like a pain in the ass," he grumbled as he typed.

She loved the play of his muscles under her fingers as the knots melted away. Massaging him this way reminded her of all the ways she liked to touch and be touched by him. Especially naked. Maybe this wasn't a good idea, not if either one of them wanted to get any work done.

That didn't mean it would be easy for her to let go and walk all the way back to the sofa without him. She eased her hands down the front of his chest and rested her head next to his. "Feel better?"

"Actually, quite a bit."

She could feel him smile. "Want to take a break?"

"I could use one. Just let me finish this search first."

"Perfect, I'll make a fresh pot of coffee."

Before she could back away, Grey suddenly tensed up and craned his head forward toward the screen.

"Bloody fucking hell!" He slammed his hand down on the table hard enough to rattle the dishes left over from their dinner. "I cannot believe this!"

"Grey?" she asked.

He jabbed a finger toward the e-mail on the

screen. "I talked to this wanker right before I picked you up at school. And did he bother telling me that he was here in Seattle? No. In fact, hell no!"

She held on to the back of Grey's chair with a death grip. "Who is it?"

"Lawrence Harcourt, a first-class prick who is currently at the top of our list of suspects and is apparently already here in Seattle."

"And that's a bad thing." It wasn't a question.

Grey turned bleak eyes in her direction. "He's a self-righteous prig, but the bastard served in the SAS. I'm betting he could blow us all to hell and back again without breaking a sweat. Grab your things. We're going back to Kerry's."

Chapter 14

Ranulf stood in front of the door to the Thorsens' private quarters, putting himself between her and any threat that might come her way. Grey couldn't fault his intentions except that the Viking was also blocking Grey's access to the Dame. If the berserker thought Grey was the enemy, then there was no hope of him keeping her safe.

"I need to talk to Kerry, Ranulf."

"No, you don't. I'll relay any messages."

Okay, so that's the way it was going to be. He fought for control before speaking again. "As Consort, your job may be to support your wife, but it's sure as hell not to restrict my access to the Dame. Now move out of my way or I'll move you." He would, too, no matter the cost.

"You mean you'll try." Ranulf widened his stance and clenched his fists.

As tempting as it was to throw a few punches, that

wouldn't get them any closer to finding the real villain in this mess.

Grey tried for diplomatic. "Only a few hours ago we pledged to end this mess together. Now you're treating me as if I'm the enemy. What happened since then?"

"We got an interesting e-mail from Adele Harcourt. At her suggestion, we checked your bank records. You've been receiving regular payments from her father since you arrived here. We'd initially suspected you came here as a spy, but we were willing to give you a fair chance. Now we know you've been in the employ of Lawrence Harcourt. How much have you told him?"

Ranulf's smile turned nasty as he continued, "I bet you weren't at all pleased with your partner in crime when it was you who almost got blown to bits the other day. What's the matter? Did the two of you have some kind of falling out?"

All right, obviously Little Miss Adele has been busy stirring up discord. Clearly, she wanted to turn the Dame against him. The question was why?

"I've already told Sandor that I used Harcourt's interest in Kerry as an excuse to come to Seattle, but I don't know a damn thing about any payments. I'm guessing the same person who has been manipulating our e-mails has something to do with it. Divide and conquer, and all that. But no matter what you think, I am not now, nor have I ever been, anything but loyal to the Dame of our people."

His skin burned with the need to strike out at

their unseen enemy. "As far as the money goes, you can ask Harcourt about it yourself as soon as I find him. It shouldn't take long since the bastard is here in town."

Ranulf sneered. "Yeah, and how long have you known that? Adele's worried about her father because he came here to meet *you*."

"The hell he did. I found out he was here thirty minutes ago when a search of his finances showed a ticket to Seattle. I came straight here, stopping only long enough to print out his records in my office. Ask Piper. She was with me at the hotel when I found out."

If the Dame and her Consort chose not to believe him, there wasn't much Grey could do about it. That didn't mean he wouldn't do his job. He'd prefer not to get physical with Ranulf, but the Viking wasn't leaving him much choice. It also didn't help that Piper was already in there with Kerry, so he couldn't get to her either.

"I repeat, as Chief Talion, I'm requesting an audience with the Grand Dame of our people." He drew himself up to his full height, his hands flexing with the familiar burn of energy. "Stand aside, Viking, and let me pass."

Before Ranulf could refuse yet again, the door behind him opened. Kerry didn't try to push past her husband, probably knowing it wouldn't do any good.

"Ranulf, let him in. He deserves a chance to defend himself. Other than those two payments, there's nothing to indicate he's done anything wrong. Until now we've had no reason to doubt him."

Her husband growled, "That we know of."

"True, but we won't learn anything if we don't let the man explain."

Finally, Ranulf moved to the side—only far enough to allow Grey to barely squeeze past. Then, of course, the big jerk followed him inside.

Grey had never been invited into the Dame's personal quarters before. The furniture—obviously chosen for comfort—made it clear that this was where Kerry and Ranulf really lived. She plopped down on the closest chair. Ranulf stood beside her, still looking as if he'd rather be swinging his sword than exchanging words.

"Have a seat, Grey." Kerry waved him toward the other chairs in the room.

Time to get down to business. "I understand that Adele Harcourt has e-mailed you, Grand Dame. I regret more than I can say that I didn't come to you before this about the exact circumstances of my arrival here."

"Why didn't you?"

She put a little heat behind the question, the small blast of energy pressing him against the back of the chair. Clearly, Kerry wasn't as calm as she appeared. But then she'd already been blindsided with one unexpected revelation today.

He considered his choices and settled on blunt. "For this exact reason. I figured if you found out, you wouldn't trust me. I realize now that I had it backwards. If I had come clean from the beginning, you'd have no reason to doubt me now. I should've told you that I was asked to come, not just by Lawrence Harcourt, but by a group of Kyth in the UK. They wanted me to meet you in person and offer my opinion of how suitable you were to replace Grand Dame Judith. You can understand their concern when you were thrust into the job with little warning and no training."

He shot his cuffs, using the gesture as a distraction. "Your unexpected ascension to the throne sent huge ripples of unrest throughout our kind. Harcourt had hoped that his daughter Adele would be Judith's heir, and he took it particularly hard."

Kerry sat forward, gold sparks swirling in her eyes. "Some of the memories I inherited from Judith were muddled. Harcourt and his daughter definitely ring a bell, but the details are vague. Was she really qualified for the position, possessing all the gifts needed to rule?"

Which answer was Kerry hoping for? That there was someone else she could hand off the baton to or that she alone had the ability to serve their people as Grand Dame?

He could only report what he'd heard. "Adele's repertoire was said to lack several key ingredients, although she tested high in the gifts she did have."

Kerry's normally expressive face was remarkably stoic at the moment. "How did she feel about being replaced?"

"We never discussed the matter. She's always followed her father's dictates, and he definitely wanted her to take the throne. I met with his cousin Reggie this afternoon, and he confirmed my suspicions about Lawrence."

Ranulf finally entered the discussion. "Why do you think Adele chose to reveal his unannounced arrival in Seattle? Is she hoping to protect him by giving us a chance to catch the bastard before he does anything else?"

Grey had been wondering about that himself. "That's definitely one possibility, but somehow that doesn't ring true. Maybe she's in on it with him."

The Consort's eyes were finally starting to thaw when he looked in Grey's direction. "What do we do next?"

"Several things. First of all, I want Sandor and Lena take the three kids out of town until this is settled. That will leave six fewer targets for whoever is behind this."

Piper joined the conversation. "You must be tired, Grey. Check your math. Two adults and three kids only adds up to five."

Her smile faded as soon as he looked in her direction. "Oh no, you don't. I am not being packed off to god knows where right before finals. You have no right to make that decision for me."

Yes, he damn well did, but he'd save that argument when for when they were alone. He shot her a smile that was all warning and little warmth. "Maybe they'll let you make up the tests."

She met him glare for glare. "It's not happening, so move on."

They'd see about that. For now, he turned back to Kerry. "Harcourt won't be able to stay hidden for long. I'm monitoring his phone records and credit cards.

Eventually something will pop up, and then we'll have him.

"Dame Kerry, I ask that you leave town as well. I'd suggest your mountain retreat, because Ranulf's wards—combined with a team of my Talions—will keep you safe."

Before she could respond, he looked to Ranulf for support. "Afterward, I'll bring the Packard back and park it out front."

"To make it look as if we're still at home." Ranulf winced, no doubt already seeing where Grey was headed with this.

"Yes. Then you'll disguise someone to look like the Dame, and send her back here so it will appear that Kerry returned home without you. If the enemy sees that as a weakness, it might draw them out of hiding."

Piper butted her pretty nose right back into his business. "I could pretend to be Kerry. Our hair is similar enough in color if I cover up the pink."

He wanted to argue against it, but she was right. She wasn't just the best choice, but the only one.

Piper echoed his thoughts. "Who else do you have? Besides, she's not just Dame to me, Grey. She's my sister. I will do what it takes to keep her safe."

"Fine, but as soon as you come down off the mountain, you're going back into hiding." The whole idea made his gut ache. "I'll also need to pull the Talion guards back, again to weaken the appearance of our defenses. Any suggestions for how to keep the Talions close by while keeping them out of sight at the same time?"

Ranulf looked toward Kerry. When she nodded, he said, "There's a secret entrance to the house. The guards can come back in that way. As long as they're careful, no one outside will know they're in here. We can slip Piper back out to safety the same way."

Grey nodded, fighting hard to hide his growing frustration. When had they planned on telling him about the secret entrance? He choked back the urge to read Ranulf the riot act. Now wasn't the time.

He deliberately met the gaze of each person in the room. "I would suggest that we all be ready to leave first thing in the morning. The earlier, the better."

As Grey rose to his feet, Ranulf sighed loudly. "Damn, I'm going to miss that car."

Grey didn't blame him. The Packard was a classic beauty. He'd almost rather sacrifice his Jaguar. Almost. "I'll try to keep it safe. For now, I'll have two of my men go over the car with a fine toothed comb and then stand guard to make sure no one gets close to it during the night."

But there could be no promises, and they both knew it. Not when the bomber had already declared it a target. If it came down to sacrificing Ranulf's beloved car in order to keep people safe—and especially the Grand Dame herself—there was no contest.

"Now, if you'll excuse me, I'll get to work." He bowed to his Dame and then her Consort.

Kerry nodded and stood, her expression solemn. "Grey, as your Dame, I grant you and your men authority to do whatever you deem necessary to stop this threat against our people."

Then Kerry's eyes flashed burning hot. "But let me make one thing clear: If that bastard blows up the Packard, it will mean war."

The meeting broke up after that, and everyone scattered to start their preparations. Piper quickly took her leave of Kerry and Ranulf and headed for her office. No doubt Grey would have something to say about her upcoming role in getting Kerry out of the line of fire. She understood his reluctance, but she was an adult and capable of making her own decisions. Why couldn't he accept that?

Grey was waiting for her.

As soon as she crossed the threshold, he slammed the door closed behind her. She'd been prepared to be civil, but really, this was just too much.

"Grey Danby! What is your problem?"

"You are."

He snapped his arms around her as his lips came crushing down on hers before she could protest. His tongue swept into her mouth, stealing her objection and her anger. How was she supposed to think clearly—or at all—when he did that?

She gave herself over to the moment, well aware that Grey wasn't happy with her. He thought nothing of thrusting himself into potential danger but wouldn't allow her to make the same decision for herself. Granted, he was the trained warrior, but she had her own vested interest in keeping Kerry safe.

Gradually, Grey eased back, changing the whole

tenor of the embrace to one of gentle comfort. How was a woman supposed to stay mad at the man?

"I'm still not going into hiding, Grey."

The jerk actually laughed, although it had a definite edge to it. "You think I don't know that? I'm surprised I survived the daggers you shot at me when I dared to suggest it."

Okay, so that much was settled. "If we're going to get anywhere with this relationship, you've got to stop making decisions without consulting me."

Some of the humor in his eyes faded. "I don't have to remind you that I'm the Chief Talion, Piper. It's my job to protect our people from any threat. That alone would make me want you out of the line of fire."

He kissed her again, a soft brush of his mouth across hers. "But it's more than that, and we both know it. Look at Ranulf. He's going crazy, wanting a hard target that he can fight to protect Kerry. Sandor feels the same about Lena, and we all feel protective about the kids. I can assure you that Sean's going to be royally pissed about being forced to leave town right when things are going to get interesting around here."

Another kiss, this time at her temple. "I worry that my focus will be fragmented with both you and Kerry in danger. My honor and my duty demand that I sacrifice everything to keep the Grand Dame safe."

He studied her face for a few seconds. What was he looking for? Finally, he nodded as if finding an answer to his unspoken question. "The problem is that my heart has a different set of priorities."

As the meaning of his words sank in, her knees melted. If not for the strength of his arms supporting her, she would have sunk to the floor in a puddle of—what, she didn't know. How was she supposed to respond to a statement like that? Especially when she hadn't yet figured out exactly what she was feeling for him, except that it was good and it was strong.

The mental replay of that bomb going off continued to haunt her, along with the image of Grey lying on the ground, still as death. Did she have enough courage to watch him put himself in danger over and over again?

Maybe not. She gave him the only answer she had.

"I want to have a say in things that concern me directly, Grey, but I'm not stupid. I can and will take orders without demanding explanations when the situation calls for it."

After she spoke, she buried her face against his chest, not wanting to see if she'd hurt him by not owning up to her feelings for him.

Bless the man, he held her close with such tenderness. "Let me give the men their orders, and then we'll head back to the hotel."

"I can't wait."

Wes tossed Adele a knit cap. "This is for later."

She immediately rejected the hideous thing. "No, thanks. It doesn't go with my outfit."

He rolled his eyes. "So? It's not like we're going to be parading up and down the street for the world to see. But the Dame *will* have her men watching for suspicious-looking people. The last thing we need is for you to be recognized."

Maybe he was right. "The only one who knows me well enough to recognize me is Grey Danby."

"Not true. You said your old man used to drag you here every year. Someone might remember you, especially that Ranulf Thorsen or his buddy Kearn."

"Oh, all right. I take it we're going to drive by the house." She tucked her hair up inside the hat. One look in the mirror told her that it looked every bit as bad as she'd feared.

"Yeah, but later, just before dark. There's less chance of us being spotted that way even if they have no way of knowing what kind of car you're driving." He looked up to offer her a tentative smile. "That is, if that's all right with you."

She liked that he asked. Most of the time he was too lost in his formulas and projects to take note of anyone else, but once in a while he surprised her. Even now Wes was carefully braiding strand after strand of wire into a colorful, but deadly, work of art.

Would a red bow on the box be over the top? Probably. Besides, no one would see it once Wes attached it to the Packard. She would have loved to have seen the expression on Ranulf's face as he watched his car exploding into little bits in that e-mail. Well, the reality would far outshine the preview. That pleased her on so many levels, and Wes was the one who would make it happen.

There was no harm in tossing him a few crumbs.

"Good plan. Right now Grey and his buddies should be busy hunting for my father. We certainly wouldn't want to distract them."

Wes snipped the last wire and stepped back to study his creation. After a second, he made one final adjustment and then nodded. "I'll have to watch for a chance to install this, which will only take a couple of seconds. I'm using a remote detonator, but I've got a small camera mounted to a tree across the street so we'll have a front row-seat when the fireworks start."

Adele beamed. "Good on you, Wes. We wouldn't want to miss a minute of the excitement."

She had to give him credit for always thinking ahead, which reminded her how much she'd regret his imminent demise. After all, how could a ruler trust someone who showed a definite flare for assassination? She studied him as he carefully packed his creation away, admiring the fit of his jeans and the smooth line of muscle under his T-shirt.

Hmmm. This far north, the sun didn't completely set until very late in the evening. That left them with several hours to kill. And she knew just how she wanted to spend them.

She waited until Wes closed the box and stepped back before sidling up behind him. He tensed briefly as her hands expressed admiration for his backside before sliding around to the front of his jeans.

Before she could do more than give his package a quick squeeze, he turned the tables on her, pinning her against the wall. In other areas of her life, she liked to be in control. But when it came to sex, she was more than happy to let Wes take charge.

As his tongue plunged into her mouth, she gave herself up to the moment, determined to make his remaining days on earth unforgettable for them both.

Sean stood in Sandor's garage, his duffel at his feet. He'd already stuffed everyone else's bags in the sedan's trunk. Lena, Tara, and Kenny were inside finishing up breakfast. The crunch of gravel warned him that Sandor was back.

The Talion set a small cooler by the car. "What's the matter? Isn't there room for your bag?"

"Yeah, there's room, but I'm not going."

Sean braced himself for a blast of power from Sandor, willing to take whatever punishment the Talion dished out. After all, Sean had sworn to take orders from the man without question. Now here he was, openly defying a man who could squash him flat with little or no effort.

When he didn't immediately get crispy-crittered, Sean gathered up the ragged edges of his courage and faced his mentor. Sandor stood a short distance away, his eyebrows drawn down over his eyes, his mouth a straight slash of pure frustration.

"Care to explain yourself?" Sandor's voice sent a chill up Sean's spine.

Not particularly, but that wasn't an option. Okay, if he was going to fry, it might as well be for speaking the truth. "I'm supposed to be training as a Talion, not hiding at the first sign of danger. That's not what I signed on for."

Sandor's hand snaked out to grab Sean by the front of his shirt. Suddenly, his feet were dangling in the air as he got up close and personal with one pissed off Talion.

"Fuck that crap, kid. A Talion's job is to keep our people safe. If that means making sure innocents are out of the line of fire, so be it."

Sandor dropped Sean as quickly as he'd picked him up. "Unless you think I'm a coward for protecting Tara, Kenny, and Lena. Or for following the Chief Talion's orders."

Holy shit! All this time he'd been thinking about how he felt being banished from the front lines. It hadn't occurred to him that Sandor might be having the same problem with their orders.

"Oh, hell no!" Sean managed to stammer. "That's not what I meant at all."

"Then why don't explain exactly what you did mean? And don't think I've forgotten about your promise to follow orders or the consequences if you don't."

Sean forced himself to look Sandor in the eye. "I'm not some little kid who needs to go hide under the bed when the boogeyman knocks at the door. I understand everyone wanting to keep Kenny, Tara, and even Lena out of the line of fire, but I want to do what I can to keep the Dame safe. I owe her just like I owe you."

Sean hated—*hated*—that his voice cracked a little as he spoke, but he meant every damn word he'd said. Following that geeky guy around the neighborhood had been his first taste of what it was like to serve the greater cause, and he'd liked it. But this was more than that.

"Somebody needs to help Grey Danby take down the bastard who sent that bomb through the mail. We both know Ranulf won't leave Kerry's side, and who can blame him? You've got Tara, Kenny, and Lena to worry about. That leaves me to help Grey." Honesty made him add, "And maybe Piper."

"And what can you do that those other Talions Grey brought in can't do?"

Okay, that was a fair question. "I know the city. They don't. I've had years of sneaking around without being noticed. Most of them look like you."

There went Sandor's eyebrows diving down again. "What the hell is that supposed to mean?"

"You know, all polished and pricey. I bet you can't go anywhere without making women drool."

Finally, Sandor's mouth quirked up in a half smile. "What's it worth to you for me not to tell a trained pack of killers that you think they're nothing but a bunch of pretty boys?"

Sean wished he'd kept his mouth shut, especially when he'd be hard pressed to cough up more than ten bucks at the moment. "Uh, Sandor, I'd rather you just kill me now than throw me to the wolves."

"As tempting as that is, Grey wouldn't appreciate me slaughtering his new sidekick." Sandor pulled out his cell phone. "I'll ask him, but if he says you go with us, you go."

"Yes, sir." Sean nodded and crossed his fingers in his pocket, both for luck and because he had no intention of keeping his promise if the Brit said no.

"Grey, change of plans. Sean wants to hang with you. Says he can make himself useful. That okay?"

Sandor had a real knack for hiding his thoughts behind a blank expression, a talent Sean really hated right then. What could Grey be saying that took so long?

Finally, Sandor hung up. "Congrats, kid. You've been promoted to the big leagues. And once we get through this, Grey and I are going to drag your ass down to the local recruiter's office. You can pick which branch of the military you want to enlist in, but that's as much say as you get in the matter. If you're going to serve the Dame, you need to learn discipline as well as the weapons and tactical training that a stint in the service will give you. Got that?"

Memories of living on the streets, desperate to keep his stomach filled and his energy tank topped off, flashed through Sean's mind. The man standing in front of him had offered him the chance to have a real life, one with meaning and purpose. If Sandor said the military was what he needed now, Sean believed him.

He threw his hand up in an awkward salute, "Yes, sir. Message received, sir."

Sandor rolled his eyes in mock disgust and then

surprised them both by giving Sean a quick hug, pounding on his back with a heavy hand.

"I'll make you proud," Sean promised.

"You already have." Sandor tossed him the keys to his sports car. "Get your stuff and head on back to Kerry's house."

Sean stared at the keys. "I'll take good care of it."

"I'm not worried about the car. Take good care of my friends."

"Yes, sir, I'll do my best."

"I know you will."

Chapter 15

"*A*re you sure about this?"

Piper smiled at her sister's worried face and nodded. "I'll be fine. Grey left a couple of his men back at the house. When we get back, Sean and I will slip out through the secret entrance, and he'll drop me off at school in Sandor's car, not the Packard."

"Are you sure it's safe for you to go to school?"

"Yeah, it is." Although she'd argued long and hard with Grey about it, she didn't admit that to Kerry. "Because of finals, classes are running on a completely different schedule, making my routine unpredictable. After I finish my exam, I'll check in with Grey and then head straight for a new hotel. He thinks I'll be safer in a public place than I would be in my apartment."

Kerry held out her arms for a quick hug. Piper closed her eyes, fighting off tears. Even without the blood connection, she would have loved Kerry.

"Good luck with your test," Kerry said. "And while we're on the subject, we have to talk about what you want to do after you graduate. I don't want to lose you to some big corporation. Now get going before I break down completely."

Kerry rejoined her husband as two Talion guards moved up to flank them on the porch of the cabin. Despite how Ranulf physically dwarfed Kerry, Piper knew the two were equal partners. It was hard not to be a bit jealous of the happiness they had found.

"You ready?" Grey asked as he opened the passenger door of the Packard for her.

"As ready as I'll ever be." She softened the remark with a smile. "I'm terrified of the test I have this afternoon."

Grey carefully maneuvered the Packard across the uneven ground back toward the road, stopping to speak to one of his men before continuing. Just as they reached the edge of the pavement, a wave of energy washed over them, leaving Piper dizzy and nauseated. It felt like a roller coaster ride but without the thrill.

Through clenched teeth, she asked, "What on earth was that?"

"Ranulf reinforcing his wards on the property." Grey shot a dirty look back into the rearview mirror. "The bastard could have waited a few seconds longer until we were in the clear."

The unsettling sensation was rapidly fading. "He's worried about Kerry."

"I get that," Grey snarled. "It's the only reason I'm not going to flatten the bugger next time I see him."

Piper laughed. "I'd pay to see that."

"Why? Because you don't think I can take him?"

She studied her lover. "Actually, I think it would be an even match. He might be bigger, but I have a feeling you'd fight dirty."

Grey looked pleased by her assessment. "Thanks for the vote of confidence, but they didn't call Viking warriors berserkers for nothing. I might hold my own with Ranulf, but he hasn't survived a thousand years by losing many battles."

She reached over to squeeze Grey's bicep, not that she wasn't already intimately acquainted with every bit of the man's incredible body. "I'm still betting on you."

"Thanks, luv," he laughed.

Piper smiled back at her lover and settled back to enjoy the ride.

Time was passing too quickly as they barreled down the mountain back to civilization. At that thought, her stomach cramped into a painful knot. She'd lied to Grey. Her history final was small potatoes compared to what he would be facing.

It was only because she knew him so well that she could sense his growing tension. Grey might be calm, but he definitely wasn't relaxed.

"So tell me, how bad is this going to be?"

His knuckles whitened as they grasped the steering wheel. "It all depends."

"On what?"

"On how fucking crazy Adele, her father, and

whoever is helping them are. You can depend on warriors to keep casualties to a minimum. Fanatics, on the other hand, tend to revel in blood."

The sick feeling was back in full force, although this time she couldn't blame it on Ranulf's words. One only had to watch the evening news to know that Grey was right. Considering the nutcase had already mailed them a bomb that could have gone off at any time, there was no reason to think the next attack would be less dangerous.

His hand caught hers in a tight squeeze. "I'll be fine, Piper. We all will be."

"You can't know that. That bomb almost killed you."

His eyes were alight with blue flames. "True enough, but we weren't expecting an attack. He'll have hard time sneaking up on any of us now that we know he's out there."

"He? So you think it was this Harcourt guy who sent the bomb?"

Grey shook his head. "He might be footing the bills, but the bomber had to be close by at the time, and Harcourt only just got into town. Whoever is behind this either hired local talent or brought someone in. Besides, Harcourt isn't the type to want to get his own hands dirty."

Unexpectedly, Grey grinned. "Unlike me. I'm a street brawler by both birth and preference. When I find the low-life bastard behind these attacks, he's going down."

Piper believed him. She thought back to the day they'd met. The first thing she'd noticed was his hand-tailored suit, but it hadn't disguised his true nature at all. He was a powerful warrior and that was a good thing right now.

Still, she had to ask, "How can you be so matter of fact about all of this? You can't possibly be happy about this mess."

Grey drove in silence for a few seconds before answering. There was more to Piper's question than just idle curiosity. She'd obviously picked up on his growing excitement. He could lie to her and hide his true self, but he had too much respect for her to settle for half truths.

"Moments like these are what I've trained for since I first found out what I was. Trust me, if Kerry wasn't the target, Ranulf would be acting the same way. Sandor, too, although he's had more practice at acting civilized. We are born of warrior stock."

They were nearing Kerry's home. "That doesn't mean I wouldn't prefer to grow old never facing another renegade in a fight to the death. Even if my target deserves to die, it leaves its mark on a man."

She had to be wondering how many of those battles he'd already fought. The question was there in those pretty dark eyes of hers. If she had a problem with him being willing to kill to defend his people, then she'd be better off walking away now.

Piper stared out of the window. "You might not wear a uniform, but you and Ranulf and Sandor are the equivalent of the Kyth military."

He nodded. "That and law enforcement, including judge and executioner, all rolled into one. Is that too much for you to deal with?"

Before she could answer him, he noticed the front gate was standing open. Had someone been careless or had the house been breached?

"What's wrong, Grey?"

"Maybe nothing, but the gate's open." Nothing looked out of place, but he couldn't shake the feeling that something was wrong. "Piper, lock the car doors and stay down while I check things out. Follow me when I give you the signal."

Drawing his gun, he approached the house. Pausing at the threshold only long enough to make sure that Piper was staying put, he tried the door and found it unlocked. It hadn't been that way when they'd left earlier. He pushed it open and eased inside.

His first impression was silence. Closing his eyes, he concentrated hard, trying to pick up any heartbeats inside the house. The nearest rooms were definitely empty. He moved farther into the house, turning his head to the left and then the right, reaching out with all his senses.

There. He caught the briefest whiff of a pulse, distant and muffled by the solid walls of the house. He kept moving, finally coming to a halt at the top of the basement steps. Turning the knob slowly, he pulled the door open just enough to slip through. As soon as he did, he knew exactly who was down there.

He holstered his gun and pounded down the steps, ready to wring someone's scruffy neck.

"Damn it, Sean, you little bugger! What's up with leaving the gate open and the front door unlocked? Do you want to get yourself killed? Because I'm telling you right now, if the bomber doesn't do the job, I will."

Accompanied by a pair of Talions, Sean appeared in the door leading to the shower with a towel wrapped around his hips. The three of them looked puzzled.

"What are you talking about? We haven't gone near the front door or the gate because we're supposed to stay out of sight. Besides, Ranulf threatened to kick my ass if I set foot out of the house before you got back. I was getting cleaned up after my workout so I could take Piper to class."

The hair on the back of Grey's neck stood up as a cold trickle of dread slithered through his veins. If Sean hadn't unlocked the door, who had? And why?

He started back up the steps, slowly at first, as his mind struggled to connect all the pieces. He hated the picture forming in his head. There was only one reason someone would have left the gate standing open and that was to lure him inside, away from the car.

Away from Piper.

Bloody hell! Grey charged up the remaining steps, screaming a warning that Piper didn't stand a chance of hearing from inside the Packard.

Suddenly the front door and the windows exploded inward, showering the entry hall with razor sharp fragments of glass and splintered wood. The basement door provided some protection, sheltering him and Sean from the worst of the blast, but the front rooms of the house weren't so lucky. He'd survived the explosion, but that didn't matter. He had to get to Piper.

Dimly aware of someone yelling, Grey stumbled past the shambles of the front hall and out to the porch. He raised his arm over his face, trying to see past the flames and the twisted metal that was all that remained of Ranulf's beloved Packard. Running down the steps and across the lawn took only a few seconds, but he already knew it was too late.

Numb from the inside out, he stood staring at the flaming car. At all that was left of Piper Ryan.

Someone was screaming; Grey's ears pounded. He looked around, ready to shoot the culprit if that's what it took to make it stop. Then he realized he was alone and the agonized screams were his.

And he couldn't stop. Didn't want to stop. Ever. He fell to his knees at the edge of Piper's funeral pyre, not caring if he was burned, painful blisters rising on his tear-soaked cheeks. If Piper was dead, so was he. He might still breathe, but only until he found her killer.

Talions swore to serve justice on behalf of the Dame, but they also understood vengeance. An eye for an eye was what "Talion" meant. When he got his hands on the fucker who'd done this, he would shred the bastard into bloody pieces with his bare hands.

"My God. Was Piper in the car?"

Grey jerked his head in a short nod.

Sean's young face was blank as he stared at the horror in front of them. Grey forced himself back up to his feet. To give the kid credit, he stood his ground despite Grey's obvious rage. Ripping his shirt open, Grey pointed at the symbol burned into his skin right over his heart.

"See this, kid? Do you know what it means?" he demanded, his voice a raw growl.

Sean swallowed hard and nodded. "It's a Thor's Hammer like the one Ranulf wears around his neck. Sandor has a brand like yours on his arm. It's the mark of a Talion."

The other two Talions crowded closer, each displaying his own badge of office. Grey pointed at theirs and then back at his own, as the emblems flashed brightly.

"And you want to be one of us? Because I'm telling you right now, once you choose this path, there's no turning back. They've killed Piper. They've drawn first blood. They will die for it. This I vow."

The kid didn't hesitate to join in as the other warriors echoed Grey's words. Sean jerked himself to attention and nodded. "She was one of us. They deserve to die. This I vow."

His voice sounded years older as he repeated the Talion oath. Grey grabbed Sean's hand, pressing it against the emblem burned into his own skin as he concentrated his power on that one spot. Instantly, it burned as hot and painfully as it had the day he himself had been marked as one of the Dame's own.

Sweat poured off Sean's face as he endured the pain

that would connect him, not only to the Grand Dame of the Kyth, but also to every other Talion. When the power surge ended, Grey released him. The teenager stared down at the raw burn that had appeared on his forearm, his mouth turning up in a grim smile at what his life had now become.

Finally, he lowered his arm to his side. "What do we do next?"

The sound of sirens made that decision for Grey. "We get the hell away from here before we're tied up for hours answering questions. We'll go out the secret route to avoid neighbors and police. Then we'll find someplace to set up temporary headquarters and regroup."

Once they put some distance between themselves and this clusterfuck, he'd contact Ranulf and Sandor. Then he'd gather the remaining Talions and establish a control center somewhere nearby.

"Everybody haul ass. Grab whatever gear you need from the house on the way through."

Sean nodded and took off through the rubble. Grey stared once more at the tangled mess of metal and laid his hand over his brand again. He drew comfort from the knowledge that his was the blood of warriors. Even with his heart shattered and his soul dying, he would find the strength to end this fight once and for all.

As Chief Talion, he was sworn to bring the renegades to justice, and he would do his duty. But when the verdict was handed down by Kerry Thorsen, Grand Dame of the Kyth, Grey would carry out the executions by right of vengeance for the loss of his lover. On that day, he would look straight into their faces and let the guilty see their deaths in his eyes.

He murmured his vow one last time and then followed Sean into the house.

Sean sat in the corner of the hotel room, out of the the Talions way who'd been pouring in since Grey sent out the alarm. They setting up computers and checking their weapons. Until they gave him something else to do, he studied the stylized burn on his arm. It hurt like a bitch, but he wasn't about to complain. Not around Grey, and especially not now. He was stunned the man could function at all. It didn't take a genius to know that Grey had it bad for Piper.

Hell, whenever the two of them were in the same room, the temperature jumped at least twenty degrees from the looks they gave each other. It was the same way with Lena and Sandor, not to mention the Dame and her Consort. *And they talk about teenagers having raging hormones!*

He cringed. Now wasn't the time for such thoughts. There would be no more looks for Grey and Piper. His eyes sought out the Chief Talion, watching for signs that Grey was finally going to crash and burn. Damn, that was a poor choice of words, but it had to be coming—soon.

Sean couldn't imagine how he'd have reacted if it had been Tara in the car when it exploded. Not that Grey wasn't suffering. He was; he *had* to be. Maybe it was all his training that kept him focused on the big picture.

"Hey, kid!"

Sean glanced toward the nearest Talion. Normally, he would have resented being the designated kid in the room, but now wasn't the time to argue.

"Yeah?"

"Can you give me a hand hooking up these cables?"

"Sure thing."

Finally, a chance to be useful. Anything was better than just sitting there wondering what happened next. Grey had already called Ranulf and given him orders to keep Kerry at the cabin. Several more Talions were about to be dispatched to stand guard.

One of the new arrivals held out his hand when Sean reached his side. "Sorry I didn't catch your name. I'm Rolf."

"Sean."

Rolf spotted the raw brand on Sean's arm and grinned. "Welcome to the club. When we go out for some food, we'll pick up some salve for that."

"It's not that bad."

Rolf laughed. "Yeah, sure, tough guy. I said the same thing when I got mine. It was a lie then and it's a lie now. Let's get these cables connected before Grey kicks both our asses."

"Sounds like a plan."

Adele stood back and studied the unconscious woman they'd tossed on the bed.

"Do you think she's pretty?"

Wes stepped closer to Adele, shaking his head. "Pretty enough, I guess, but a bit old. Nice legs, though."

Not exactly what Adele wanted to hear, but Wes was often oblivious to such things. At first, she'd thought the woman really was the Dame. Certainly there was a superficial resemblance, which had her wondering exactly who they'd captured.

Maybe she should have gone with her first impulse and left the woman in the Packard when they'd detonated the bomb. But Wes had pointed out that a hostage had more value than a casualty. Judging by Grey Danby's response to the explosion, Wes might be right.

Maybe. And besides, the prisoner's status could change at the drop of a hat—or the press of a detonator.

"The purple bruise on her temple goes well with the streaks in her hair, though." Wes winked at Adele.

"Who should we e-mail about her? It might be fun to hear what that Danby fellow has to say. He seemed pretty broken up over her death."

It served the blighter right. His screams had been music to her ears as she and Wes had watched the aftermath on a laptop in the safety of their car, several blocks away. Wes had positioned the cameras and microphones perfectly. The fireball had been impressive; the explosion itself reverberated through the neighborhood and rattled windows for blocks. She'd almost come from just watching the excitement.

"The show was perfect, Wes. Exactly what I had imagined." She was in the mood for something besides talking. "Let's celebrate first. Then we can decide what to do with—*that.*"

She kissed her lover, well aware that their captive was starting to stir. That the woman might wake up enough to watch only added to Adele's pleasure. It might be different if she lived long enough to talk about it. After all, the future Dame shouldn't have a reputation for being a slut. But neither their guest nor Wes would be around to gossip.

She eased his zipper down, slipping her hand inside those tacky cotton boxers he liked. Silk would show so much more class. He groaned and thrust his cock more firmly against her hand.

Then he gently pushed down on her shoulders. "Down on your knees, sweetheart. Use that talented mouth to show me some gratitude."

How dare he? When she resisted, he shoved her down to the floor. "Now."

Before she reacted, someone pounded on the door. Just that quickly, the mood dissipated, and for the first time, Adele tasted fear. Wes yanked her to her feet, fastening his pants on his way through the living room.

"Who could it be? We've been so careful."

Wes shot her a disgusted look. "Only one way to find out, luv. Open the fuckin' door."

Orders again. For now, she'd let it slide, especially since he suddenly had a rather impressive gun in his hand. Another frisson of heat settled in the core of her body. She hoped whoever was at the door didn't stay long.

After waiting until Wes positioned himself for a clear shot, she kept the door between herself and the intruder as she turned the handle.

"About time you let me in, daughter."

She sighed heavily. Her father—the absolute last person she needed butting into her business right now.

"Come in," she said reluctantly.

At least Wes had the good sense to keep his gun aimed right at dear old Dad's head. She stood by her lover, making sure not to get between Wes and his target.

Harcourt bristled at her unspoken declaration of loyalty. Bloody prig that he was, Harcourt's lip actually curled in disdain as he studied the two of them.

"I did not raise you to be a fool *or* a tramp, Adele."

"No, you raised me to be Dame. Seems you failed all around."

She wrapped her arm around Wes's waist and pressed a wet kiss to his cheek, knowing how much her father hated PDA. Wes responded by squeezing her ass with his free hand as he grinned at her father.

"Do you want to hear what this wanker has to say, luv? If not, let's kick his arse back out the door and pick up where we left off."

She laughed at the outraged expression on her father's face. "You did show up at a particularly inopportune moment. Another few seconds, and we probably wouldn't have answered the door at all."

Harcourt stamped his foot. "This is not the time, Adele. You have no idea the hell your actions has unleashed on all of us."

"You mean other than sending the usurper diving for cover and blowing up the Viking's beloved car?" She frowned. "I think that about covers it. Did I leave out anything, Wes?"

His eyes had that lovely crazed look they always got when he thought about making things go boom. "There was the bomb we shipped to the Dame's house, but that was more of a preview than an actual event."

By now, Harcourt was shaking with fury. "You idiots! Don't you get it? You've signed your own death warrants and maybe mine, too. Even if Dame Kerry and Ranulf could forgive the loss of the car, do you actually think Grey Danby will ever quit hunting for us?"

"I'm not worried about him. He's little better than a street thug, after all."

Her father looked at her as if she'd lost her mind. "Grey Danby has fought his way up from those streets, Adele. Nothing and no one ever stopped him from getting what he wanted. You might have a better pedigree, but you've always had everything handed to you."

He pointed toward the window. "Out there the strongest Talion since Ranulf himself is on the hunt for you. And once Grey Danby gets us in his sights, your boy toy there will die begging for mercy, and the two of us will follow. All because you two are greedy and stupid.

"You've never seen a Talion execution, but I have." He shuddered in revulsion. "The renegade deserved to die, but don't think for a minute that it was anything as merciful as a hanging or the electric chair. He died screaming as blue flames burned through his skin while Danby squeezed every drop life energy out of the poor bastard. When it was over, there was nothing left but a pile of ashes to be swept up."

He gave her one more hard look. "That's the future you've chosen for yourself, my dear. Well, you're welcome to it. For myself, I'm choosing to go home on the next flight and pray that Grey never connects your actions to me."

Okay, he'd succeeded in scaring her. Time to share the joy. "Too late."

"What do you mean?"

She smiled sweetly. "Grey already knows you're in town."

Her father paled. "How?"

She marched over and got in his face. "I told the usurper, and then hinted that Grey was on your personal payroll. The payments into his accounts can be traced right back to yours. If Grey's as good as you say he is, I'd guess you have only hours before he tracks you down."

The crack of flesh against flesh rang out as her father slapped her across the face. The shock of being smacked for the first time in her life left Adele standing within striking with tears streaming down her face. When her father raised his hand for a repeat performance, Wes stepped forward.

"That's enough."

Wes pulled Adele behind him. "Touch her again and it will be the last thing you ever do."

Her father focused on the barrel of Wes's gun, aimed squarely at his face. Realizing it was more than an idle threat, he backed toward the door.

"You want her? Well, congratulations, kid. She's all yours."

Then he looked past Wes to her. "As of this minute, I have no daughter. You are no longer mine. And as soon as I can reach my solicitor, you will no longer be my heir."

"Fine. You were never much of a father anyway." She pushed the bitter words out through her swollen lips. "Start running, coward. Grey's coming for you first."

Her father had gone but two steps toward the door when Wes cocked the hammer on his gun, freezing Harcourt in his steps. "Do you want him dead, darling girl?"

It was tempting. So very tempting, but no. She had bigger plans still in play.

"Let him go." She made sure her father was listening when she added, "For now. As long as Grey is hunting him, he won't be looking for us."

When the door was firmly locked between them and the world outside, Adele considered her options. For the moment, there was nothing to be done except play the cards they'd been dealt. That her father would abandon her wasn't much of a shock. She'd always known he was a coward.

Wes, on the other hand, was turning out to be quite a surprise. She definitely owed him for standing beside her against all comers. Time to show him a little appreciation. She stepped in front of him and ran a finger down the barrel of his gun before dropping to her knees.

Ignoring the pain that lingered on her face, she smiled up at him. "Now, where were we?"

Chapter 16

*P*iper licked her lips and tasted blood, which added to the acid burn in the back of her throat. What a fool she was! She'd been so worried about Grey's headlong rush into Kerry's house that she'd forgotten to worry about herself.

By the time she'd looked up to see the gun pointed at her head, it was too late to do anything but follow orders. All things considered, she didn't regret not screaming for help. That would've only brought Grey charging to her rescue at the exact moment her captors had detonated the bomb. She hated knowing that Grey thought she was dead, but better that than him dying for real.

She listened carefully, trying to make sure she was still alone in the room. The only voices she could hear were some distance away in the next room. By the sound of it, things were heating out up there.

She flexed her wrists and ankles, testing the

strength of the rope that bound them. It was hard not to cry remembering the crazed look in that man's eyes right before he'd stuck a needle in her arm. She'd almost been grateful for the darkness that washed over her, temporarily delivering her from this nightmare.

The drug had been working its way out of her system for some time, but she'd instinctively hidden that from her captors. Her blood had run cold as they'd discussed her death. Adele and Wes were scarily pragmatic, more worried about the effect bloodstains would have on his damage deposit than the thought of killing another human being.

Score! The rope knotted around her wrists had a little bit of give to it. She closed her eyes to concentrate better. From there, her plan for escape was pretty nebulous, but she'd take it one step at a time. Only she could save herself; everyone else thought she was already dead.

God, it had been agonizing to hear Grey's screams as he stared helplessly at the inferno that engulfed the Packard. If she'd had any doubts about the depth of his feelings for her, they'd died in that blast. And, coward that she was, it had taken a disaster to make her face up to her own love for him.

Please, God, let me live long enough to tell him.

The push and pull against her bindings left her skin raw and bloody. Fine. The blood would only serve to make the ropes more slippery if she could loosen them enough to pull a hand free.

It was time to figure out what was going on with

her captors. Earlier, she'd been stunned—and grossed out—by the realization that they were going to have sex right in front of her. Even the nearly silent slide of the guy's zipper had made her want to puke.

A door in another room opened and then slammed closed. It was to much to hope that they had suddenly decided to make a quick trip for lattes.

A low moan dispelled any chance of that. They were at it again. Hoping the guy had enough staying power to let her break free, Piper hurried her efforts to work the rope. Of course, if she succeeded, how was she going to get past them?

Maybe her room was on the first floor. Or perhaps there was a phone handy, so she could call Grey. Then he and the cavalry could come riding to her rescue. That is, if she could figure out where she was. She knew only one thing for certain: Grey was resourceful. Given even a vague hint about her whereabouts, he'd find her. She loved that about him. She loved everything about him.

With that comforting thought, she gave her right hand another hard yank.

Grey stared at the computer and ignored everyone else in the hotel room. Harcourt hadn't changed his airline reservation, which meant he was still in Seattle. Eventually, he'd light somewhere long enough for Grey and his men to scoop him up.

"I've almost got you, you bastard!"

For the first time in hours, Grey felt something

other than cold rage and grief—anticipation. Once he'd gotten Sean safely away from the Dame's house and rounded up the troops, he'd done his damnedest to crack down on every thought or feeling that interfered with his concentration on the hunt. He was slowly making progress.

He'd managed to report in to the Dame with cold dispassion. The call to Sandor had been just as succinct. The hardest part was ignoring the backwash of grief when they learned that Piper had been the first casualty in this war.

He keyed in another search, well aware that someone was about to make an attempt to distract him. So far, Grey had successfully deflected all offers of food, rest, or any kind of comfort, all the things he didn't deserve. Not yet. Not until the enemy was found and engaged.

He'd sorely underestimated their foes. They all had, but it wouldn't happen again. Not on his watch. He did his best to ignore Sean, who hovered a few feet away. The kid was nothing if not stubborn. Maybe that's why he reminded Grey of himself so much.

"Not now, Sean."

The newest Talion obviously wasn't lacking courage. So far, he'd been the only one who'd actually defied Grey's orders to leave him the hell alone.

"Sorry, boss, but your phone is ringing again. It's that detective calling. He's taken to dialing your number every five minutes."

"So?"

"It's driving the rest of us crazy, and I need to know what to do about it. Do you want me to answer it?"

"No."

"Okay, so then can we shut the fucking thing off?"

Okay, so the kid had Grey's temper as well. "Not until everyone has been notified of my new number."

"When will that be?"

Grey's hands itched to lash out, to rip into the kid, but Sean's only crime was being there, alive and breathing when Piper wasn't. Grey forced himself to back away from his rage. He rubbed his temples, trying to ease the pain long enough to be civil.

"We've all switched to throwaway phones to keep the authorities—and our enemies—from tracing us easily. I disabled the GPS in my phone, but not everyone has the new number yet."

He held out his hand. "Besides, sooner or later, whoever detonated that blast will call to gloat. There's no way I want to miss a chance to track that bastard down."

Sean stepped closer. "Okay, I get it. Here."

But instead of dropping the cell into Grey's outstretched palm, Sean handed him a plate piled high with food. "I'll watch the phone while you eat that. By the time you're finished, Sandor will be here and can take over. We all think you should get some sleep, too."

Sean walked away without giving Grey a chance to react, or to ask why Sandor hadn't stayed with Lena and the other two young Kyth. Grey felt an odd sensation and the realized he'd actually smiled. He had to hand it to the kid; it had been a gutsy move. Sean was going to make one helluva Talion warrior. He was sneaky and had the right bad attitude.

He studied the plate. He hadn't been hungry in all the hours since the explosion. The truth was, he hadn't felt much of anything except for chilling pain. For a few seconds, he held the plate over the trash can, but tossing it wouldn't accomplish anything. Even he had to admit that he should keep up his strength. Besides, he had the suspicion that Sean already had a second plate ready just in case. That's what Grey would have done if the situation were reversed.

Conceding the point, Grey picked up half of a sandwich and took a bite. It tasted like dust dry dirt, but he choked it down anyway. When he had trouble swallowing, a bottle of water magically appeared on his desk.

"You're welcome," Sean muttered and walked away, leaving Grey no chance to say thanks.

Yeah, he really liked that kid.

A few minutes later, he finished the sandwich and the water. Time to get back to work. But before he could start another search, a knock at the door cut through the air like a knife.

"Do you want me to open it?"

Grey rose to his feet as he drew his gun, aware of half a dozen others being readied at the same instant. Chances were that it was someone on their side, but he wouldn't risk another mistake.

He crossed the room and pressed his palm to the

door, concentrating all of his senses on the person standing on the other side. He recognized Sandor's energy pattern immediately, but there was someone else standing too far back for Grey to get a reading.

"It's Sandor, but he's not alone. Open the door slowly and stay the hell out of my line of fire."

Sean nodded and did as instructed. Sandor held up his hands to show he was no threat. When Lena moved into sight, Grey immediately lowered his weapon and motioned for the two of them to come in. Tara and Kenny filed in right behind them.

Sandor took a quick look around Grey's makeshift headquarters before speaking again. "How badly was the house damaged?"

Grey shrugged. "The front took the biggest hit, mostly broken glass and the like. But we're also dodging Detective Byrne and company."

"Good thinking." Sandor shot his companions a disgusted look. "Sorry to take so long getting here."

Lena punched him on the arm. "Don't blame us. You were the one who wasted all that time arguing even though you knew I wouldn't let you come by yourself. Besides, Tara and Kenny wanted to be here with Sean."

"And I wanted all of you out of the danger zone."

Personally Grey agreed with Sandor, but he recognized an uphill battle when he saw one. "Lena, why don't you see if you can book another room on this floor for you and the others."

"Already did. We've got the three rooms next to this one."

A sick feeling churned in Grey's gut. There could only be one reason they'd reserved so many. "Ranulf and Kerry are on their way back to town. How soon will they be here?"

"Soon enough. Ranulf said once they heard about Piper, there was no keeping Kerry up on the mountain. She's promised to be reasonable about flying under the radar, but Kerry's definition of reasonable isn't always what it should be."

Great. Just bloody fucking great.

There was nothing to do except get on with the matter at hand. "Why don't I bring you up to speed?"

Lena raised up on her toes and gave Sandor a quick kiss. "We'll get out of the way. Keep me in the loop, and let me know if I can do anything."

Before leaving she surprised Grey with a hug. "I'm sorry, Grey. She was a wonderful woman and deserved better."

As Lena walked away, he decided he agreed. She might have been talking about Piper dying the way she did, but the truth was that she'd also deserved better than Grey. If he'd left her on the mountain with Kerry instead of giving in to his selfish need to keep her close, she'd still be alive. Or if he'd thought to take her in the house with him instead of leaving her in the car—easy prey for an enemy.

Enough of that. There'd be plenty of time later for recriminations and regrets. Grey noticed the look of impatience on Sean's face. So the kid really did expect Grey to hand over the reins to Sandor for a while. Fine. But only long enough for him to catch his second wind. After a quick nod in Sean's direction, Grey led Sandor over to the bank of computers Rolf had set up.

"I'm tracking Harcourt. It shouldn't be long before we find him."

"So you think he's behind the attack that . . ." Sandor's voice trailed off, clearly unwilling to finish his sentence.

Grey ignored the flash of pain in his gut. "No, not really. Harcourt might want the throne for his daughter, but I still think he and his cousin Reggie would've tried legal channels first if they thought they could build a case against Kerry. I'm not saying he couldn't have turned violent if things didn't go his way, but Harcourt wouldn't have started off that way. However, he wouldn't be trying to hide his tracks so carefully if he didn't know something about the real culprit and wanted to protect her."

"You really suspect his daughter Adele?" Sandor sounded doubtful.

Grey didn't blame him. It was hard to reconcile his memory of Harcourt's daughter with the image of a stone-cold killer. But once he'd started digging into her lifestyle, he'd found enough evidence to make it seem at least possible, if not likely.

"Let's just say that I won't be surprised to find out she's the one behind the scenes pulling all the strings. She has her father's fastidious nature, but all along I've suspected there was at least one complete unknown involved. Bomb makers of that talent aren't very common."

After they had talked for a few more minutes, Sandor gave Grey a hard look. "How long since you've had any downtime?"

"God, not you, too. I thought Sean was our resident nursemaid."

The teenager had been talking to Tara, but he obviously had a Talion's enhanced hearing because he immediately protested. "Hey, now!"

Grey exchanged a weary smile with Sandor. "As I was saying, I was told once you got here to take over, I should rest. Who am I to argue?"

He was only doing it because he couldn't bear another minute of everyone watching him. Half the men in the room kept him in their peripheral vision as if they expected him to explode. The rest, Sandor included, stared at him with so much sympathy it made him physically ill. Pretending to sleep would at least give him a few minutes of relief.

"We have these two adjoining suites for a command center, but I also booked one across the hall for whenever someone needs sleep. I'll be in the bedroom on the right. Anything breaks, send the kid to get me."

He started to walk away. "I mean *anything,* no matter how small. I . . . I need to . . . I just need to, that's all."

"Will do."

The room across the hall was blissfully quiet. Despite Grey's reluctance to leave his post, he was running on a combination of adrenaline and caffeine. If he didn't downshift soon, he'd risk total burnout at a crucial moment.

He kicked off his shoes and stretched out on top of the comforter. Concentrating on relaxing one muscle group at a time, he ratcheted his tension down to a more manageable level. Gradually, his eyes drifted shut.

Floating just short of slumber, there was nothing he could do to keep the memories of Piper from slipping in, filling his mind and breaking his heart. He needed to rest, but even more, he craved something to soothe his soul. If he couldn't sleep, maybe he could still dream; rather than fight the images, he let them come. Remembering. Cherishing. Loving.

And if a few tears slipped down his cheeks, too damned bad.

Piper bit back a cry and cursed under her breath when she ripped another nail off. What kind of criminal would do such a crappy job of tying her wrists together, but then use the grandfather of all knots to bind her ankles? She probably had minutes at best to make good on her escape, so she did what she could to block out the pain, as well as the knowledge that her captives were just in the next room.

If there had been a phone anywhere in sight, she could have wormed her way across the room to call Grey and pray he reached her before her captors decided she'd outlived her usefulness. Not that they'd used her for anything at all. If they were going to hold her for ransom or for leverage, why hadn't they put their evil plan into action? She had an awful feeling that her time was running out.

Frustrated with her lack of progress, she looked around. If worse came to worst, she could always wrap the rope around her wrists and pretend to be unconscious. It wasn't much as plans went, but it was all she had.

She eased her legs over the side of the bed and stood up. It was difficult to balance as she inched her way across the floor to the window. The thick carpet helped muffle any noise. At the window, she braced herself and looked out.

Whoa! She was on the first floor! If she could get the window open and her feet free, she could reach the neighbor's place in a few seconds. The lock creaked as she turned it. Despite the noise, the small victory spurred her on. She threw all her strength into opening the window and got absolutely nowhere. After three more tries, she dropped her head against the glass. The darn thing was painted shut.

Across the room, there was another window. What were the chances of it being any different? She'd never know unless she tried. The shortest route was across the bed. Easing herself back down on the mattress, she started to roll.

A noise caught her attention—footsteps. She quickly wrapped the rope around her wrists and assumed the position she'd been in when her captors left her. Hopefully, whoever was about to come through that door wouldn't pick up on her racing pulse.

A finger poked Piper's shoulder.

"Wes, how much of that stuff did you give her? I thought she was waking up a while ago, but she's still out. Should we dump water on her head or something?"

Her boyfriend yelled from the other room. "Give it another thirty minutes. I followed the guy's directions, but he also said that it's different for everyone. Maybe she's extra sensitive to the stuff."

"Okay, fine, but then I want her awake or it will mess up my plans. Grey already thinks she's dead. Think how much fun will be to let him find out his lover is very much alive, only to have her die again, but for real."

Wes's voice came closer. "Adele, have I ever told you how much I love the way your mind works?"

"Several times. All right, thirty minutes and then the games will begin, with or without Grey's plaything's cooperation."

As soon as they left the room, Piper yanked the ropes off her hands again. She stared at the closed door, her entire body shaking with fury. What had Grey ever done to this woman to make her want to torment him? Obviously there was some history there, something to ask him the next time she saw him.

With that thought in mind, she started for the second window again. No way did she want to stick around and be a part of any games that Adele and Wes had planned.

• • •

"Grey! We need you."

The note of excitement in Sean's voice bounced Grey to full awareness. He rolled off the bed to his feet.

"What's up, kid?"

"Sandor has a lead on Harcourt. We're getting ready to roll and figured you'd want to lead the charge."

"Damn fucking straight. Let's go."

The tension in the suite across the hall had ramped up to a new high, but the aura was different. Now that the Talions had a live target, their sense of purpose was back. Each man had his weapons out, checking them over, pocketing extra ammo clips, his game face on—as the Americans would say. Grey drew strength from their excitement, the extra hit of energy bringing his own warrior instincts into sharp focus.

Sandor looked up from the computer screen. "Ah, there you are."

"What have you got?"

"A couple of things. Ranulf called a few minutes ago to say they'd be here within the hour. And Harcourt just made a call to the airline, probably to change his flight. I've narrowed his current position to a hotel near the airport."

Grey stared at the map on the screen, memorizing it. "Let's go get the bastard."

He snapped out orders. "Rolf, you've met Harcourt. Pick a team and go hang at the airport in case we miss him. Station men near both check-in and security. Keep it low key because we need to snag him without anyone noticing."

He looked at the other Talions. "The rest of you will stay here and continue to monitor the situation until we need you. Rolf, check in regularly."

"Will do. Let's go," Rolf said, nodding to several of the others. As his team prepared to file out, they all stopped and looked back at Grey. They placed a hand over their brands.

Rolf gave voice to their thoughts. "Here's to good hunting, sir. This we vow."

Sandor, Grey, and even Sean echoed their sentiments. The Talion connection made Grey grateful to be part of such a dedicated group.

Grey and Sandor were preparing to leave just as Lena joined them, a grim expression on her face. Sandor reached out to touch her cheek.

"I know you hate this. I wish it could be handled differently, but—"

Lena's shoulders sagged. "It's how Talions protect their people. I might not like it, but I understand it. Be careful out there, big guy. Don't show up back here sporting any new scars."

Grey winced and looked away, unable to see the love the two had for each other without being reminded of what he'd almost had. He turned his attention to the one other person in the room.

"Sean, I know you resent being left behind, but I need you here. Hang out with Lena, and watch my phone. If it rings and it's anyone other than the cop, answer it and then report to me. Can you handle that?"

"Yeah."

He was obviously disappointed, but at least he didn't argue. Instead, he looked Grey straight in the eyes and echoed Rolf's words. "Good hunting, Grey."

"Thanks, kid."

Outside, Sandor tossed Grey the keys to his sedan. "You drive. I'll navigate."

Soon they were on their way to Harcourt's hotel. Sandor kept his eyes on the computer screen, watching for any more hits.

"I'm going to kill him." There. It had to be said.

Without looking up, Sandor asked, "Even if it's Adele behind the attacks?"

"Even if. The bastard knew what she was up to and didn't warn us. If he'd called us, we would've been able to track Adele down before it got this far."

"Adele is his daughter, Grey. I'm not defending his actions, but maybe he thought he could stop her himself."

"She might be his daughter, but Kerry is his Dame. That's treason any way you look at it."

"Maybe, but you'll need to wait until Kerry issues the order. If she does, I'll be right there beside you."

There wasn't much Grey could say to that. Even if Kerry hesitated, there was no way he could leave anyone who was responsible—even partially—for Piper's death breathing.

Luckily, the traffic gods were smiling on him. They made it to Harcourt's hotel in record time. Sandor shut down the laptop.

"Nothing new."

They both stared at the hotel. "Got any ideas about how to find him? There must be a hundred rooms in that place."

A slow smile spread across Sandor's face. "You might as well put that snooty British accent of yours to good use. American women seem to have a real thing for it. Tell the clerk at the counter that you're Harcourt's driver and ask her to tell him know that you're here for him."

Grey was mildly insulted, but he was willing to try anything. "And if he won't come down?"

Sandor shrugged. "At least we'll know he's still here and then we wait."

Grey got out of the car and headed for the door, pausing to make sure his shirt was tucked in and his jacket hid his gun. Inside the lobby, he headed straight for the desk, glad to see that a woman was on duty. He doubted a man would have succumbed as easily to his charm.

The woman looked up as he approached. "Can I help you, sir?"

"Yes, I'm here to pick up Lawrence Harcourt to take him to the airport. Can you give me his room number so I can help him with his luggage?"

She looked puzzled. "I'm sorry, but he called a shuttle to take him to the airport. They couldn't have left more than five minutes ago. The van stops along the way, so he would have been better off waiting for you."

Grey quickly switched gears, trying to look disappointed. "I knew I shouldn't have picked up a quick bite on the way. My boss is *not* going to be happy. Mr. Harcourt isn't the type to ignore poor service."

The clerk smiled sympathetically. "But he makes up for it by ignoring good service, doesn't he?" Then she glanced back toward the office door behind her. "Whoops, I probably shouldn't have said that. Sorry."

"Nothing but the truth. Well, I guess I'll go face the music." He took a step back, looking worried.

The woman took pity on him. "Listen, if your boss calls, I'll tell him that Harcourt decided to leave early and didn't bother to cancel your services. That much is true."

"Thanks, luv. I appreciate it." Grey winked at her.

"You're welcome." Her smile heated up a notch. "And by the way, I love the accent."

Chapter 17

*G*rey slid into the car and started the engine. "Call Rolf and warn him that Harcourt took a shuttle to the airport. They unload on the lower level of the parking garage."

Sandor hit Rolf's number on speed dial. "Do you want them to snatch him or save the fun for you?"

"We can't afford to make a public spectacle of this, not with that detective already on us. If they can get a clear shot at grabbing him, tell them to go for it. Otherwise, keep him in sight until we get there and figure something out."

"Will do."

While Sandor relayed the instructions, Grey maneuvered through traffic quickly, but without drawing unwanted attention. In his head, he imagined the sweet taste of Harcourt's fear even as he maintained outward control. Later, when they had the man in custody, Grey would harvest all the information the elitist snob had on the attacks.

Once Grey had learned everything he could, Harcourt's fate would be in Kerry's hands. Would she be able to take the hard stance required by Kyth law? God, he hoped so. If she couldn't, if she wavered at all, she might as well paint a target on her chest. Even if this current rebellion failed, it wouldn't be long before some other fool tried the same thing.

"Tell me, is Kerry up to this?"

Sandor didn't pretend to misunderstand. "She's stronger than you think."

Which didn't exactly answer his question. "This is going to get bloody before it's over. We have to handle it right or every Kyth out there with a God complex will be making a play for the throne."

"Kerry's smart enough to know that. She may have had the role of Dame dropped in her lap with no warning, but she's a fast learner. She could've walked away and didn't. With Ranulf beside her, they would've given Judith and her Consort a run for their money even back in their prime."

Sandor paused. "And with Piper being . . . well, Kerry's out for blood. We all are."

The mention of Piper's name cut through Grey's chest, but it strengthened his resolve. Sandor's conviction that Kerry would see justice done was also a comfort.

"Better call Rolf for an update. We're here."

•　•　•

In the end, the hunt was disappointingly short. Grey and Sandor parked in the garage and ran for the sky bridge while Rolf and his men blocked the terminal side. Even though the aristocrat wasn't yet in sight, Grey could sense the man's turmoil and savored the pungent spice of his fear. He inhaled deeply, drawing power from Harcourt's churning emotions. This was going to be good.

Grey stopped himself, not liking where his thoughts were taking him. No wonder they had laws forbidding feeding off the darker, more addictive emotions.

His cell rang. Rolf gave him a brief report and hung up. "They've spotted him just ahead."

Sandor smiled. "Let's get the bastard."

As yet unaware that he was being tracked, Harcourt started across the sky bridge toward the terminal. When he was about halfway across, Rolf and the others stepped out to block his way. Looking for an escape, he wheeled around only to find Grey waiting only a few feet away.

"What's the matter, Lawrence? Don't you have a minute for an old friend?"

Harcourt didn't answer, but once again tried to reach the terminal. Grey walked in step with him as he headed for the escalator behind Rolf, probably figuring the Talions wouldn't risk a major incident if he could reach the main concourse. Wrong. This time, they'd do whatever it took to get the job done.

"Get your men out of my way, Danby. I have a plane to catch."

Grey reached out to brush a speck of imaginary dust off his quarry's shoulder, enjoying watching Harcourt flinch. "There, that looks better. I have to ask why you're in such a hurry to leave Seattle. I can't tell you how hurt Grand Dame Kerry is that one of her faithful retainers was in town and didn't stop by."

Grey crowded closer. "You *are* a faithful retainer, aren't you, Lawrence? I would hate to learn otherwise."

Now in a state of near panic, Harcourt shoved past Grey and retreated back across the bridge, heading for the questionable safety of the garage. He skidded to a halt when Sandor stepped into sight. Slowly the Talions all started forward, herding Harcourt right back toward where Grey waited.

"What are you doing, Danby?"

"We're still waiting for your answer, Lawrence. Are you loyal to our Dame?"

Harcourt's blood ran cold. Oh, God, he was a dead man. They already knew the answer to that question. It was there in the brittle anger flaming hot in their eyes. How had they found him?

Like that mattered. His chance of escaping was nil; his chance of surviving only slightly better. He had to try, though.

"You have no right to interfere with my plans, Danby. Call off your dogs."

Rather than look insulted, a young Talion coming from the other end of the sky bridge smiled. "Woof, woof."

His companions laughed and joined in, barking softly as the pack closed the circle around Harcourt. He spun around, looking for a weak link in the wall of angry warriors or, failing that, some hint of sympathy for his plight. He didn't find it.

"I didn't do it, Danby. I swear it wasn't me."

Ice-colored flames danced in Grey's eyes. "You didn't do what, Lawrence?"

He fumbled for an answer that wouldn't sentence him to death. "I'm not the one behind the attacks on the Dame. I swear it."

The whole group took another two steps toward him, causing his knees to buckle. "Please, Grey. You know me. I wouldn't do something like that."

"Like what, Lawrence? Mail a letter bomb? Send threatening e-mails? Blow up Ranulf's Packard? Kill Piper Ryan, the Dame's assistant? Tell me, Lawrence, did you know Piper was also Kerry Thorsen's sister? Though she was much, much more than that to me."

The Dame's sister? Dear God, what had Adele done? He'd heard tales about the terror of being hunted by the Talions, but never expected to experience it himself. "Please. I'm not the guilty party."

Grey moved closer so Lawrence could feel the rage flowing off him in waves. "You know, Sandor, I think I believe our good friend Lawrence. He's too much of a coward to attack the Dame or her people directly."

Grey brushed his hand over Lawrence's shoulder again and then straightened his tie, tugging it a bit too tight. "So, no, you're not guilty of any of that."

Grey stepped back, but Lawrence's relief was short-lived, because the Talion's open hand lashed out and collided with his face, jarring his teeth and drawing blood. "But you bloody well know who *is* behind the attacks and you did nothing to stop them. For that, you will face the Dame's justice."

Grey shoved Harcourt stumbling back into the waiting arms of his fellow warriors. "Rolf, take our friend here back to the hotel and lock him in. I'll deal with him later."

Hands latched onto Lawrence's arms with bruising strength. Desperate to escape, to live, he fought to break free. "Wait! Please, for God's sake, listen to me. I can help you, Grey."

Sandor answered instead. "How could a sniveling coward like you help us, Harcourt?"

There was no hope, none at all. Better to throw Adele and her boyfriend to these wolves than face the Dame's justice alone.

"It's Adele. She's gone stark crazy. I came here to try to stop her, but she won't listen. Adele and that street scum she's been fucking are behind all of this."

Neither Sandor nor Grey looked shocked by the revelation. Holy hell, they'd played him. The Dame's pet killers had known all along that Adele was the culprit. Obviously that bit of information wasn't going to earn him any kind of a reprieve.

But maybe he had one more weapon in his arsenal.

"I know where they are."

• • •

Piper wanted to stomp her feet or throw something in pure frustration. The second window was sealed shut, too. She didn't have time to chip away decades worth of dried paint.

Looking around the room, she considered her options. She could always break the glass in the window, hoping to draw the neighbors' attention. Her captors would also come running, so it would have to be a last ditch effort.

Next on her agenda was to check the drawers. Surely there had to be a blade of some kind—a razor, scissors—anything she could use to cut herself free. She started with the bedside table. Nothing in there but a half empty box of condoms. She shoved the drawer closed.

Moving on to the dresser, she had better luck. Under a jumble of socks and dingy underwear, she found a small pocketknife. Hopping her way back to the bed, she began sawing on the rope. The knife finally cut through the last strand, and she ignored the painful tingling as normal circulation returned. Then she started chipping away at the paint on the windowsill.

She'd no more than scratched the surface when the bedroom door banged opened, and her captors filed into the room. Piper backed up at the sight of a pair of guns pointed at her.

Wes motioned toward the knife in her hand. "Toss that over here."

She did as he said, knowing the small blade would provide no defense against bullets.

He smirked and said, "See, Adele. Just like I said—thirty minutes and she's as good as new."

Adele rolled her eyes. "Yes, well, another job well done, Wes. Now what? I can't wait to let her lover know she really didn't die in the Packard. Imagine his joy, up until we kill her. It would be more fun in person, but safer over the phone."

Her utter calm made Piper ill. This woman had more than a few screws loose. How on earth could she look like the quintessential ingénue and talk about death and destruction as casually as she would the latest sales at the mall?

As for Wes, he smiled at Piper, obviously considering the possible ways to murder her. Piper rubbed her hands up and down her arms, trying to ward off the chill of his dead eyes. The way he got off watching things explode was seriously twisted, but then his girlfriend wasn't exactly normal either.

While the two of them pondered her fate, Piper did her best to ignore them, concentrating instead on something positive, something good. She'd found her sister, which was definitely good, although she dearly wished she'd told her sooner. From the first, Ranulf had treated her as a little sister, all gruff and protective. She'd never thanked him for that. Sandor and the others had made room in their lives for her without hesitation.

God, but if this was to be her last day on earth, she'd give anything to go back in time and tell Grey that she loved him.

She couldn't just stand there waiting for these

sickos to decide how she was going to die. If she had to go, it would be on her terms, not theirs.

In the space of a heartbeat, she lunged for the bedside lamp and heaved it at Adele. With aim so perfect it was almost uncanny, it hit the woman right on the temple, driving her straight to the floor. All her years of playing softball finally paid off.

"Adele!"

With Wes's attention temporarily diverted, Piper sprinted out of the room, her whole being focused on escaping. She made it across the living room, and her hand was reaching for the door when, for the second time in two days, she slammed into an invisible wall. Adele's doing no doubt. Then Wes grabbed a fistful of Piper's hair and yanked backward, throwing her to the floor.

Piper came up fighting, swinging her fists and kicking Wes in the shins. When he caught her right hand in a painful grip, she went after his eyes with her left. Then the press of cold metal against the back of her head brought it all to a complete stop.

The click of a gun being cocked echoed in the sudden silence. Piper froze.

"It's the blue house at the far end of the block." Harcourt pulled out his cell phone. "Drop me at the corner. If I can catch a cab back to the airport, I may still make my flight."

Oh, this was going to be good. Sandor looked at Harcourt as if he'd grown a second head before meeting Grey's eyes in the rearview mirror. "Do you want to tell him?"

"Tell me what?" Harcourt was already reaching for the door handle as Sandor slowed for a stop sign.

"Our plan, Lawrence. You see, it involves you."

Grey smiled and pressed the barrel of his gun against their prisoner's head. Harcourt immediately slumped in his seat. Good. Now that he had the man's attention, Grey slid across to the other side of the car and watched Harcourt's expression.

"You see, Lawrence, Sandor and I figure Adele won't be inclined to invite two Talions in for tea and biscuits. But how could she possibly turn her own father away? Especially since he's had a change of heart and wants to help her."

Harcourt's face turned ashen as he sputtered, "But Adele is just as likely to kill me. And I've already told her that I wouldn't help her, that she was on her own in this."

"That's a real shame, because you really have no choice in the matter. You see, Adele only *might* kill you, but I *definitely* will unless you do exactly as I bloody well tell you. Your choice."

Harcourt looked toward Sandor. If he hoped to find sympathy there, he was sadly mistaken.

Grey prodded him again with the barrel of his gun. "So what's it going to be? Are you going to settle for the sure thing and stay in the car or go for the long shot and knock on your daughter's door?"

"I'll knock on the door, but this is little better than cold-blooded murder."

Grey had had enough. "Look at this way—if Adele isn't the forgiving type, it will save you standing trial before the Dame and her Consort."

Sweat was pouring from Harcourt, despite the day's cool temperature.

Sandor added, "You know Adele and her boyfriend are both crazy for thinking that this has any chance of ending well for them. They might prefer to go out in a blaze of glory together, but somehow I doubt it. Adele is obviously pretty damn driven to succeed, and it's not likely she'd do anything to interfere with that."

That was pretty much what Grey had been thinking and said so. "On the other hand, she *is* likely to sacrifice her lover in a heartbeat. If he's smart enough to realize that, he might have his own opinion of how this should play out."

If anything, Harcourt looked worse. He twisted around in his seat to face Grey, and for the first time he sounded like a distraught parent. "You know Adele. How did I miss seeing this side of her?"

Grey had a momentary flash of sympathy for the man. He was about to pay a pretty steep price for his elitist attitude and his greed. "She either hid it well or you've had your head stuck in the sand."

Harcourt shrank into himself, clearly beaten down. Even if he survived the Dame's justice, which was unlikely, his life would never be the same. Status was everything for the aristocrat, and his peers would cut him adrift as soon as the truth came out. And Grey would make damn sure it did to send a warning loud and clear to anyone else who thought to threaten the new Dame.

Grey's cell rang, interrupting his train of thought. He checked the number as he flipped the phone open.

"Yeah, Sean, what's up?"

"A woman named Adele wants you to call her. She said she has something you want."

"The fuck she does! Unless she's decided to surrender and face justice." He fought to keep his temper under control. "Sorry, kid. Give me the number."

Before calling her, Grey said, "Sandor, drive past the house and circle the block. Evidently Adele wants to *talk*."

Harcourt straightened up in his seat. "What about? Do you think she's come to her senses?"

Grey didn't hesitate to rain on the man's parade. "Hell no. She says she has something I want."

Sandor pulled into the parking lot of a small neighborhood park. "Any idea what that could be?"

"None. Right now all I want from her is her surrender." And death, but he kept that last bit to himself. "There's not much chance of that happening, though."

Sandor nodded, his dark eyes filled with bursts of hot energy.

Grey braced himself and punched in the number Adele had given Sean. She answered on the second ring.

"Greyhill Danby, how *are* you doing?"

He stared at his phone for a second before replying.

She was smug and sure of herself, definitely riding a high. No way he was going to feed her ego.

"Cut to the chase, Adele. What do you want?"

She actually giggled. "Why, Grey, you sound upset. Did you lose something important?"

Yes, he had, but this wasn't a discussion he wanted to have with Piper's killer. "Get to the point, little girl. I've got a job to do, and you're wasting my time."

That did it. When she spoke again, all traces of good humor were gone.

"Don't call me a little girl, Grey. We both know I'm the rightful heir to Judith's throne. If you'd done your job and rid us of that usurper, none of this would have been necessary."

"Tell me something, Adele. I get that the letter bomb was just intended to get our attention. No hard feelings for putting me in the hospital. Bygones, and all that."

He infused his next question with a whole lot of temper. "How was blowing up the Packard with someone sitting in it supposed to help your cause? Someone who'd never lifted a finger to hurt you?"

"Oh, is that what's got you all in a dither? Well, that god-awful Packard simply had to go. It was in the way of where I plan to park my Jaguar when I take over. Something in a nice silver, you know, like yours. After all, you won't be needing it."

Then she laughed. "But you don't want to hear about that, do you? Seriously, Grey, there must have been some kind of misunderstanding. I didn't kill your little friend. I kidnapped her."

Grey's world stopped turning, his mind and body completely devoid of sensation. Finally, he managed to whisper, "Piper's alive?"

Sandor whipped around in his seat, his shocked expression reflecting Grey's.

"Well, of course she's alive! I wouldn't waste a valuable asset for no reason."

Grey's profound relief made his hands shake to the point where he almost dropped the phone. Ignoring the roaring in his head, he concentrated on regaining control and reestablishing contact with the world around him. As if sensing his need, Sandor held out his hand, offering Grey a hit off his energy supply. It helped some. Finally, he remembered how to talk.

"Adele, don't fuck with me. If she's alive, I want to talk to her."

"*Tsk, tsk*, Grey. Your lack of breeding is showing again. Hang on a second."

Adele whispered something on her end not meant for his ears, but she didn't allow for a Talion's enhanced hearing. She was telling her friend Wes to take the gag out of Piper's mouth. He heard a rustling and then the sweetest sound he'd ever known—Piper's voice as she argued with her captors.

"Why should I do anything you two want?"

Bless the woman, his Piper was alive and feisty. He was damn happy about the first part, but the second might just get her killed for real.

Something sounded like a slap and Piper yelped. Adele's next words confirmed his worst fear. "Because, bitch, if you don't do exactly what I say, you won't live long enough to regret it. Now talk to your loverboy before I kill you both."

"Grey?"

"Piper, honey, are you all right?" She had to be. The gods couldn't be so cruel as to give her back to him only to snatch her away again.

"I've been better." Her voice caught when she continued. "I'm so sorry they let you think I was still in the car when it blew up. They made me watch."

She yelped again. "Quit pulling my hair, you jerk! You wanted me to talk to him. What did you expect me to say?"

Energy, dark and lethal, writhed under Grey's skin. They were hurting his woman, and there was nothing he could do to stop it. Not yet. But, by god, there would be a reckoning—and soon.

"Piper, can you hear me? Do exactly what they say. Don't fight them, not alone. I need you to promise me that. Please." Because if she didn't, she might not survive long enough for him to get her away from those two monsters.

"I will."

"Good."

"And please don't let these two use me as a weapon against Kerry."

"I promise to keep the Dame safe."

"Thank you. There's one more thing. I love you." She choked on a sob. "I wish I'd told you before, and I was so scared I'd never get the chance."

"God, honey, I know. I love you, too." He savored the sweet truth of her admission. Even so, the knowledge scared him down to the core because it was another weapon Adele would use to manipulate him. "Piper, please be careful until I can get there."

"Now wasn't that just so sweet." Adele had taken the phone back. "Here's how this is going to play out, Grey."

"Before you say another word, Adele, know this. You hurt her or anyone else, and you're dead. If I don't get the job done, Sandor or Ranulf will. You won't ever be able to stop running. You're already breathing on borrowed time. Make it easier on everybody and turn yourself in."

Her laugh had a note of hysteria.

"So I take that as a no, then." He leaned back in his seat, proud of his new sense of calm. "Okay, little girl, we'll play this your way. Don't keep me in suspense. What's your evil plan?"

And while she told him, he plotted her death.

Chapter 18

Grey slammed his hand down on the coffee table. "This is absolutely insane. You're not about to abdicate, and Adele knows it. You know it. So there's no reason to put yourself in danger."

Ranulf said, "He's right, Kerry. The whole idea is effing crazy."

She glared right back at her husband and then at Grey. "Yes, I do know that. If anyone has a viable option that doesn't result in my sister getting killed, speak up now. I just found her. I won't risk losing her, not like this."

The silence was answer enough.

Grey tried again. "Kerry, no one wants to get Piper back more than I do, but my first duty is to keep you safe. Ranulf's duty is the same."

He pointed around the room at the group of warriors who surrounded her. "We Talions all swore an oath to protect the Grand Dame of the Kyth, even if it means protecting her from her own folly. Piper will never forgive any of us if we put you in danger to save her."

Adele had insisted that they convene at the Dame's house, saying the place was her rightful home. He pointed out how unwise that would be considering she'd drawn the attention of god knows how many law enforcement agencies by blowing up the Packard in the driveway.

Finally, she'd reluctantly given in, agreeing to meet sometime after sunset to discuss Kerry's abdication. She'd call back with the location later. Grey hung up satisfied with the confrontation. As long as the woman thought she was running the show, she had no reason to hurt Piper. What she didn't realize was that he knew exactly where she and Wes were holed up.

The situation was far from perfect, and the element of surprise was the only factor that played in their favor. Wes's house sat on a fairly big corner lot, but that translated to too many potential witnesses. It didn't help that Kerry wanted a shot at talking Adele down off the ledge before unleashing the Talions. No one thought that negotiating would work, but their Dame insisted on trying. He wished he knew if it was weakness or compassion that was driving her decision.

Kerry reached out and took Grey's hand, sending a high-powered jolt of energy up his arm. "I'm going with you, Grey. I know you hate it, but deal with it."

He gauged her resolve. The woman's warrior spirit glowed brightly in her eyes. "Yes, Dame Kerry."

After releasing him, she crossed the room to her husband. "And you hate it most of all, but I won't be the kind of leader who huddles in the basement while my people are in jeopardy. It would be different if I had no powers of my own, but I've already proven myself in battle, if it comes to that."

Turning back to Grey, she continued. "Make your best plans, but make sure I'm part of them. Now, if you'll excuse us, I have a feeling my husband has a few things he'd like to say to me in private."

As the two walked out of the hotel room, Grey smiled. On the whole, he thought the Viking had shown great forbearance by waiting until they were in the other room to start railing at his wife. Grey and the rest of the Talions did their best to hide their smiles as the deep, angry rumble of Ranulf's voice increased in volume as the seconds ticked by. They all knew he was going to lose the argument—including him—but no one blamed the man for trying.

"Sandor, tell me you've learned more about the layout of Adele's house than the few scraps Harcourt could tell us," Grey said, getting focused.

The Talion nodded and held out a stack of papers. "Original floor plans."

Grey nodded his approval. "Nice job. Everybody take one and memorize it. The countdown has started, so we don't have any time to waste."

Piper refused to let her captors see how scared she really was. Instead, she concentrated on being mad at herself for letting them manipulate her into becoming a weapon against the one person she needed to protect. No, make that two people. She cared about Sandor and the others, too, but right now she knew that Kerry and Grey were going through an even deeper hell.

Of course, if she'd stayed tucked safely behind Ranulf's wards, maybe Adele and her sicko friend would have blown up the Packard with Grey in it. Any number of scenarios could have played out. Hindsight was getting her nowhere.

Right now, she had a few demands of her own. "Hey, you two, I'm getting pretty hungry in here."

Adele had ignored Piper since she'd hung up with Grey. Right now, she and Wes were across the room whispering. From what Piper could gather, they were busy stripping the Harcourt family holdings of all liquid assets. They'd spent half an hour arguing over which offshore bank offered the best protection.

They sat there, quibbling over interest rates, as if they didn't have a care in the world. Did they really think they stood a chance against Grey and his men? Wes might have a talent for explosives, but she suspected Talions knew more ways to kill an enemy than Wes could even imagine, and they wouldn't play by the rules Adele had laid out.

She tried again. "Hey, I said, *I'm hungry!* I doubt I'm the only one. Besides, I think there's a rule somewhere about the condemned getting a last meal."

Wes looked up from the mess of wires he'd been

working on. "What do you say, Adele? Want to order something in or do a drive-thru thing?"

Piper rolled her eyes. What a wimp! What kind of villain had to ask permission to buy a hamburger and fries? His partner in crime didn't even look up from her notepad to answer. "I don't care if she's hungry."

The muscles in Wes's jaw tightened up. "What if I'm hungry?"

Adele evidently realized that his question was laced with subtext. She reached over and brushed her fingertips across his cheek. "Of course that's different, Wes. You know that." She gave him a sweet smile. "Fast food sounds good. I'd love a burger and a chocolate shake."

"Good. I'll be back in plenty of time to finish wiring all this." He closed his tool kit and stood up. "See you in a few."

Once Wes was gone, Piper might as well have been dead for all the attention Adele paid to her. She passed the time wondering if she could sow some seeds of dissent among the troops. When she heard Wes pull up in the driveway, she broke the silence, hoping Adele wouldn't hear him come in.

"So, tell me, Adele. Have you written your will? Your heirs will appreciate your leaving everything in good order for them."

Nothing.

"And I was wondering, did it hurt your feelings when your father left you to face the music alone? Well, not *alone*. After all, you've got good old Wes to stand with you. But I've got to tell you, he doesn't strike me as the kind of guy a Grand Dame would pick for a Consort."

Adele finally looked up. "Wes has his uses."

"I can only imagine." She was definitely on to something here.

Adele shot her a suspicious look. "What's that supposed to mean?"

"Well, we both know that image is everything. Wes is perfect if you're looking for a mad bomber, but then he doesn't exactly scream leadership material, does he?"

"And you think Ranulf Thorsen is any better?" Adele sneered. "The man should still be wearing animal skins and a horned helmet."

Piper shook her head. "I hate to nitpick, but Ranulf's tribe didn't wear horned helmets. Still, I get what you're saying. He's a warrior, not a politician, hence his jeans-and-flannel look. However, no one questions his ability to fight, and Kerry knows he'll do whatever it takes to keep her safe. That's important to a Dame.

"Besides, it's Sandor who acts as her ambassador, and you've got to admit that he looks hot in a suit and tie. Personally, I think Grey Danby has him beat hands down, although I might be a little biased."

She offered Adele a sympathetic smile. "But then, Wes is just an ordinary human male, isn't he? I suppose comparing him to the prime quality of Talion warriors isn't really fair. You can't expect him to measure up to the special Talion abilities the past two

Consorts have had. Somehow I just can't picture Wes standing there at your side as you rule."

Maybe she'd pushed a little too far because Adele began toying with the barrel of her gun. "Bloodlines are everything in our world. I can trace my family back for generations, but mutts like you and Kerry wouldn't know anything about that. When I rule, I will restore the purity of the Kyth gene pool. The taint of human blood has already diluted our strength too much. Wes will understand. If not—" She just shrugged.

Enhanced Talion hearing wasn't necessary when the man in question stood right there in the doorway. Just as Piper had hoped, he'd overheard their conversation. The only question was what he was going to do about it.

Unaware they had an audience, Adele went back to making notes. "Wes does have his uses, though. He has a real talent for explosives, which you've already seen firsthand."

The man stalked into the room and tossed a sack full of burgers and fries on the table. "I'm good for a helluva lot more than just explosives, Adele, and you know it. It doesn't take brains to swing a sword, just gorilla-like strength. And I'd like to see one of your precious Talions best me in a cyber war."

He was wrong about that, too. Piper would put her money on Grey and Sandor anytime, but she kept her opinion to herself. Far better that they underestimated the men who would be coming after them.

Piper shivered. It was one thing to know that Grey

was capable of violence, and quite another to witness it. Still, these two had drawn a line in the sand and dared the Dame and her warriors to cross it.

And lucky her—she'd been caught in the crossfire.

"Here." Wes tossed a cheeseburger in Piper's lap and set a shake on the small table beside her chair. At least they'd tied her hands in front this time, making it possible for her to feed herself.

"Eat up, you half-breed bitch. We wouldn't want you to die on an empty stomach."

Piper ignored Adele's taunt. Fine. She might not make it through the day, but she was damn sure she wouldn't be the only one who'd breathed her last before the dust settled. Closing her eyes, she choked down her meal.

In her heart, she knew Grey was coming for her, his blue eyes ablaze with battle fever. And there would be hell to pay. How could Adele have known Grey this long without realizing that the man would crawl through broken glass to protect what was his? Well, she'd learn soon enough.

Drawing comfort from that thought, the pain in Piper's chest eased.

"Okay, everybody clear on their jobs?"

Each of the men surrounding Grey nodded as they checked their weapons one last time. They'd taken several cars to the Adele's stronghold, slipping through the gathering shadows to meet up a short distance away from the house.

Sean, trying hard to look like he belonged, checked the slide of his knife in its sheath. He was too damn young to be there, but Grey knew they'd have a fight on their hands if they tried to leave him behind. With Sandor's approval, he'd assigned the kid the job of driving one of the cars, hoping that would keep him out of the line of fire. He was under orders to keep the engine running in case they needed a fast escape for any wounded, or to get the two women to safety.

Grey stuck another loaded clip in his pocket just in case. The last thing they needed was for this to turn into a shootout on the streets of Seattle, but it was his job to be prepared. Finally, he checked the charge on his cell phone in case Adele called.

All set. "Let's roll."

His men fanned out, preparing to approach the house from all directions and ready to keep innocent bystanders out of the way. They'd planned for every scenario they could think of, but he couldn't shake the sense of impending disaster. There was no way this was going to go down clean and tidy. Adele would never play by the rules or stick to the plan she'd outlined over the phone. No, he couldn't see her leaving the relative safety of her current location to meet him out in the open.

Despite her considerable ego, Adele had to know that she was up against warriors schooled in both combat and tactics. In some cases, that meant decades of training or even centuries, as in Ranulf's case. Most Talions had also served in the military, naturally gravitating toward the highly specialized forces that taught urban combat techniques.

"What's wrong, Grey?"

Kerry moved up beside him, her dark eyes narrowed in concern. "You're not happy."

Well, no shit! Her sister—his lover—was already in the hands of two certifiable crazies, and now leader of his people insisted on putting herself in danger. What was there to be happy about?

He kept that particular summation to himself. "I think—no, I know—we're playing right into Adele's hands. She's expecting us."

"She said she'd call with the meeting spot after sundown, but you don't believe her. Why?"

"Because she's not stupid. She had to figure we wouldn't wait around until she crooks her finger to come running. By now, she's confirmed that her father didn't make his flight back to London, which means we have him in custody. Adele knows the first thing Harcourt would do is sell her out to save his own worthless hide."

Ranulf entered the discussion. "So she's spun her web and is waiting for us to show up to spring the trap."

Grey nodded. "All things considered, it feels right."

"Okay, so how does that change anything? We can't sit here and wait for her to come to us."

"No, we can't. The longer we wait, the more likely it is they'll decide to make an example of Piper."

And if that happened, hell would rain down, secrecy be damned. Grey would raze the whole fucking house if that's what it took.

"Sandor will take out the power grid for the entire neighborhood in the next few minutes. Adele's bound to think we're up to something, but having the whole area go dark may buy us a few precious seconds."

He pegged his leader with a hard look. "You *will* hang back. You're our last resort, got that?"

"Yes, Grey, I've got it. Now go save my sister."

"I will. This I vow." He gave his ruler a solemn nod. Then, unleashing the full power of his Talion senses, he walked away and faded into the growing darkness.

When the lights all around him blinked out, he smiled. *Let the hunt begin. May the gods above help them all.*

The lights flickered once, twice, then stayed on a few seconds, and then everything went dark. Piper flinched at the sudden change, but then drew immediate comfort from the blanket of darkness that surrounded her. She blinked, giving her eyes a chance to adjust.

She was looking directly at the front window when a quick movement caught her attention. It was too dark to see any details, but she could have sworn she spotted two small circles of blue light aimed straight at her. Her heart did a slow roll. It had to be Grey. He was the only one she knew with eyes that burned that exact shade when his emotions ran hot. As quickly as they appeared, the twin lights blinked out, making her wonder if her imagination was just working overtime.

Wes's laptop cast a soft circle of light at the table, but the glow didn't extend much past the center of the room. Neither Adele nor Wes seemed upset about the power outage, which meant they were expecting it.

Wes scooped up his computer and closed it, blanketing them in darkness. Piper thought she saw him palm his gun before dropping down out of sight of the windows. Adele followed suit.

When the lights didn't immediately come back on, Adele rose up to peek out the window. "And so it begins."

Fed up with the woman's theatrics, Piper sighed loudly. "Tell me, Adele, could you *be* more melodramatic? A car probably hit a transformer, and you make it sound like a bad horror flick."

"Do shut up, Piper, or I'll make you. Your buddies are out there staging a rescue. How very heroic."

"It is." Okay, so she wasn't supposed to say anything else, but someone had to speak up for them.

"I'm very disappointed in Kerry Thorsen. A Dame is supposed to keep her word, yet she sends her thugs after me rather than negotiating with me directly."

Personally, Piper would kick Kerry's butt up and down the street if she was stupid enough to come within ten miles of Adele.

When Adele's cell phone rang, she answered it and then hit speaker phone. "Kerry, I was just going to call you."

"I'm sure you were. But as Dame, I have a rather busy schedule. I can't always wait around until it's convenient for my subjects. Are you ready to meet or not?"

Piper didn't need to see Adele to know the woman was vibrating with fury. "I am *not* one of *your* subjects. I refuse to acknowledge a low-bred stray as the Grand Dame of *my* people."

When Kerry spoke again, she sounded every inch the ruler of the Kyth. "Regardless of how you might personally feel about it, Adele Harcourt, I *am* your Dame, and you are still subject to my rule and my justice. This night will not end well for you unless Piper is released unharmed. I order you to lay that gun down now, and walk out the front door with your hands up. That goes for your companion as well."

Adele sounded unnaturally calm when she responded. "I don't know where you got the idea that you were in the position to do any bargaining. Will you really force the Talions to die for you? Because that's what's going to happen if you insist on sending them after me. Think about that. How will you sleep at night when Grey, Sandor, and your precious Ranulf all die defending a piece of trash like you? Because, make no mistake—they will."

There was an ominous silence on Kerry's end of the conversation. The next person who spoke was definitely male and it was a voice Piper recognized immediately.

"Adele Harcourt, this is Sandor Kearn speaking on behalf of Greyhill Danby, Chief Talion to Grand

Dame Kerry Thorsen. Remember this when you face justice: you were given ample opportunity to halt your treason against our people. It is now too late to recant and request mercy. You stand charged with attempted murder by sending a bomb to the Dame's Home.

"Furthermore, you are charged with assault on the Dame's home and property for destroying a highly valued automobile belonging the Dame's Consort. You stand charged with the kidnapping and unlawful imprisonment of Piper Ryan, with intent to do harm. And finally, you have been charged with the crime of high treason against the Kyth nation. Stand ready to surrender and face judgment. We await your decision. Failure to comply will result in grave consequences."

As the list of charges was being read, they heard cars pulling and then speeding off, followed by footsteps pounding on the sidewalk. Both Adele and Wes ran across the room to look out the front window.

Piper felt a slight stirring in the air coming from behind her. She looked at the door to the kitchen just as a section of shadow broke away, forming a dark figure that loomed over her.

Before she could scream, a hand clamped over her mouth, and Grey whispered in her ear, "Hush."

She recognized his voice, but there was something wrong with his face. When he cut the ties on her hands and then her feet, she realized he was wearing night vision goggles.

"Go. Get out."

She didn't want to leave him behind, but he left

her no choice. If she stayed, if she protested, she would put them both in greater danger. Grey positioned himself between her and Adele and Wes. For the moment their attention was directed toward Sandor's disembodied voice.

Only a few more steps and they'd be in the clear. She reached out to touch to the doorframe, feeling her way along. Her heart pounded in her ears, her breath so loud she was sure the neighbors could hear it. The comforting presence of Grey right behind her was all that kept her from panicking.

She glanced back at him only to be blinded by a flash of light. Grey immediately whipped off his goggles, pointing his gun at Wes and Adele. Wes was aiming a battery operated lantern at Grey with one hand, but it was the gun in the other that destroyed any hope Piper had left. She reached for Grey's hand and held on for dear life.

"Bloody damn hell" Grey cursed, as Wes's finger hovered over the trigger of his gun. Grey stared at the twin model Adele held. Not for a single second did Grey think they were bluffing.

Grey gave Piper's hand a quick squeeze before letting go. He had to get her out of the line of fire. He stepped in front of her, hoping to buy her a few seconds.

"Run, Piper. I'll deal with this."

Her eyes pleaded with him. "Grey!"

He risked a quick look back at her, drinking in

the bright glow of her fierce love for him. "Damn it, Piper, get going!"

Wes joined the conversation. "Gee, Grey, let her join our party if she wants to."

Grey ignored him. "Now, Piper." Before it was too late.

There was only a small chance that he'd be able to put a lid on the conflagration that Adele and her lackey were likely to start. If he couldn't pull it off, he didn't want to lose Piper. Not again. Not for real.

Adele evidently had other plans. "We said to let her join the party."

Suddenly she flung a bright burst of energy across the room, trapping Grey and Piper in an invisible web. *Son of a bitch!* At the last second Grey lunged toward her, taking most of the hit himself. He strained against her hold with no success.

"Surprised, Grey? You shouldn't be. The ability to control others is part of the whole Dame package. But either way, your little friend there isn't going anywhere. Not until Kerry takes her place."

He sensed Piper fighting against the wards. It might be wishful thinking on his part, but he was pretty sure she'd just snapped one tentacle of Adele's web. Good. Adele wasn't the only one with hidden talents. Maybe Piper could actually make it to the door if he kept Adele occupied.

"Kerry won't be coming, Adele. We both know that."

Another broke. This time he was sure of it.

"She gave me her word. I knew she wasn't up to

the job of Grand Dame. It's nice to be proven right, isn't it, Wes? The taint of human DNA she carries weakens her. That's why the purity of the race will be my first priority. There will be no more diluting our heritage with genes from an inferior species. I will seek my Consort from among the strongest of our race."

She gave Grey an assessing look. "Too bad that you've eliminated yourself from the competition, Grey."

From Wes's expression, he didn't appreciate being considered her inferior. Grey could work with that. "So, Wes, I guess we're both out of the running."

"Shut up!" Adele snapped.

He offered the fool a commiserating smile. "I'm betting you were the one behind the pyrotechnics and all that fancy hacking?"

Wes nodded and set the lantern down on the table. "Yes, it was *all* me."

Adele's eyes narrowed. Clearly she didn't like sharing the spotlight. When her focus was split between Grey and Wes, the bonds were further weakened. She might have the gift, but it was nowhere near as honed as Kerry's. He used some of his own energy to deplete it further.

Grey broke his feet free and sidled over to stand more solidly between Piper and Adele. He was hoping that Piper would be able to tear herself free in the next few seconds. Time to fan the flames a bit more.

"Well, I've got to tell you, Wes, it took Sandor Kearn and me hours of damn hard work to figure out how to back trace your e-mails. We're not without our own talents in that area, so that's quite a gift you've got. Kudos."

He stopped to look from Wes to Adele and back. "With all the work you've put into this operation, I'm guessing you were hoping to end up Adele's Consort."

He was right on the money. Grey recognized the same powerful emotions that he himself had for the woman standing beside him swirling behind Wes's eyes.

"But it sounds like the best you can hope for is Chief Lackey. Must be hard to sacrifice everything for such an ungrateful bitch."

"Adele? What's he talking about?" But Wes knew. It was there in his desperate expression.

The soft squeak of the hinges on the kitchen door set Grey free to finish this once and for all. He sensed Sandor adding his own pull to break the last of Piper's bonds. They needed only a few seconds more to clear the danger zone. He'd buy that time for Piper even at the cost of his own life.

"Go ahead, Adele. Tell him. Or better yet, let me."

Rather than respond to Wes's questions, Adele went on the attack, throwing another bolt directly at Grey. Suddenly, her jaw dropped in surprise. Piper had slipped free of her bindings.

"Where did she go? How did she break free?" The woman was actually shocked that someone would disobey her.

"Guess what? Piper is Kerry's sister and shares some of her abilities, but you weren't clever enough to figure that out." He countered her blast with one of his own as he taunted her. Not expecting the backlash of energy, Adele stumbled sideways.

Wes caught her arm and jerked her upright. She tried escape his grasp. "Get your hands off of me, Wes. I have to go after her!"

Wes hang on with surprising tenacity. "You're not going anywhere until you answer me. Is he telling the truth? Were you only using me?"

Adele sneered at him. "Did you really think I would marry someone like you? Could you possibly be that stupid? Me, marry a loser whose entire ambition consists of playing with computers and fireworks?"

"I just wanted to hear it from you." Wes looked almost at peace as he held up the detonator for Adele to see.

Adele's eyes flared wide in panic. "Wes, no! We can work this out! Please!"

"Show me, Adele," he demanded and pulled her up against his chest.

"I'd do anything for you, Wes." Adele kissed him with a considerable amount of heat. "Tell me what you want and I'll do it."

Wes smiled down at her tenderly and whispered, "I want you to die for me."

Then he pushed the button.

Piper's image filled Grey's mind and his heart as he dove through the kitchen door, throwing every ounce of his Talion energy into controlling the wave of destruction that rolled through the room. It was a lethal explosion that shattered everything in sight, including Grey.

• • •

With no warning, a wave of molten energy picked Piper up and slammed her to the ground. She and Sandor bounced across the yard, finally coming to rest at the back edge of the property. There, they held on to each other and waited for the world to come back into focus. They watched in horror at the clouds of smoke that poured out of the house.

"Grey!"

She lurched to her feet, determined to find him, to save him, just as he had come for her.

"No, Piper! It's too dangerous."

"Let go! I won't let him die in there."

"At least wait until help arrives. The last thing he'd want is for you to get hurt because of him." Sandor was already punching keys on his cell phone.

She waited until he was busy barking out orders to take off running for the back steps of the house. It might be more sensible to wait, but Grey was in there.

At the top of the steps, she yanked open the door. The room inside smoldered with thick smoke that left her choking. She dropped to her knees where the air was clearer and started forward, hoping that she would find Grey before she passed out from lack of oxygen. On the other side of the kitchen, the refrigerator had fallen over at an odd angle, blocking the way into the living room. She was about to climb over it when she realized she felt a body.

"Grey?"

He moaned softly as she pulled him away from

the fridge. Moving Grey was probably not the right thing to do, but if she didn't get them both out into the fresh air, they'd die from the smoke. She dragged him across the floor in fits and starts, coughing to clear her lungs and then straining to gain another few inches.

"Here, let me help."

Sandor shoved past her and picked up Grey by his shoulders as she grabbed his ankles. They maneuvered him through the door and into the yard, both choking on the smoke they'd inhaled. Grey was unnaturally quiet.

Sandor placed his hand on Grey's chest. "I can't tell if his heart's beating."

She knocked the Talion's hand out of the way to check for herself, burrowing her hand under Grey's torn shirt. As soon as she settled it over the warm brand on his chest, she was rewarded with a slight flutter of movement.

"It is, but barely. Where's Kerry? He needs her."

"On her way. Before Grey went in for you, he ordered everyone to pull back if the two of you weren't out in five minutes. He figured something like this would happen."

Piper gathered Grey closer, keeping her hand centered over his heart.

"Grey, come back to me. Please."

She felt a soft vibration where her hand connected to the symbol of his power. As she focused her full attention on that small sensation, it rapidly increased in intensity.

Grey's eyes fluttered open long enough to recognize her. "Piper?"

That small whisper was all it took to open the floodgates. She poured everything she had into their connection, using her own life force to restore his. Nothing mattered except dragging Grey back from the darkness.

Suddenly, Piper was no longer kneeling in the damp chill of the grass. Instead, she floated in a heavenly glow of warm light. Maybe it *was* heaven because Grey was there with her, unharmed. She took his hand.

Grey looked sorry as he tried to tug free of her grasp. "Let me go, Piper. It's not your time."

"Not without you, Grey. I love you too much to go back alone. I need you to live for me."

He cupped the side of her face. "And I love you too much to let you die for me. When I thought you were dead—"

She kissed him, letting him feel her desperation. "Then we're at an impasse, big guy, because whether we stay or we go, we do it together."

"You're one stubborn woman." He smiled and shook his head. "But that's just one thing I love about you."

Then he pulled back, this time successfully breaking their connection. Her eyes burned with grief as Grey started to fade away.

"Please, don't—" Before she could finish, she screamed as she was ripped away from the warmth and tossed back into cold reality. When she opened her eyes, she was wrapped in a pair of flannel-clad arms right next to Kerry and Sandor as they knelt over Grey's body.

Kerry looked up long enough to bark some orders. "Get the next donor over here. Ranulf, keep her hand on his. Her touch seems to be helping."

Piper blinked up at the Viking warrior, glad for his warmth. "What's she doing?"

"Finishing what you started." Ranulf stared down at her. "Somehow you stabilized Grey long enough for Kerry to get here, but you almost killed yourself in the process. She nearly sucked me dry to give you back some of what you gave him. Now she's using Sandor's energy to heal Grey. The rest of the Talions are all waiting to donate energy too."

Ranulf looked at Grey in awe. "He saved more than just you. We have no idea how he did it, but somehow he contained the explosion Adele and her boyfriend set off. The neighbors may have heard the rumble, but the damage stayed inside the house."

She wanted to ask Kerry if Grey was going to make it but didn't want to interfere with her sister's fierce concentration. Two more Talions came and went, staggering away in exhaustion before Kerry finally sighed and moved back.

"Kerry? Is he—?" She couldn't even finish the question as fear warred with hope inside her.

The Dame finally turned her dark eyes to Piper. "Give him another minute or two to absorb that last batch of energy and then you can fuss over him all you want. Sean is bringing the car around for both of you. I'm guessing Grey will be back on his feet in a couple of days."

Piper looked up into the night sky and smiled.

"Piper?" Grey twisted his head around until he spotted her. She looked like hell—but so beautiful to him.

"I'm right here." She leaned in close, her gentle fingers soothing him with their touch. "Don't try to talk yet. Your body is still absorbing the energy it needs."

He struggled to say one more thing, something she needed to know. "Together. Us. Always."

Her smile lit up the night. "That's right, Grey. Together. Always."

Satisfied he'd gotten his message across, he settled back and watched as the two sisters fell into each other's arms and cried.

Epilogue

*G*rey eased down on the swing in the Dame's rose garden and pushed off with his right foot. It had been a long two days since he'd died, and he was still coming to terms with it. If he closed his eyes and concentrated, he could almost feel the comforting warmth that had greeted him on the other side. Not that he had regrets about coming back. This world held the one person who loved him enough to offer up her life for his.

But now came the hard part. He'd spent the past forty-eight hours rebuilding his strength and weighing his options. He stood poised at the crossroads of a difficult decision, one he couldn't make alone. For the first time in his life, his future was entwined with someone else's. He wouldn't make a move of this magnitude without consulting her first.

And that someone had just stepped through the door. Piper smiled and headed his way.

"Ranulf said you were out here. How are you feeling?"

He stood up. "Better now that you're here. Would you mind if we walk a bit? I'm stiff from sitting so much."

"Sure, as long as you don't tire yourself out."

He wrapped his arm around her shoulder, breathing in her scent. He waited until they'd reached the far end of the rose garden before speaking.

Turning to face Piper, he gently brushed a lock of her hair back from her face. "I'd like to talk about where we go from here. I've been giving it a lot of thought."

He felt a shiver of apprehension ripple through her and he hated it. After everything that had happened, her fear would take a long time to fade.

Her dark eyes were worried. "What's the matter, Grey? Having second thoughts already?" she asked.

"About us? No, never. I can't imagine my future without you."

Judging by the sudden tension in her body, his words, the ones meant to reassure her, had failed miserably. "Okay, then what are you having second thoughts about if it isn't us?"

"My job." He put several steps between them, needing space in order to say what had to be said. "I wanted to tell you first, but I'll be offering my resignation to Kerry, effective immediately."

He held his breath, waiting for her response. It didn't take long.

"Okay, what's really going on?" She put her hands

on her hips and stared at him as if he'd just sprouted a second head. "My sister needs someone she can trust to be her Chief Talion, and don't try to deny that it's what you've trained for your whole life. Why are you doing this?"

Okay, time to roll the dice. "Because, Piper Ryan, I love you, and I'm asking you to marry me—to be my wife. What I won't do is ask you to spend the rest of your life living in fear."

There, he'd said it. All he could do was wait.

What an amazing, sweet fool. There he was, offering to give up everything that he'd ever lived for just to be with her. No wonder she was head over heels in love with the man. She reached up to cup his face in her hands.

"Greyhill Danby, yes, I will marry you, but only if you promise to keep your job. I fell in love with you as you are—a man born to serve and defend our people. Yes, it will take some getting used to being the wife of a Talion warrior, but I'm strong, and your love will only make me stronger."

Drinking in all the emotion shining there in his handsome face, she said, "So here's the way I see it. I love you and you love me. All that matters is that we cherish each other and make the most of every day we have. God willing, we'll grow old together. If not, no regrets ever, no matter what."

Grey's amazing blue eyes lit up with enough heat to melt her bones. His voice grew thick as he answered her. "Piper, your love *is* my life, and every day I live is yours to share."

Then he took her hand in his and held both of them over his brand. "Always together, luv. This I vow."

They sealed the oath with a kiss.

Turn the page
for a special look
at the next irresistible Paladins novel
from
Alexis Morgan

BOUND IN DARKNESS

Coming Soon from Pocket Star

"Are you hurt?"

He reached out to brush her hair back from her face, but jerked his hand back when she flinched. Fine. Her reluctance pissed him off royally, even if he understood why she felt that way.

The sooner he got her back topside the better. "Come."

"You're one of *them*, aren't you?" Sasha shrank away from him.

He ignored how much her reaction hurt. "Right now, what I *am* is your way out of here."

She backed away another step. "But where are we going? The elevators are back that way."

He snagged her arm before she could take off and glared down at her. "So is the fighting, Sasha. Too many from both worlds are already bleeding and dying, and I'd rather not kill any more of my people because of your foolish behavior. Now, follow me or not. It's your choice."

He let go of her, hating the fear in her eyes and hating himself even more for his part in putting it there. Then he walked away, stopping to retrieve his knife before moving on. Surely she'd show the good sense to stick with him. If not, he'd force the issue. But he really hoped she'd find it in her to trust him enough to get her to safety.

Sasha stared at the four bodies scattered nearby. So much blood. Too much blood, its bitter copper scent filling her head, overloading her senses. Her stomach churned and a foul acid burned the back of her throat. God, would this nightmare never end? She leaned against the wall for support and retched dry heaves.

Please, let it stop. She needed to follow Larem even if he was one of them. Kalith, Other, the name didn't matter. If she lost sight of him, her life might very well end right here in this hellish passageway. She tried to straighten up between heaves, but that only made the pain worse. After stumbling forward only a few steps, she had to stop and close her eyes to ward off the dizziness.

As she did, she felt someone beside her and panicked. "No, please no! Get away!"

"Sasha, calm down. It's me."

She sagged in relief at the sound of Larem's deep voice. Despite everything, he hadn't abandoned her.

"Hold still and don't fight me."

His accent was more pronounced, but his voice was far gentler than it had been before. His hand, cool and soothing, rested softly on her forehead, and his arm slid around her waist, supporting her weight.

He murmured something softly. The words were unclear, perhaps his native tongue, but their effect was immediate and miraculous. The nausea disappeared almost immediately, as did the cramping. When he removed his hand, she looked up at his pale gray eyes.

"Better?"

She nodded. "Much."

The chill came flooding back into his gaze as he stepped back and picked up his sword. "Let's get out of here."

What choice did she have? She glanced back toward the other end of the passage, careful to avoid looking at the bodies scattered along the way, and then followed Larem around the corner. He was moving fast enough that she had to almost run to catch up.

She had so many questions, now that her brain was starting to function again, but she suspected she wouldn't like the answers she got. Why had he let her think he was human? She'd known there were Kalith living among the Paladins, but no one had even hinted that they had the run of the place. What was Larem doing prowling around the lower levels?

But now wasn't the time—not when her life depended on his skill with a sword. Her eyes strayed to the bloody blade he'd wielded with such skill and terrible grace. Would she ever get over the horror of seeing four lives ended right in front of her? Or the knowledge that she'd come so close to being . . . No. Don't go there. She slammed the door on that thought.

Larem came to an abrupt halt. "Quiet, now. We don't want to draw attention to ourselves. Wait until I make sure the way is clear."

Sasha froze, her ears ringing with the ragged sound of her own breathing and the pounding of her heart. Gradually, other sounds began to make sense. Horrible sense. Swords banging and clanging. Screams of pain and, worse yet, weak whimpers of agony. Larem moved forward a few feet, holding his sword out to the side as if expecting to be attacked any second.

Finally, he motioned her forward. "Don't look."

But of course she did. The ground was littered with bodies. She watched as a line of Paladins slowly pushed forward, forcing the ragged band of Others to retreat back across the barrier. Men in guard uniforms were dragging the dead and wounded Paladins back out of the way, leaving the Others where they'd fallen.

Larem fell back beside her. "Sasha, snap out of it! We've got to get the hell out of here. Those guards might not hurt you, but they're likely to come after me, given half a chance. I'd just as soon not die because of your stupidity."

Larem all but dragged her along until finally he stopped outside of an elevator. As soon as she saw the number pad next to it, her heart sank.

"Larem, my code won't work. We're trapped down here until Devlin sounds the all clear." Her voice went up an octave as she spoke, the thought of spending one unnecessary minute trapped in this hell absolutely unbearable.

Larem was already punching numbers into the security system. "This one will work."

Sure enough, she felt the small blast of air from the doors announcing the elevator was on its way. She leaned against the wall, relieved beyond words. As fried as she was feeling, it still occurred to her to wonder why an Other would have been trusted with a high level security code.

The more she thought about it, the answer was obvious. It wasn't his code at all. Someone had broken protocols by giving it to him, most likely one of his friends among the Paladins. Under the circumstances, she wasn't about to complain.

She stepped to the back corner of the elevator. "Please thank whoever gave you his number to use. Tell him there will be no repercussions for the security breach."

Her good intentions seemed to only make Larem angrier. "That's awfully generous of you, considering he did so hoping to save your life."

"I didn't mean it like that. I understand why he gave his number to a . . ." She stopped. She would do better to just keep her mouth shut.

But it was too late. Larem immediately snarled, "A what, Sasha? An alien? An Other? An animal? How about a monster?"

Each arrow-sharp accusation hit its target—her conscience. "I'm sorry, Larem. I was trying to do the right thing."

He turned toward her, his eyes burning with fury. "The right thing would have been to stay the hell out of places you don't belong. Because of the threat to you, my friend delayed his arrival below in order to share that number and the location of this elevator with me. There are damn few enough of the Paladins as it is to hold back the invasion. How many were placed at extra risk because he was late to the fight, or because they were concerned for your safety and not focused on the battle they faced?"

Dear God, she hadn't thought about that. Stricken with remorse, she said, "I never thought . . ."

He stalked toward her, dropping his bloody sword to the floor as he cornered her. "Exactly. You never thought."

"None of this was supposed to happen. I'm so sorry."

"That doesn't change a damn thing. Because of you, I betrayed my vow to protect my own people. Those males died at my hand, and I have to find a way to live with that."

He was standing so close that she could feel the tension pouring off his body. This was no time to notice how long his eyelashes were or how they framed those intense gray eyes.

Her hand lifted to touch his cheek. "But you're not like them."

"No. I'm not. Because they were sick with the need for light. That's the only difference."

At her touch, he tangled his fingers in her hair, tilting her face up toward his. "One thing you would do well to remember, Sasha Willis. I might not be human—but I am a man."

His angry mouth crushed down on hers. When she gasped in shock, his tongue swept past her lips. She'd never tasted pure fury before, but she had no doubt that's what flavored Larem's kiss. She should push back, should fight to wrest control from him— but rather than feeling threatened, she felt safe. Larem's kiss wasn't a claiming but a cleansing, washing away some of the fear and horror of the past half hour. A small voice in the back of her mind told her this was crazy, that she should be revolted by the prospect of kissing a Kalith.

Larem ripped his mouth away from hers and lurched back to the other side of the elevator, breathing hard. His mouth, which had felt so soft and forgiving against hers, was now a straight slash of anger.

He scrubbed at his mouth with the back of his hand as if to wipe away any taste of her. The soft ping of the elevator finally reaching its destination echoed in the heavy silence between them.

As the two of them stalked out, she said, "This didn't happen."

He smirked down at her. "Do you really think Devlin Bane won't find out that you were down there? Or that you almost managed to get not just yourself, but me, killed?"

"Not that, you big jerk!" She waved her hand between the two of them. "I mean this—us. *This* didn't happen."

"Why? Afraid what will happen to all your plans if it gets out that you've been sullied by the likes of me?"

Okay, that did it. "Could you be *any* bigger a jerk?"

She marched away, her shoulders squared. Darn that man anyway! How had all of this gone spinning so far out of control? No matter how hateful Larem had been, he'd still risked his life to save hers. Her father might think all Others were a substandard life form, but she now knew better. Clearly he was a man of honor, one who was suffering because of what that honor had just demanded of him. All because of her.

Okay, so she'd try one last time. But when she looked back, he was already walking away.

"Larem? About what you did—thank you."

For a second she thought he slowed down, but maybe she was only imagining it—because he never glanced back. It was surprising how much that hurt. She ignored it and moved on herself. She was done for the day. The stack of work on her desk would still be there in the morning. Flipping open her cell phone, she texted her assistant that she wouldn't be back today.

Without waiting for a response, she hurried out of the building and hailed a cab. With luck, she'd be able to hold herself together long enough to reach her suite. After giving the driver the name of the hotel, she leaned back and closed her eyes, glad she didn't have far to go to where a stiff drink and a shower would be waiting.

Sometimes love needs a little help from beyond…

Bestselling Paranormal Romance from Pocket Books!

JILL MYLES
SUCCUBI LIKE IT HOT
The Succubus Diaries

Why choose between the bad boy and the nice guy…
when you can have them both?

CARA LOCKWOOD
Can't Teach an Old Demon New Tricks

She's just doing what comes supernaturally….

GWYN CREADY
FLIRTING *with* FOREVER

She tumbled through time…and into his arms.

MELISSA MAYHUE
A Highlander's Homecoming

Faerie Magic took him to the future,
but true love awaits in his Highland past.

The darkness hungers...
Bestselling Paranormal Romance from Pocket Books!

KRESLEY COLE
PLEASURE
OF A DARK PRINCE

An *Immortals After Dark* Novel

Her only weakness...is his pleasure.

ALEXIS MORGAN
Defeat the Darkness

A *Paladin* Novel

Can one woman's love bring a warrior's spirit back to life?

And don't miss these sizzling novels
by *New York Times* bestselling author
Jayne Ann Krentz writing as

JAYNE CASTLE
Amaryllis   Zinnia
Orchid